LOVE & STONES

SALLIANNE HINES

GRASSLANDS PRESS

Love & Stones

Copyright ©2020 Sallianne Hines

All rights reserved.

Dedicated to Jonathon & Rocky

A GRASSLANDS PRESS PUBLICATION

ISBN: 978-1-7333844-2-1 (print); 978-1-7333844-3-8 (ebook)

Cover design by Sallianne Hines and Rachael Ritchey (rachaelritchey.com)
Front cover photo by Wendy Mathers
Back cover photo & interior design by Sallianne Hines

This is a work of fiction. Names, characters, places, brands, and incidents are either the product of the author's imagination or are used fictitiously. Any resemblance to actual persons living or dead, events, business establishments, or locales is entirely coincidental.

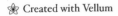 Created with Vellum

SONNET 116

Let me not to the marriage of true minds
Admit impediments; love is not love
Which alters when it alteration finds
Or bends with the remover to remove.
O no, it is an ever-fixèd mark
That looks on tempests and is never shaken ...

WILLIAM SHAKESPEARE

ABOUT OUR HEROINE

No one acquainted with Cathryn McNeil would fancy her a heroine. Her situation in life, the character and position of her parents, her own person and disposition—none bespoke a heroine. Her father was taciturn and less than encouraging; her mother was effervescent but bewildered by Cathryn, who floated a bit 'out there' in the family constellation. Some thought her a complicated creature. Others found her quirks endearing. Grandma Esther called her tenderhearted, and had probably known her best.

A great reader, Cathryn was often absorbed in the adventures of Jane Austen's heroines. Truthfully, Cathryn may have had more difficulty separating herself from Austen's world than she was aware of, or would care to admit. That world was her sanctuary when adult life proved beyond the pale.

As an animal lover and active sort of person, riding horses was a passion Cathryn still enjoyed long after many women had given up the saddle. However, being a woman of 'a certain age,' Cathryn had lost her bloom. She wanted to believe in happily-ever-after, but was her chance for romantic love too long past? Would fate step in? For if a lady, of any age, is to become a heroine, something surely must occur to send adventure—and a hero—her way ...

CHAPTER ONE

*C*athryn McNeil parked her truck and hurried over the blistering blacktop to the cool refuge of the brick building. *Are we really meeting at funeral homes now?*

She contemplated this prospect while frowning into the hallway mirror, tucking stray locks back into her French braid. A good hair day was impossible in this humid weather. She smoothed the wrinkles pressed into her sundress during her two-hour drive from Quinn to Fullerton and took a last look. This would have to do.

After rounding the corner she stopped to survey the visitation room full of people gathered for the memorial. Her chest tightened. She had never been one to converse easily in society. Sometimes she berated herself for not being more open; at other times she wondered why others made such little effort to know her. But all that was of no matter now— today she was here for Lisa. Spotting her friend, Cathryn took a deep breath and strode over to join those who'd come to pay their respects; Lisa's mom had died.

Cathryn and Lisa had grown up in Fullerton and shared a long and winding road from junior high through high school, college and beyond: dances, slumber parties, new loves, marriages, children, grandchildren, and divorces. And now here was a new kind of loss.

Lisa reached out and threw her arms around Cathryn. "Dad says he'll never set foot in the house again."

Cathryn was moved. "It must be devastating, after so many years together. It's a big change to live alone. For him, home will never be the same."

Home. It struck at her heart. She shifted uneasily.

"But it's not like this was sudden," Lisa protested. "Mom was sick a long time; we've known for months. He's had some time to get used to the idea."

The corners of Cathryn's mouth twitched. "Yes, but Lisa, reality is very different from an idea. From now on, being alone will color every single minute of every single day."

Lisa sighed. "Dad's been staying with me, and doesn't seem to have a plan. I'm worried."

Cathryn wrapped a comforting arm around her friend. "Give it some time. You'll work things out. Loss is always a shock, even when it *is* expected." She winced. And more so when unexpected. As a children's therapist, Cathryn had often helped kids cope with loss. But that skill didn't necessarily translate to dealing well with one's own losses.

Today's scene lent a sharper bite to her sense that time was on the wing. Cathryn and her friends were nearing the end of the 'sandwich years' during which they'd cared for their children *and* their parents. They were now on the brink of being the older generation themselves. It seemed impossible. It was most unsettling, if one dared think about it at all.

As she strained to refocus on the conversation between Lisa and the others a man strolled over and joined them. After a second look, she recognized Jack Stone, the younger brother of her classmate Joe. Jack spoke well. When he turned his easy smile her way, she squirmed at the blush she knew brightened her cheeks. As he talked with the group, she found the twinkle in his eye appealing, which only managed to unnerve her. She struggled to maintain her countenance until the group disbursed to visit with others.

After a sigh of relief, she chided herself for such a schoolgirl response to the mere presence of a man. It was most disconcerting.

She retreated to a quiet corner to watch the video loop of Lisa's family pictures from the past. It brought back memories of her own, fond and otherwise. Cathryn and her contemporaries were the tail end of the baby boom generation. They had grown up when the small post-war bungalows in neighborhoods like Valley View were packed with kids— often twenty or more kids to a city block. It didn't seem that long ago.

"Those were good times, weren't they?"

She turned toward the voice and quelled a flutter. Jack? She couldn't recall ever talking to him, although she'd spoken to his older brother on occasion. She knew the three brothers by sight but they had not been part of her social group. In fact, she couldn't remember them socializing much at all; they had been painfully shy.

Jack did not appear so now.

Cathryn cleared her throat. "Yes, Valley View was a great place to grow up." She returned his smile, uneasily aware of being drawn into his gaze.

He had a lanky build and moved with purpose. His angular face, etched by the outdoors, was framed by dark hair shot with silver. He was handsome, in a rugged 'everyman' sort of way that she found very agreeable.

Jack and his brothers had lived on a small farm at the edge of the Valley View neighborhood. They'd always had horses and for that reason Cathryn had always found them interesting. Lisa's family lived next door to Jack's back then. During junior high his family moved farther into the country; she wondered if the two families kept in touch.

He commented on most of the pictures in the video and turned for her response, making a marked effort to engage her. Such attentiveness was flattering. Dismayed to find herself blushing again she scrambled for something to say.

"You're a doctor, right?"

His body stiffened and his demeanor chilled. "Uh, yeah.

Pediatric orthopedics." His eyes narrowed and he looked across the room.

Alarmed, she hastily regrouped and tried another approach. "Are ... both your brothers still here in town?"

His eyes found hers again. As he warmed to the new topic, his body relaxed.

"Joe and his wife have a ranch out west, in the Wyoming foothills. But Jeff's here. He's a professor at the community college. Biology. Actually, I live next to Jeff and his wife on Potter's Lake ... you know, just north of town. We all get together several times a year."

So the brothers were still close. She smiled to herself, pleased at such sibling solidarity. In her experience it signified good character, usually.

"Last fall the three of us packed into the mountains on horseback from Joe's ranch. We said we were going to hunt elk, but we really just wanted to ride and camp together. The elk lucked out." He chuckled.

Horses. Her pulse quickened. Now she was intrigued.

"Do you do any other riding?" She hoped she had adequately disguised her breathless intensity.

His face brightened. "Yeah, I play polo."

She blinked. She knew little of the sport, beyond that scene in *Pretty Woman*. Was it all so highbrow here on the prairie?

Their mutual passion for horses absorbed them for some time, sharing tales about those they'd owned, places they'd ridden, breeds they liked—in short, all the details that interest those enamored of everything equine. He leaned close as he described the places he'd traveled for polo and trail riding. His eyes repeatedly sought hers, and she eased into the rhythm of his rich voice carrying her along on his equestrian exploits. For a while, she was charmed enough to forget her underlying qualms.

Some time later, a commotion near the door startled them. People were leaving. They both stood and looked around in a self-conscious way.

"I guess it's time to go," he mumbled.

She wished she could prolong their visit but didn't know how. To her surprise—and relief—he did.

"Seriously, as a horsewoman you should give polo a try. I could set it all up, show you the basics. You could ride one of my horses."

Her heart leapt at the offer. His grin was inviting and her pulse raced. "I'd like that."

He looked down and fumbled for her hand, enfolding it in both of his. "I'm glad we had this chance to talk, Cathryn."

Her body stirred at the warmth and strength she sensed in him. His touch kindled a feeling she'd nearly forgotten. Their eyes locked and they lingered over awkward parting smiles, neither knowing what else to say.

As he made his way to the door, he glanced back at her—first with a lopsided smile, and then again with a short wave.

Is he as reluctant to part as I am? Is he thinking about more than a polo lesson?

Then Lisa was at her side again. "You two sure had a lot to talk about."

Cathryn could only stare at her friend.

"It looked like some pretty captivating conversation," Lisa continued with a sly smile. "Or was it the company itself that was so captivating?" As college roommates, they'd been each other's wingman on many a social foray. How easily that role was revived, even after so many years.

"Lisa, did he ever marry?" Cathryn had forgotten to look for a ring; but with men, lack of a ring wasn't a sure sign of anything. How odd. Even today marital status did not define men as much as it did women.

After a pause Lisa said, "No, I never heard he'd married, although he's been linked with a few different women over the years. His brothers are married and have kids."

Cathryn looked at Lisa. "Maybe he's ...?" She raised a brow.

"I've heard rumors of that too," Lisa mused. "No one seems to know. It's not like you can just ask someone that."

Cathryn's eyes wandered back to the doorway, moved by a sense of wonder and spurred on by a spark of hope.

Maybe it's not too late to become a heroine after all?

The evening clouds gathered at the horizon, spreading a haze across the western sky. As Cathryn cruised along the four-lane her thoughts took the reins. Her life had not played out as she'd expected. Lately each day seemed a quick succession of busy nothings, dying away with no more significance than the day before. Although she tended to dodge change, lately she had grown impatient with the dullness of her own existence. This ignited a sense of urgency that increased daily, but she didn't know whether to shield herself or fan the flame. Meeting Jack had set it ablaze. In the darkness of the pickup, she savored the memory of his voice, his eyes, and especially his warm, strong touch. On paper, he was perfect for her: the right age, fit and attractive, with an admirable career—and he loved horses. Best of all, he wasn't a complete stranger. He was a tempting yet comfortable combination of the unknown and the familiar.

Romantic scenarios prodded at her imagination as she sped along the highway. Today's encounter had loosed a small stone that could release an avalanche if she wasn't careful. She had all but given up on men, and on romantic love. Like Austen's *Sense & Sensibility* heroine Marianne, Cathryn felt that she herself required so much. Too much. Although she would absolutely preserve a better balance of sense and sensibility than Marianne had.

Surely at my age I can do that? I *must* do that. Love is too easily entangled with loss.

Those tears still stung.

But was Jack even available? Why had she not asked him about marriages or ... partners? She bit her lip. And why had he not asked for her phone number? Had his offer to ride been tossed out with no serious intention of following up?

Her heartbeat quickened. First impressions could be misleading. Unreliable. There was one truth Cathryn universally acknowledged: when things seemed too perfect, loss and sorrow were sure to follow.

A single ray of the setting sun pierced the cloud cover ahead. She blocked it with her hand.

And what was the meaning of Jack's obvious discomfort when she'd asked about his profession? He'd been all ease and affability with every other subject. Why would a man of sense and education, who has lived in the world, feel ill qualified to recommend himself … ?

The sun sank, pulling the clouds with it and the evening star rode alone in the sky.

Darkness fell and Cathryn's fancy took flight.

CHAPTER TWO

Cathryn slipped out the door as the gray sky surrendered to dawn. A townie since her last divorce, she now boarded Henry, her old gelding, at a farm a few miles south of Quinn. Although early rides held a certain magic, the timing of today's adventure was dictated by the insufferable heat.

By the time horse, rider, and trailing dogs returned to the barn, the temperature had soared. Cathryn swirled the currycomb over Henry's lathered coat, breathing in the lovely scent of horse. Keeping up her usual one-sided natter with her four-legged friends she asked them, "What do you think, will it storm?"

The air was thick. Henry stomped his foot at a fly. Her dogs lazed in the dust under the nearby lilacs. Pushing back her damp hair, Cathryn scanned the sky. Not a cloud. In the distance the horizon shimmered in the heat. Even the relentless prairie wind offered no reprieve—it was as suffocating as the air itself.

Henry rubbed his head on her arm and she patted his clammy skin. "Let's get you a drink, huh boy?"

He nickered at her while she checked the water tank in his tree-shaded paddock.

"Don't worry, I haven't forgotten." She dug in her pocket

for a piece of carrot and he lipped it nimbly from her outstretched hand.

"Now that's what I call gentlemanly behavior. Mr. Darcy has nothing on you."

She ruffled the horse's forelock with affection, then kissed his soft muzzle. They'd been together nearly twenty years, she and Henry; longer than she'd spent with both of her husbands combined. She'd been the one to leave those marriages—her only regret being the time wasted. Other losses had left deeper wounds. She now chose to remain on safer ground. Detached ground.

She left Henry in shady repose and drove back to her cottage in Quinn. It was not a cottage by Austen standards, being much smaller than Barton Cottage in *Sense & Sensibility*. Rather, hers was a modest bungalow and very snug indeed.

It was past noon but the heat had dulled Cathryn's appetite. After a cool shower, she situated herself on the sofa with a book, a glass of lemonade, and a big bowl of popcorn. The heat was oppressive. The only fix for weather like this was a raging storm. She grimaced and opened her book. With Quinn being a small prairie town, Cathryn spent a good deal of time reading. There wasn't much else to do, especially if one was single and of a certain age.

Today she was finishing Jane Austen's *Sense & Sensibility*, again. Although Cathryn had read the novel many times with great fondness, on completing it today she realized—with no little shock—that it was now *Mrs.* Dashwood's age and situation that most closely resembled her own. Mrs. Dashwood was forty and widowed, with two eligible daughters—heroines Elinor and Marianne. But no love interest was written for *Mrs.* Dashwood. No hero was in want of such a wife.

Cathryn slammed the book shut, startling her gray cat who jumped to the floor and scowled."Sorry, Marianne."

Leaning back on the sofa, she pondered the disturbing literary parallel to her own life.

Marianne groomed herself with detached calm, proving nothing could disrupt her composure for long.

Cathryn envied her cat's equanimity.

"So, what happens to *Mrs*. Dashwood, huh Marianne? What is *her* happily-ever-after?"

The cat looked up, annoyed at another disruption, then resumed licking her paw and cleaning her face. After tucking her paws under herself like a sphinx she blinked at her mistress with disinterest.

Cathryn stared at the book in her lap, as if an answer might leap from the pages and set her at ease, but the book remained stubbornly silent. Her gaze darted to the window as a huddle of worried clouds skidded across the sky at the mercy of the east wind. An east wind signaled rain, or maybe even a storm. She disliked storms. They disturbed *her* equanimity. She only wished to be left in peace. There'd been enough disturbance in her life.

Both of her marriages—first to Steve, and then to Barry—began starry-eyed but rapidly declined into vexation and shattered dreams. She always clutched at hope for too long. She'd never had an equal partner in life; never known a deep connection with a man of good character—not for long anyway. In her younger days, she'd assumed such a match would magically happen. Pairings like Austen's Elinor and Edward or Anne and Frederick came to mind. Wasn't there someone for everyone? She'd come close once, with Bob, until she pushed him away. Why had she done that? The reason still eluded her—and she'd never dug for deeper understanding. Digging was painful. Even if he was the great love of her life.

When she and Steve divorced—years before cell phones or social media—she had tried to find Bob, with no success. Then when her marriage to Barry crashed and burned, she searched the internet with determination until she hit the ultimate roadblock—Bob's obituary. Stunned, shocked, and grieved, even now she found it hard to believe he was gone from the world, that she would never see him again. Only Henry had witnessed her tears.

Gentle *woofs* now penetrated her reverie. The sun had set. Her dogs stared at her, tails wagging; they knew the time.

"I certainly don't lack for good company, do I? At least not of the four-footed variety."

The first rumble of thunder rolled through the sky. Cathryn rose and called the other cat, who emerged from the bedroom, then handed out the much-anticipated bedtime treats to four appreciative creatures. She made herself a piece of peanut butter toast and tidied the kitchen.

Her own bedtime treat was always a book. There was such comfort in a good book. With each successive reading, a different self was brought to the page and something new was learned. But the book itself never changed. It was 'an ever fixèd mark.' Something to count on. Cathryn liked things, and people, she could count on.

She reached up and pulled the chain of the ceiling fan, then propped herself on her pillows. Thunder echoed back and forth across the sky, punctuated by flashes of lightning, but the storm was still at a distance. As the fan began its lazy spin she opened *Northanger Abbey* and settled in to enjoy Henry Tilney's teasing wit. The familiarity of the book was soothing, but vicarious romance was growing stale.

The nights were lengthening and another summer waned.

CHAPTER THREE

*S*omething had changed upon meeting Jack. More than a week had passed—eleven days to be exact—and Cathryn could no longer ignore the question that had been simmering beneath her well-composed demeanor long before he strolled into her life at that funeral home. Her discontent was now drawn to the surface, her mask of serenity twisted loose. It was the question she'd dared not ask herself seriously, or even consciously—was it too late for love?

Cathryn paced from window to window, her eyes blind to the kaleidoscope of late summer color adorning the yard. Her body was tense, knotted, teeming with an energy that could find no release. Imaginary encounters clogged her mind. It was difficult to concentrate on life's mundane details. *Discomfited.* Yes, that was Austen's very apt word.

Elinor, her calico cat, jumped to the sill and condensed her body to fit the narrow ledge. Cathryn mindlessly stroked the silky fur and muttered, "I should do something. But what?" She wrung her hands, then paused as a little voice whispered *you could call him.*

"*Shall* I call him?" Her breath caught in her throat at speaking the very idea aloud. "Lots of women do the calling now," she said, attempting to reason with herself. Wrinkling her brow, she contemplated the idea for a minute, but then cast it firmly away. No, it felt too ... assuming. Bold. But not in a good way. Desperate. And just a little sad.

Only one action seemed logical. She reached for her phone and tapped in a number.

Lisa's familiar voice was comforting, but her immediate question only served to increase Cathryn's vexation.

"What have you heard from Jack?"

"Nothing. Nothing at all. What do you make of that?"

"Oh," Lisa said, a little subdued. "I'm surprised. Didn't he say he would call?"

Cathryn thought for a moment. "No. It was implied, but never actually promised. He did say he'd teach me to play polo; that he'd set everything up. It sounded like an invitation, but he didn't mention a day or time. He didn't ask for my number either and I didn't think to ask for his. I suppose I could call his office ..." She groaned. "Oh Lisa, I really hoped this would go somewhere!" Disappointment rang in her voice. "Jack is the only interesting man I've met who's anywhere near my age. Plus, he's a horseman. It would be so amazing. And you know—other than Jack—when I look at men now, it's the much younger ones that catch my eye. Help! I'm trapped in some kind of romantic time warp."

Lisa chuckled. "Wasn't your last husband ... wasn't Barry younger than us?"

"Well, yes. He was born the year the Beatles came to America. But the only Beatle he could name was Ringo."

They laughed at that. The music of the Beatles had been the soundtrack to their own coming-of-age journey.

"It's only been a week or so since you saw Jack. Maybe he got busy, or had to go to a conference or something. Where's your professional detachment?"

"My prof—come on, Lisa, you know we all lack an objective view of our own situation. That's why I called *you!* I'm so confused. It's like junior high all over again. I think I've forgotten how this dating thing works," she admitted with a rueful laugh. "I don't even know if it was a date he proposed, or what."

Despite a long talk with Lisa, Cathryn remained frustrated at the effect Jack was having on her peace of mind. He crept into her thoughts more often than she wished. She ached to see him again. How long was long enough to gauge if he had any real interest, or honorable intentions?

But what Lisa had said did make sense.

Cathryn slumped back onto the sofa, wishing a relationship could just magically coalesce. Oh, for the convenience of a ball or an assembly! Why did they ever stop having those anyway? How were people supposed to meet one another nowadays? It was all very vexing.

Her ring tone interrupted her meandering thoughts.

"What are you up to, girl? Are you off Monday? It's a mail holiday you know. Let's ride." It was Deb.

"I'd love to. But I don't think Henry can haul there and back *and* trail ride all in the same day. He's an old guy now."

"No worries. Plenty of horses out here. Seems we're a retirement center for my niece's old show horses. You rode Mac before, right?" Her congenial voice made Cathryn smile.

Cathryn and Deb had little in common. Deb ranched with her husband and rode regularly with a small group of ranch women, usually while Cathryn was stuck behind a desk at the law office where she now worked after the 'to-do' at the counseling agency.

The two women were as different in looks as they were in personality. Tall with dark hair and eyes, Deb had a no-nonsense attitude and a big, easy laugh. Horses *and* people knew exactly where they stood with Deb. Cathryn was introspective with a small, athletic frame and pleasant regular features lit by a gentle smile. Their unusual friendship was fostered by a shared passion for horses, and cemented by a keen love of the land.

What a propitious invitation. A ride would be the perfect diversion from dwelling on Jack. She must not allow herself to act like Harriet Smith in *Emma,* mooning over a man who may not be thinking about her at all.

～

Monday dawned appreciably cooler in the wake of Sunday's brief storm. After lunch Cathryn aimed her pickup west for the twenty-mile jaunt to Bill and Deb's. Situated at the end of a long gravel road, the ranch nestled into the Vision Hills, a geologic formation hewn by glaciers in ages past. The hills flanked the ranch on the west, running north to south for miles along a broad section of the prairie. It was a beautiful place—primitive, wild.

Once her truck left the houses of Quinn behind, her dogs paced the back seat in anticipation. Cathryn had ridden with Deb often over the years.

Within minutes of parking her truck the whole group was on the trail. There was no dilly-dallying with Deb.

As Cathryn got the feel of the horse under her, Deb and the now-combined troop of dogs led the way. Having ridden for years on the prairie, Cathryn appreciated how the land—which might appear flat and boring to the casual observer—was actually quite rolling, with some deep ravines cut by creeks that were now parched and silent in the heat of late summer. A quiet rustle was the only token of their passing as the riders moved through the tall grass.

"How is your old guy anyway? You still ride him?" Deb asked.

"Oh, sure. We've explored a lot of prairie roads this summer. I warm him up for longer than he likes before I let him canter. He'd go and go, but then suffers for it the next day—all stiff and sore—unless I hold him back. I guess that's the Thoroughbred in him," Cathryn said as they trotted side by side along the edge of the meadow.

"Likely. Never had a hot-blooded horse before I rescued Crystal here; she's half Arab." Deb patted her horse with affection. "She needs a special touch, but I adore her. She's like that too—never wants to quit. I admire that."

Cathryn smiled to herself. Yes, that was definitely a trait Deb would admire.

They kept to the meadows and the base of the ridge—challenging enough to be interesting but easy enough to be relaxing.

"These oldsters do pretty good, don't they?" Deb observed. "Sometimes I think they do better than we do. You know, in horse years, they're about the same ages we are." She laughed heartily, a laugh so contagious that Cathryn found herself joining in. It felt good to release her worries and abandon herself to the moment. Long ago she'd discovered it was pretty much impossible to dwell on the past or fret about the future while on the back of a horse.

They slid their way down into a deep gully with a sandy bottom and rode along quietly, hearing only the whispered footfalls of the horses' hooves. After a time, Deb found a path to take them back up to the meadow. The horses scrambled and lurched their way upward among the loose stones as their riders leaned forward to reduce the burden.

When they gained the top Cathryn patted her horse in appreciation. "Good boy," she murmured.

Mac nodded his head as if in reply.

Deb shaded her eyes with her hand. "This field has good footing to the north. Ready to run?"

"Let's go!"

Off they galloped, the dogs following, excited by the sudden change of pace. After the exhilarating run, Cathryn breathed deeply as they walked on; the air carried just a hint of approaching autumn. The open space around her, the big sky above her, and the rhythm of the horse beneath her revived a sense of life's possibilities. Her knots had unraveled, her mind had cleared, and her worries had evaporated into the golden glow of late afternoon. Watching the dogs chase rabbits and each other through the ditches made for an amusing sideshow. The ride had provided more laughs and companionship than she'd had in some time and she was grateful.

The sun was dipping behind the farthest ridge when they returned to the barn. Quickly they unsaddled the horses, turning them out just before mosquitoes invaded.

"Run for it or they'll eat you alive," Deb yelled.

They sped to the house.

After kicking off their boots at the door, the women settled themselves in the screened porch to chat over slices of watermelon.

Deb planned to enter some photos in a local show and wanted an opinion, so Cathryn examined those set up at the back of the well-worn table. The shots were impressive and reflected Deb's love of the land. She always rode with her camera. And she rode almost every day.

Cathryn envied her—out on the land with her animals, in charge of her own time instead of submitting to some employer's time clock.

"You realize how lucky you are, don't you?" Cathryn asked between bites of watermelon. "Why, you're the mistress of your own modern-day manor."

Deb hooted. "I suppose that's from those books you read. You really get lost in those, don't you? I did read the one, let's see, it was *Pride and* something ... why, Bill even sat down and watched the DVD with me. It *was* pretty good. Funnier than I would've guessed. Maybe I'll read another one this winter, when we're snowed in."

Deb and Bill were happy together, real partners in life. They had married right after high school, decades ago. Observing the wildflower bouquet on the table, Cathryn gave her friend a knowing look.

Deb laughed merrily. "Yes, Bill still picks flowers for me. I admit ... he's a treasure."

A sharp pang stabbed at Cathryn's heart. That's all I want —a real partner, someone I can count on. A true gentleman, in the best sense.

Scooping out another spoonful of watermelon, she

reflected on the few couples she knew who actually had that. Would I have it too if I'd listened to my heart? Hastily she brushed the wistful feeling aside, then stood and crossed the room.

"This ride was just what I needed, Deb," she said, scraping her watermelon rind and seeds into the compost bin. "It gets boring riding alone. Not that Henry isn't good company ..."

"I'll haul over and ride with you one of these days," Deb said in reply to the unspoken invitation. Then she eyed Cathryn curiously. "Is it just riding alone that's ... boring?"

Cathryn froze. She refused to be one of those insufferable singles that whined to their friends about being lonely or alone. There *was* a difference. She didn't want anyone's pity.

"Well, Deb, I'm a bit ... in the doldrums," she admitted, staring out the window. "Feeling restless, you know? Like I need a change, but I'm not sure what."

Deb narrowed her eyes.

Cathryn shifted uneasily. Elusive didn't cut it with Deb.

"Okay, and ... well, I met someone—this guy, a polo player —at a funeral home, of all places. I thought we kinda clicked. He offered to teach me polo. Which of course I wanted to do, especially with him. But ... well ... I haven't heard from him since." She sighed.

Deb listened in thoughtful silence to the rest of the tale about meeting Jack. When Cathryn had finished, Deb still didn't speak.

"So?" Cathryn prodded. "Inquiring minds want to know."

Deb's face eased into a smile. "Give it some time. People get busy. Seems you don't like riding on a loose rein." After a bite of watermelon she said, with an arched brow, "Seems you might wait for someone else to take the reins."

Cathryn looked at Deb. That last comment stung, but she couldn't argue with the truth.

"One thing ranching does," Deb continued, "it teaches you about time. Some things ya gotta deal with *right now,*" she said, slamming her arm on the table. "But other things, well, you have to give 'em their time. They'll resolve in the end, one way or another. And usually there's not a whole lot you can do about it anyway. You can't push the river, Cathryn."

They sat in silence for a while, gazing out the screened porch as the hush of evening settled over the land. Peaceful. Like time itself had paused to reflect.

Cathryn turned Deb's observations around in her mind. Why *am* I in such a rush to have things settled? And why *don't* I settle things myself? Her thoughts wound around each other until they were tangled like a horse's mane full of wind whips. Overwhelmed, she pushed the whole mess aside to deal with another time.

The last shreds of daylight had faded. It was time to leave.

"How about next Saturday, Deb? Can you haul over?" Cathryn bent down to pull on her boots.

Deb looked at the calendar by the door. "Looks clear to me. I'll run it by Bill and let you know."

"Great. Thanks for the ride. And the watermelon. See you soon."

Cathryn stepped out into the soft evening air. The silence stretched for miles, broken only by the chirping crickets. Her body softened. Their song had lulled her to sleep on summer nights when she was a little girl. Back when things were simple. After drifting a moment she shook her head.

"George. Emma. Come!" The dogs appeared in an instant, tails wagging, eager for another ride in the truck. "Load up."

After they had jumped in, she closed the door and leaned her back against it to watch the first stars pricking through the violet mantle of sky.

The stars were far lovelier than the shadows wrestling in her mind.

CHAPTER FOUR

*T*he dogs stirred as daylight filtered through the bedroom curtains. Cathryn glanced toward the nightstand. Eight o'clock. She stretched her limbs, rolled out of bed, and peered out at a leaden sky. Saturday, and it was going to rain. The wind whipped a few rusty leaves high in the air, then tossed them ruthlessly across the yard. With a sigh she headed to the kitchen.

She let the dogs out and back in, then fed and watered them and the cats, grounding herself in the daily ritual of loving care. It was nice to be needed and to feel adored. And those feelings were definitely mutual.

At least she didn't have to work weekends anymore—no more being on call as she had been at the counseling agency. But the grind of clerical duties at the law office was tedious compared to her former job as a children's therapist, a position she'd resigned some months back when the new director's want of integrity made it impossible to serve her families effectively—or honestly. Misappropriating children's funding was something she simply would not do. Eventually the scoundrel was indicted and fired but his minions remained in power and she could not, in good conscience, return.

Carelessly she pulled on jeans and an old sweater and gathered her hair back in a barrette. Her heart wasn't into fussing much these days, but she'd agreed to meet Gwen for coffee at Brews. In ten minutes! She grabbed her raincoat and ran out the door.

∼

"It's worse than ever," Gwen moaned, referring to the counseling agency where they had worked together for years. "There's no leadership and the minions are rising up!" She contorted her face in mock horror and then laughed, but the tinge of bitterness in her voice was not lost on Cathryn. She knew exactly who those minions were.

Jobs were scarce in a small town like Quinn. At times she thought about leaving. Moving away. Starting over, again. But where would she go, all alone? And at this age, what would starting over even mean? Her kids and grandkids were spread across the country. The logistics of moving her dogs and cats, and finding a new place to board Henry—it all seemed like a lot of work and expense for an uncertain reward. She set her discontent aside and ordered a latte.

Rain drummed at the window. Across the table Gwen Somerset sipped at her mug of coffee. With intense eyes and a runner's build, Gwen was the picture of brisk efficiency except for the wild blizzard of white hair that circled her head like a halo. One of those people who somehow seem ageless, she was an old soul with a generous heart. She'd been with the agency more than thirty years.

Gwen spoke again. "Too bad for this rain, though we do need it. I wanted to walk a good ways with you and your dogs today." She stared at the rivulets running down the glass.

At work, Gwen had often requested Cathryn's expertise concerning the younger children in her caseload; and Cathryn had sought Gwen's insight when dysfunctional parents kept messing up the lives of the kids she was trying to help.

"I could have used the exercise too," Cathryn said, pushing back her sodden hair. "Something to shake me out my doldrums."

Gwen eyed her keenly. "So are these doldrums about the guy who hasn't called? Or something else?"

Cathryn's mouth curved in a wry smile. "Partly about him, I guess. But I think 'him,' or the idea of *a* 'him,' and the role he might play in my life, or not, well ... it's all triggering a sense of ... I don't know, frustration? I seem to be hitting dead ends and brick walls. I want something to change. I'm just not sure what." She took a drink of her latte. "Of course, adding a man to my life is not at my sole command. And a man isn't the whole answer either," she said with a slow shake of her head.

Gwen's eyes twinkled. "Dead ends and brick walls usually mean you're on the wrong path."

Reaching for Cathryn's hand across the table, she squeezed it and added, "I know you miss working with kids. I know your current job isn't challenging or fulfilling. That's got to be tough."

Then she sat back, took a bite of her muffin, and chewed thoughtfully. "It will come to you, what you want to change. The muse will speak. Just give it time."

Cathryn snapped off a bite of her scone at this echo of both Deb's and Lisa's advice. 'Give it time' they say. But I feel like time is running out. Are all my chances spent? Maybe this is it for me. Her chest tightened.

Then she looked at Gwen and her heart yielded. Gwen's husband had died a few months ago. Wayne had been seven years older but the heart attack wasn't anticipated.

"How about you, Gwen?" she asked, her voice now softened. "Is there anything I can do?"

Gwen stirred her coffee, took a sip, then set the mug down with great purpose and looked Cathryn squarely in the face. "Actually, I'm thinking about making some changes myself. Without Wayne, this town has lost its luster for me. His kids are grown and have their own lives. I'm totally fed up with the agency, and convinced staying there is a big negative." She paused for a deep breath.

"I'm thinking of selling my house and moving away."

The scone fell from Cathryn's hand. "What? But ... where would you go?"

Grinning inscrutably, Gwen leaned back, seeming amused at Cathryn's shock. "At Wayne's funeral, my niece and her husband invited me to move in with them, up in Granite City. With them *and* their three kids *and* new baby. I've never been around kids, as you know, so I'm not sure ... but their new place has a mother-in-law unit on the lower walkout level. I'm seriously considering it."

Quinn without Gwen? Cathryn shuddered. Inconceivable. "So will you retire? What will you do?"

"I'm not sure. Sometimes I think it would be fun to do something completely different, like work in a coffee shop or bookstore. I'm enjoying playing with the possibilities." Serene and unruffled, Gwen finished her muffin.

Cathryn couldn't swallow. The breath had been knocked out of her. Since she'd started at the agency twelve years ago —newly married for the second time—Gwen had been an anchor in her life.

Floundering for words of support, Cathryn could only come up with, "Well, it does sound exciting, a fresh new start and all. Just don't leave town without saying goodbye."

"Don't worry. I won't do anything too quickly."

But Cathryn knew Gwen. Once she made up her mind, she was as good as gone.

～

Autumn draped Quinn in vibrant color. The crisp dry air was ideal for riding. This was Cathryn's favorite season, although it made her restless. It held a bit of melancholy too. She had often moved in the autumn; moved with great hopes that crumbled all too quickly.

One autumn morning she and Henry wandered along a prairie road that wound past an old settlers' cemetery. Cathryn paused to stare at the headstones that marked lives that ended long ago.

Endings.

"Henry, what will I do if Gwen leaves?"

Henry tossed his head.

Gwen was the only single woman near Cathryn's age in Quinn. In a small town, being single usually meant being alone—a lot. And besides, no one could replace Gwen.

Then there was Jack. Or wasn't Jack. She pressed her lips into a hard line. *Was I just building a castle in the sand?* She'd had no word from him, and felt the snub with no small sense of bitterness. The Sunday school song said the wise man built his house upon the rock. Not the sand. She sighed. *I seem to be forever mired in the shoals.*

And, winter loomed. The season of ice and snow lingered long on the prairie. That thought alone was disheartening. She cued Henry to walk on.

"Maybe we should move away too, huh Henry? Where would you want to go?"

The gelding tossed his head again and began prancing, eager to add some speed to the far-too-reflective ride. She laughed as she gave him his head, and he cantered happily down the road.

The colorful countryside put Cathryn in mind of a tapestry, her personal metaphor for life. She'd used the idea—and fabric samples—in her work with children to demonstrate how life can be rewoven even after it unravels. She'd known great fulfillment in her work with children. She had also loved being a mother, and adored being a grandmother. With so many areas of satisfaction and much to be thankful for, it felt wrong to admit anything was missing from her life. Was it selfish to yearn for more when others had so much less? Twinges of guilt resonated within her.

From her perch in the saddle, she surveyed the land. It actually reminded her of parts of England. In fact, her life here could be said to parallel the lives in her favorite books, set in English villages. Life in Quinn was not unlike life in *Emma*'s Highbury, where Jane Fairfax had been so misunderstood. Despite Miss Fairfax's icy demeanor, Cathryn had always rooted for her. Highbury's residents thought they knew Jane, labeled her, and that was that—until she surprised them all in the end.

Cathryn herself often felt pigeonholed in much the same way—judged by irrelevant criteria. This was not new. It had been so since childhood, when her parents had dubbed her the artistic sister and Susan the musical sister. Although Cathryn was also gifted at singing, she was only allowed art lessons, and Susan only got music lessons. Likely financial considerations played a part, but such limits had kept her childhood small and her horizons narrow.

Quinn itself had diminished since the closing of the college that once brought culture and diversity to the flat prairie town. And, though situated on the banks of the last wild river in the state, the names of the streets and parks and the largest buildings—none made any reference to the river. It was undeveloped and ignored, except when it inconvenienced the town by flooding in the spring. The rest of the time, it led as nondescript an existence as Cathryn did.

A tasty patch of fireweed now tempted Henry; it was sweetest after a frost. She allowed him a few nibbles.

Leaning on her saddle horn, she soaked in the autumn splendor. There was a rich beauty to it, but a hint of sadness. On the prairie, color was a harbinger of change, and for a moment Cathryn shivered in the diluted sunlight.

CHAPTER FIVE

The Saturday after Halloween found Cathryn in Fullerton for her mother's birthday lunch.

"I'll have the tomato soup and salad please," she told the waitress, after her mother and three friends had placed their orders. These women were a curious bunch and plied Cathryn with questions.

She was answering yet another query from the ladies when her train of thought abruptly derailed. There was Jack ... walking toward the exit with another man. He must have felt her gaze. When he saw her, he changed direction.

The older ladies tittered as the two gentlemen drew near.

"So handsome."

"Look at that smile."

Cathryn dropped her eyes, schooled her countenance, then looked up with what she hoped was a friendly smile.

"Jack! What're you doing here?"

He gave her a crooked smile. "Well, we just ate lunch." His eyes captured hers and held them in what must have been a prolonged silence.

With a bemused smile, his friend nudged him back to the moment at hand. "*Ahem*. Jack, so who *are* these lovely ladies?"

Jack shook his head and chuckled. He introduced Mike to the group, then said, "This is my friend, Cathryn McNeil."

She extended her hand. "Nice to meet you, Mike."

Jack looked around the table. "So who are you dining with here today?" His eyes stopped at her mother. "You have *got* to be Mrs. McNeil. I remember you."

Cathryn's mother's eyes lit up. "As I recall, you're one of the Stone boys, aren't you?"

He laughed and reached out to shake her hand.

Cathryn said, "Mom, ladies, this is Jack Stone. We're here celebrating my mom's birthday, Jack."

Her mother promptly took over and introductions were made. Cathryn watched with interest as Jack interacted with the ladies. He certainly was charming, when he wished to be.

As small talk ensued, a fit of impertinence swept over Cathryn. With a sidelong look at Jack she said, "It's been a nice long autumn for trail riding, hasn't it? Or is it still polo season?" She smirked inwardly at her own thrust.

"Yeah ... I, uh ... yeah, it has ..." He avoided her eye. "Say, we didn't do that polo thing yet, did we? I'll get in touch with you about it soon, okay?"

Recognition. She was almost satisfied. Adopting a breezy tone she said, "Sure, that would be great. Henry and I've had so much fun trail riding this fall. I love getting out into the countryside this time of year."

He blanched. "Henry? Who ... oh, your horse? That sounds ... nice. Yeah, trail riding is ... nice ..." He looked about the room, his eyes wide.

She sniggered. Her triumph was complete. "I hope you're able to get out and enjoy it too, Jack."

He stared at her, then recovered himself. "Well, we won't detain you any longer. You ladies have an enjoyable lunch. It was good to see you again, Cathryn. Oh, and happy birthday, Mrs. McNeil."

As the men headed for the door, Jack looked back at Cathryn with a lopsided grin, the meaning of which she could not determine. As their eyes connected, she saw—or sensed —a longing in him. Not unlike her own. She drew a quick breath and blinked, but by then his back was rounding the corner. He was gone, but her heart hammered on in her chest. What did it all mean? Was this another chance?

Reluctantly she turned back to her companions.

"So how do you know him?"

"Does he live here in town?"

It required supreme effort on her part to concentrate on the rest of the meal. She yearned to sink into daydreams about Jack, to relive and dissect every nuance of this coincidental encounter.

Her mother's voice brought her focus back to the table. "I'm so pleased you were able to come to town, dear. This was lovely. Thank you for the lunch."

"Well, I couldn't miss your special day, Mom." Cathryn gathered her things and prepared to leave. "I'll try to get here again before the snow flies," she said, giving her mother a kiss and hug. "Bye, and happy birthday. Love to Dad."

Her mind raced. Was it fate, seeing Jack again? She shook her head. Quit with the magical thinking. Had she pressed him too hard? Did he think her unkind? She walked out the door, trying not to trip over her tangled emotions. Before long she was on the highway, heading back to Quinn.

Would she hear from Jack this time?

Her practical side scoffed. *If he were interested, he'd have called before now. Look how uneasy he was. He probably regrets ever making that polo invitation. And he still didn't ask for your number.*

And she hadn't offered it. Nor had she suggested a time for the polo lesson. Was it just a repeat of an empty invitation? She cringed.

Her optimistic side stepped in. He *did* come over to the table, after all. And that longing she thought she sensed ... it fed the tiny spark of hope in her heart.

Her practical side was having none of it. *You've always waited and hoped, for far too long. Look at the price you've paid—a lost love, two divorces. Quit daydreaming. Toughen up.*

That made sense, in her head. But her heart had questions. How many chances should she give him? How long should she hope? Was there another woman? Did his romantic tendencies lean toward his own gender? Who *was* that Mike anyway? Jack had not explained their connection. She gripped the steering wheel.

Any future with Jack seemed unpredictable at best. He had proved himself unsteady, unreliable. She shifted in her seat to dodge the uneasy feeling creeping up her back and reached into the door compartment for her particular treasure: a smooth greenish stone, large enough to fill her palm. It went everywhere with her. She never tired of cradling it or tracing the intricate veins of black, tan, and blue laced across its cool surface. She'd found it on her first beach outing with Bob. Holding it, she could almost feel his presence, smell the sea, and feel the endless rhythm of the waves breaking on the shore. Such a great love they'd had—naturally born but tragically brief. Now only the green stone remained. She fingered it and let her thoughts wander onto firmer ground, back into older and deeper corners of her past.

Growing up, her family had lived next to a cemetery—one of the few places on the prairie that was truly wooded. On a gravel road at its north side, she and her sister often sat in the dust collecting stones. They washed and then polished them with clear nail enamel so they'd always look wet and pretty.

Cathryn still loved stones for their subtle beauty and interesting shapes and textures. The heft in her hand felt solid, substantial, real. Wherever she traveled, her souvenir of choice was always a stone or two, or three.

While rambling in those cemetery woods, young Cathryn had wondered about the departed souls beneath her feet, each marked by a headstone. Some of these were large and shiny, even ostentatious, with ornate carvings and fancy chiseled letters; others were rough-hewn and bore no discernible human mark. So that was it. You got one life. And what was left behind was ... a stone. It all seemed very philosophical back then, when her life was still ahead of her.

The road of the past was easier to tread than that of the future. The past was familiar. It held no surprises.

The future was veiled in mist.

CHAPTER SIX

"*My* house is sold!" Gwen's voice rang out as Cathryn slid into the booth at Casa de Rosa. "And it's a cash deal. No qualifying, no waiting. I can go as soon as I'm ready." Gwen beamed with pleasure.

Cathryn shivered. The thought of losing Gwen bit deeper than the late autumn chill.

The waiter interrupted to take their orders, giving Cathryn time to think of a cheerful response. She drew a deep breath. "So quick! We didn't even stage the house." She stared at Gwen. "What about work?"

"I'm dropping the bomb Monday at the general staffing."

They snickered, picturing the impact that announcement would have on those minions.

"I figure three weeks will give me time to work with my clients—you know, to help them process the change," Gwen said, ever thoughtful of the real reason they had each chosen their profession.

Cathryn wondered if a major change would shake up her own life, in a good way. Other than her initial move to California, her choices had not been auspicious. Perversely, each move took her further from where she thought she wanted to be. That's how she ended up in Quinn. She now knew those moves had been reactive rather than inspired, and

were usually undertaken in pursuit of—or in avoidance of
—a man.

"You *will* come and visit," Gwen said with enthusiasm,
bringing Cathryn's attention back to the present.

The conversation turned to Gwen's future home: Granite
City, Wyoming, in the foothills of the Rocky Mountains. It
seemed a world away.

It may as well have been the moon.

~

Cathryn and Gwen stood in Gwen's driveway, smarting in the
sting of winter's first blast. Their last hug was long.

"I can't believe you're actually leaving." Cathryn's eyes
brimmed with tears.

Gwen smiled and gripped her friend's shoulders. "It's
time. I'm ready." She slipped into her vehicle, the small trailer
already hooked on behind, and started the engine.

"Safe journey, Gwen. Text me when you get there,"
Cathryn called out.

Gwen's eyes sparkled. She waved a gloved hand and pulled
away. And just like that, Gwen was gone.

Cathryn attempted a brave smile to mask that familiar
ache of loss. She waved until the car and trailer disappeared
from sight. Her tears fell freely. Her friendship with Gwen
would change now—probably diminish—and that harsh
reality cut Cathryn to the core.

The bitter east wind gnawed at her back, shredding the
delusion in which she'd long wrapped herself. She could deny
it no longer. Change was upon her. Like it or not, ready or
not. She could hide from it—alone, detached. Or she could
take the reins and ride out to meet it, and create the life she
desired with the years that remained.

Like Gwen was doing.

Like she herself did all those years ago when she first
moved west.

When facing obstacles from the saddle, or in life,

Cathryn had always been inspired by the old horsemanship adage to 'throw your heart over the fence and the horse will follow.'

Was she too old to jump fences now?

She shivered and retreated to her car.

≈

Over the years, Cathryn had left Fullerton many times. The city was known for its scenic river, which twisted lazily through it from north to south. The river would always remind her of her first boyfriend, Mitch. He was a good-natured, outdoorsy guy with a tree fort by the river in a good climbing tree. Together they'd tramped through the woods, swam, skated on the river, and kissed a lot.

The breakup was tough; a tearful night at one of the boy-girl parties in someone's basement in Valley View.

The next day she and Mitch met at the river, by design. Together they cast his initial ring—which only she had worn —into the syrupy water.

Somehow through the years she and Mitch remained on good terms, and he later married one of her friends.

Now he too had an obituary, and he lived on only in memory.

≈

The river itself was the site of Cathryn's personal refuge that she called Trinity Rock.

One summer morning, seventeen-year-old Cathryn had arrived at the farm where she boarded her first horse, Trinity, a feisty tri-colored paint pony. She'd saved up her own money to buy him, and paid his board herself with her allowance and babysitting money. Her family didn't hold with horses; thought them a pastime only for the wealthy.

Trinity usually ran to her from across the field, eager for another adventure. That day, instead of Trinity she saw the farmer approaching with calm deliberate steps, his pipe planted firmly in his mouth.

When he stood in front of her he said, "I've been trying to call you, young lady." Fixing her with a grave expression, he shook his head, then gazed across the pasture. He removed the unlit pipe from his mouth and examined it closely.

"Seems your horse got hurt last night, and ... well ... probably two of them were fighting—rearing up, you know—and a steel fence post ... ah ... well ... I'm afraid your horse, he just didn't make it. Bad thing. Terrible accident. I'm more sorry than I can say."

At first she couldn't comprehend. She resisted the words. Then her mind reeled. "No!"

She tried to run, to find Trinity, but the farmer held her back.

"I have to see him!" she cried.

"Don't think you should; not up close." Still holding onto her arm he led her closer to the far paddock, but still some distance away.

There he was, her Trinity, motionless on the ground.

"No, it can't be ..." She choked on the words. "Not Trinity. I can't lose him. I can't ..." Her voice failed. Thousands of moments with her horse flashed through her mind, then shattered into shards that pierced her tender soul.

The farmer shifted uneasily and tucked his pipe into his coveralls pocket. "Want me to cut off a piece of his mane, to remember him by?"

She nodded mutely and fell to her knees. She couldn't even cry.

The farmer returned shortly with a handful of the precious mane, all three colors: brown, black, and white. She pressed it to her heart.

She had no memory of going home that day. There was no home anymore. Her fondest love, her greatest joy, her truest friend was gone. In one blinding moment, nothing mattered. All hope perished. The light of her spirit was snuffed out.

Those summer days passed in a dull blur. One hazy afternoon, her father asked her to go for a drive. They headed into the countryside and at a big bend in the river he parked the car next to a cornfield. Without a word, he led the way through the trees along a deer trail until they reached the riverbank. There, a flat shelf of rose-colored stone emerged from the water. It was large; five people could easily stand on it. Her father sat down on the rock. She sat beside him, dangling her legs. His eyes remained on the river. Neither of them spoke. The sun-warmed stone and the gentle lap of the water offered their comforts, but her wound was deep.

Her desperate heart clutched at the steadfastness of the rock platform and she adopted it as her own, spending countless hours there that summer—hours she would have spent with Trinity—watching the river flow, its virtue and strength as undiscovered as her own.

The morning after Gwen's departure, Cathryn woke to the spatter of sleet on the windows. It was Sunday. She put the kettle on, brewed a pot of tea, and curled up on the sofa with her bone china cup to gaze out at the somber day. Usually she enjoyed being at home. She'd never needed crowds and action to be content. But something felt different now.

This cottage was the first home that was all her own—no parents, no roommates, no husbands, no children. As a child, she'd always shared a room with her sister; kids didn't have their own rooms back then, unless they were an only child. She had never lived alone until now.

Cathryn had moved a lot, but not during her childhood—that was all spent in Fullerton, although in several different houses as her parents bought, fixed, and resold their way up the real estate ladder. Since leaving her last childhood home, Cathryn had lived in twelve different houses in various towns and states. Her roots were torn and scattered indeed.

She hadn't foreseen all this moving. She was not, by nature, a rolling stone. Rather, she had always pictured herself the gracious mistress of a country manor that had been, and would be, home to many generations—like *Emma's* Hartfield or Donwell Abbey. Cathryn's own nesting instinct had been strong but unfortunately wasn't shared by the partners she had chosen in the past. Truthfully, none of them had been at all suited to be head of a manor.

For her, home and love were curiously entwined. She took a sip of tea as fragments from films and songs floated through her mind: *Home is where the heart is. Love is a many splendored thing. There's no place like home. Love is all around. Country roads, take me home. Crazy love. Homeward bound. All you need is love.*

Her cottage was home, for now. But no human love waited there for her, silently or otherwise. Had she abandoned the quest for love? She squirmed. Possibly she had, but she also didn't want to be on a quest at this stage of life.

She eyed the calico cat sprawled across her lap, purring, and she petted the silky coat. Cathryn agreed with Austen that there *was* nothing like staying at home for real comfort. Though surely it might be comfier with a companion? A male human companion? She frowned. Could there be love without a quest? Could there be home without love?

The cat tipped her head back, inviting Cathryn to stroke her throat. Honored at such trust, she obliged, appreciating the softness of Elinor's multicolored fur. Marianne lay on the back of the big chair by the window, watching birds. The dogs dozed at Cathryn's feet. Her tea had grown tepid but she wasn't finished pulling at the loose threads of her tapestry.

From the moment she'd left home she'd been searching, but for what? Adventure? Love? A home? She wanted something she could count on. An ever fixèd mark. Bob had given her his love, utterly and completely, but she had seemed to want more. Something tangible. Like a home.

Was I pushing the river, even then?

She leaned against the cushions and closed her eyes, drifting back to the northern California days of hippies and flower power, when she first met Bob. Then her mind floated on to a recent visit to Marin County, when she'd found all seven houses she had lived in there. Sadly, the little cabin in Black Point that overlooked the Petaluma River was being torn down. It had been a summer retreat for wealthy San Franciscans in times past, when retreats *were* little cabins. She had rocked her first baby at that big window, watching the brackish river water empty into the bay.

When had she gotten lost?

The doors all opened so easily then. Too easily. In her big move to California she had found true love, a creative career, land she loved—all her dreams were coming true, all at once. So much happiness. Too much happiness. Afraid of losing it, she pushed Bob away—fully aware she was choosing Steve over Bob precisely because she *didn't* love Steve. No love, no loss. A tragically misguided attempt to shield herself; a preemptive strike at pain. She had never really sorted it out. She had simply buried it. Under a stone. A big heavy stone.

Jack had somehow dislodged that stone and exposed her neglected wound to the light, forcing her to look at it again. In *Persuasion*, Anne had said, 'All the privilege I claim for my own sex ... is that of loving longest, when existence or when (all) hope is gone.'

Bob was gone. So was Trinity.

Could she free her heart from that graveyard?

CHAPTER SEVEN

*G*wen called the evening of the first snowfall.

"This was the best thing I could have done," she said, referring to her move. "I've met new people and everyone is so friendly."

A twinge of envy pinched at Cathryn as the big flakes drifted against her window.

"And how is it, being around all the kids?" Gwen had no children of her own. Wayne's kids had all been in high school by the time he and Gwen married.

"Surprisingly good," Gwen replied. "Of course, when things get too loud or crazy, I retreat to my own quarters and leave it all to my niece." She laughed.

"One of the perks of being a great aunt, or a grandma—we can hand them back. So, overall it sounds like your move has been great."

"Overall, it has. Oh, there was some of the expected loneliness, and a bit of 'mover's remorse' at first, but it's all worked out."

"How is the weather there? Are you snowed in a lot?"

"Actually, no. It snows often, sometimes heavily, but it melts faster here than it ever did in Quinn. Even the climate is agreeable. I hope you will come for a visit."

"Of course I will. I can't wait to see your new life first-hand. Well, I'll *have* to wait until the weather changes."

A leaden weight pressed on her heart. She missed Gwen even more than she'd feared.

One frigid February day in the tack room at the barn, Cathryn and the vet were stomping their feet in a futile effort to warm up. The vet mentioned the upcoming horse fair in Fullerton. She was on the events committee.

"We're trying to showcase some new and different activities this year, besides the usual barrel racing and rodeo events. Any ideas? Or connections to someone who might share their less typical horse activities?"

Cathryn's mind leapt back to that hot, humid day at the funeral home. "I know someone on the polo team there. Have they ever done a demo at the horse fair?"

The vet considered. "Not for several years. Can you contact your person?"

"Sure." Her heart fluttered. A door was inching open. That little ember of hope she'd tucked away began to glow. Obviously, she would have to call Jack. Fate *was* taking a hand. Her mind flitted here and there with possibilities, but failed to light on the harsh reality that Jack had never contacted her about the polo lesson, or anything else.

The next day, as she summoned the courage to make this hopeful phone call, the memory of another hopeful phone call took her back to the Bay Area, at the waning of the Haight-Ashbury days. It was where she first met Bob, while vacationing there with his older brother, her boyfriend at the time. *Tres* awkward. As the three of them made their way over the Golden Gate Bridge and through the rainbow tunnel into Marin County, her world shifted. A veil was pulled back, revealing a whole new realm to the naive girl from the prairie. Very like *Northanger Abbey*'s Catherine Morland arriving in Bath for the first time.

That day, Cathryn McNeil fell deeply in love with Marin County—and with Bob's teasing wit and kind eyes. The mutual magnetism that flowed between Bob and herself, though wordless and unseen, was nearly overpowering. It was difficult to maintain a respectful distance during the family visit. When she returned to Fullerton, Cathryn broke up with Bob's brother. It turned out there had not been much affection in the case after all, on either side.

Wild to head west again, she worked three jobs to earn enough cash to set off in her battered car with her dog by her side. "I'm just heading west to see what I find," she told her friends. But in her heart she knew Bob was calling her home.

When she reached Marin, she had found a pay phone and, throwing her heart over the fence, dialed his number with trembling fingers. He was as thrilled as she at the reconnection. Love bloomed. Life was grand. So grand that after a short time fear gripped her—fear of losing such joy—and she stopped listening to her heart.

She looked now at her cell phone with trepidation. Could she be so lucky again—to have a second chance at such a connection? Her pulse pounded in her ears. Summoning her courage, she threw her heart over that fence again, pressed the green circle, and waited breathlessly.

"Riverside Clinic, how may I help you?" The brusque voice of Jack's secretary startled her. Was it terribly improper to call his office? It was the only number she could find.

"Oh, yes, hello. Can I leave a message for Jack … um, I mean Dr. Stone? No, I'm not a patient, this is about polo." She left her number and clicked off, surprised to find herself gasping, and more than a little shaky. Junior high indeed.

Then she laughed out loud. Suddenly she felt very young. Very alive. And exceedingly hopeful.

～

The following day her phone rang, showing a protected number. She frowned, then realized it could be Jack.

"Cathryn, how have you been? Doing much riding?"

She blinked. Riding? In the dead of winter? Overcome at the sound of his voice, she spluttered, "Well, with no indoor arena, I'm afraid not."

"Oh. How is work?" he said.

"Well, it's law, so mostly tedious."

Does he think I'm calling to chat? To ask him out?

She choked out, "Do you have a lot of patients this time of year?"

What must he think of me?

"Uh, I'm usually busy year round. It's not seasonal." He paused, then said, "And your parents? They're doing well? It was nice to see your mom."

She had to smile at his Austenesque inquiry, then took a breath and brought up the horse fair.

"We haven't been involved recently because it didn't drum up any new players like we'd hoped. But you should talk to Fielding. He's the one who'd speak for the club." He gave her Dan Fielding's number.

Then the call was over, before she'd even caught her breath. She stared stupidly at her phone. No mention of the polo invitation, or of getting together. Nothing to reward her hope. With regret she realized *she* hadn't proposed a plan either, or mentioned the polo lesson. *She* hadn't tried to resolve anything, just like Deb said. Tears pricked at her eyes. Was the polo thing just a line? Is Jack just a dream I've created in my head?

The advice given in *Emma* came to her: 'Let his behavior be your guide.'

But Jack's behavior was so contradictory—how could it possibly guide her? Or was he sending a message she just didn't want to hear? She was as vexed with herself for dwelling on it as she was with him. Like Mr. Elton in *Emma*, 'he will not come to the point ... he advances inch by inch and will hazard nothing ...' Was Jack like Mr. Elton? Heaven forbid!

But what *was* he like, really? She hardly knew. Had she taken some random snip of reality and fashioned from it a dream man who didn't exist—except in the imagination of her hopeful heart?

That evening she rang Dan Fielding. Things looked promising for the horse fair. If Jack's polo club was exhibiting, odds are he'd be there, right?

It was weak reasoning. But it was all she had.

The day of the horse fair dawned cold and cloudy, with a heavy March wind from the northwest. Blizzard warnings and travel advisories clogged the airwaves around Quinn.

Cathryn was torn. She ached to see Jack again, but had no assurance he'd even be there. Better to be housebound with her animals than stuck somewhere on the road alone.

That night the blizzard hit full force. She was snowed in for two days, safe and cozy at home, reading about *Persuasion*'s Captain Wentworth.

And wondering about Jack.

CHAPTER EIGHT

*A*pril was unpredictable on the prairie. The air might be gentle with the warmth of spring, or residents might be ambushed in a raging blizzard.

Cathryn poured a cup of tea and made her way to the glider on the porch. She settled in to enjoy the bird songs with a cat on each side of her and the dogs at her feet. Her fresh brew was crisp and bright, unlike the weather of the world. Today soft gray clouds mottled the sky, but it looked like the rain would hold off for a time.

After Jack's confusing behavior and Gwen's move, Cathryn was ready for a fresh start. Her eyes had been opened, and her interest in Jack was melting like the last remnants of snow. But when she aimed her sights toward a new future—one that might include a new love—she simply couldn't picture how that might look. Only that it must be very different from the past.

It was far easier to know what she *didn't* want. Two of her dates from the previous summer—the only two since her most recent divorce—were fine examples of that. She took a sip of tea and leaned back to reflect.

Date Number One had been a reunion of sorts with a former love who was also single again, for the fifth time. Nick was an entertaining chap and, though he would not be called handsome, had always had a certain charisma—which she had dubbed 'that musician thing.' Although she wasn't sure if playing the tambourine was all that musical. His long blonde mane and hot body had been prime attractions back in the day. The blonde mane was now a thin balding ponytail and the hot body was now slumped and paunchy. Like an older—and not improved—Frank Churchill from *Emma*.

Nick had come to visit from Fullerton and toward the end of an afternoon of chatting about old times he wheedled, "So what's for dinner? I remember you being a really good cook."

She hadn't planned on him staying for a meal. And rather thought he should take her out to eat. On the bright side, it *would* be nice to have company for dinner. Most of her meals were eaten alone while reading or watching Austen or some other beloved book or film. She rarely read or watched anything new and puckered her brow at that observation.

After scanning her pantry and refrigerator she said, "How about spaghetti and a salad?" She pulled out onion and garlic and began chopping.

Quinn, like other small towns, didn't include the unmarried in dinner invitations; at least not unmarried women. Single men—pitied as poor starving souls—were often invited for a meal as a kindness. It was assumed single women could fend for themselves. It may also have been assumed they were husband hunting, so they were kept at arm's length when husbands were around. In Cathryn's generation, women definitely outnumbered men. Sadly, sharing an evening meal with friends played no part in Cathryn's limited social life.

Although she often had lunch or coffee with her women friends, couples and singles did not mix—for meals, or for much of anything. She missed the casual society in California where people of all levels, ages, couple status, and ethnicities mingled. Was it because she'd been younger then? Had it truly been a more inclusive culture, or just a more open era? Today's small-town society did echo the nineteenth-century society of *Emma*'s Highbury in many ways. She put the sauce on to simmer and filled a pot with water.

Meanwhile, here was Nick in her kitchen, drinking her wine and plinking unrecognizable tunes on her guitar. He made no offer to help with the meal, and his music—if it could be called that—was less than entertaining.

She scowled, recognizing this once-familiar 'mothering the creative boy' routine. As the evening progressed, she became aware of how far she'd come from the past they'd shared. She enjoyed a glass of wine with dinner. He finished the bottle and opened another. Apparently Nick remained firmly lodged in Never-Grow-Up-Land.

When it grew late, Cathryn assumed another familiar role with not a little resentment. "Nick, you shouldn't drive back to Fullerton after drinking so much. You're welcome to sleep here, on the sofa, and get an early start in the morning."

He nodded and smiled.

After more wine (for him) and more guitar plinking, she announced she was heading to bed.

He stood and lunged toward her. "How about a kiss?"

She stepped back and glared at him. "Nick, we've been friends forever but I just don't think about you that way anymore."

His face was all astonishment.

He sulked, and slept on the sofa.

She slept well, and alone.

∼

Date Number Two, that same summer, had been with Karl, Georgia's husband's friend. Georgia was an acquaintance of Cathryn's, with whom she had a blossoming friendship—she thought. Georgia was gregarious in ways Cathryn was not, and had invited her to several home sales parties and introduced her to a new circle of people who mostly had a lot more money than Cathryn did. Was this how Harriet Smith had felt amongst Emma's wealthy circle of Highbury friends?

The phone rang. Cathryn cringed at the caller ID; it was Karl again. They had a dinner date—a blind date—set for next week, but she certainly didn't want to talk to him every night until then. Karl lived a couple of hours away. Cathryn was uncomfortable with his intensity on the phone but decided to stay open-minded—maybe he was just enthusiastic ... or nervous. She understood nervous.

The day of the date arrived and she watched through the window as Karl pulled up in a big boat of a Buick. He wore a clingy polo shirt and shiny pleated dress slacks. His lank gray hair was slicked back, heavily greased, definitely untouchable. She wrinkled her nose. This was not how he looked in the emailed photo, which she now guessed was more than 'a few years old.'

Her heart sank at this first impression and she struggled to maintain her countenance as she greeted him. He dressed like her grandpa had decades ago, but without the fedora. A fedora would have been an improvement. But perhaps his spirit was livelier than his appearance suggested. She could always hope. She was good at hope.

Dinner was *very* quiet—on her part. A wan smile was frozen on her face while they dined at the only nice restaurant in Quinn. Afterward they returned to her house and found seats on the screened-in porch. She made an honest effort to discover a charming personality. Karl didn't notice her silence during dinner or afterward, and seemed equally unaware that he'd droned on about himself all evening, like a modern-day Mr. Collins from *Pride & Prejudice*.

She managed to wedge a question into his monologue. "Are you staying with Ken and Georgia on this trip?"

His eyes opened wide and he stared at her. "You mean I'm not staying here?"

She chuckled. Surely he was joking.

His startled expression said he was not.

Cathryn pasted on her weary smile one more time. "Well, Karl, thank you for dinner. It was nice to make your acquaintance."

His eyes opened wider, but he followed her to the screen door. It slammed shut behind him with a satisfying crack.

Karl didn't call again.

Neither did Georgia.

Cathryn was most seriously not displeased.

She shook her head at those memories and drained her teacup. She could laugh about them now. But surely there were heroic men out there, somewhere. Or had they become extinct over the years? Were the only good men fictional?

The clouds merged and with a clap of thunder released their rain. Cathryn scurried indoors and poured another cup of tea. As she settled at the table, she recalled Lizzy's words in *Pride & Prejudice*: 'The more I get to know of the world, the more I am dissatisfied with it. There are few people of whom I approve, and even fewer that I really love.'

She knew exactly how Lizzy felt.

Was her only option to set the bar low or be alone? She wondered again if she required too much.

Then the opposite notion all but smacked her in the face —maybe she had never required *enough!* She blinked. Perhaps Emma had it right when she said, 'I always deserve the best treatment because I will not put up with any other.' Cathryn had never been that decisive in her life, especially regarding relationships. She'd been more like a small boat, buffeted about, lost at sea.

It was definitely time for honest evaluation and a new plan.

In the past Cathryn had selected men from her own sphere or below, usually fixer-uppers or charming n'er-do-wells. She was skilled at seeing potential and possibilities in people—a great asset in her work with children but a serious flaw when choosing romantic partners. It occurred to her that while focusing on the potential of a partner she had overlooked essentials.

Her parents were from an era when education and wealth formed distinctive ranks and, as members of the lower middle class, they were in awe of doctors, lawyers, and the rich. In their time, few people crossed ranks, in either direction. Her parents had happily kept to their own level, and encouraged their daughters to do the same. No 'uppity' aspirations or liaisons were tolerated.

Cathryn, now a professional herself, had friends who were doctors and lawyers, and a few friends who were quite wealthy, but they certainly did not inspire her awe. Then again, these were women friends, or married couples she knew. She had never dated such a man. Ever. Maybe she could broaden her sphere? That seemed harmless enough.

Regardless of sphere, she wanted an honorable, worthy man. One who was 'truly the best man I have ever known.' One who did not need prodding or convincing to be with her. No more pushing the river.

She sighed. Obviously this new plan excluded Jack.

But to her surprise, a sense of relief lit her from within. It became apparent that the burden need not be on *her* to find a man with potential that she would prod and shape and develop. No! This new perspective placed the burden just where it ought to be—on the man himself. He must have an admirable character fully developed, and already possess the proper essentials. He must be a hero and a gentleman.

Her body buzzed with a wild new energy. She hadn't considered romantic love in quite this way before. Bob *had* been such a man, exactly as he was—and that was why, with him, it had all been so easy, so natural. It all made sense now. Surely there must be other men like him. And she only needed one. Bob would approve this new perspective. He had always wanted her happiness.

With this fresh insight, and free of a burden that had never rightfully been hers, she was at last able to let Bob go and look forward rather than back. The fog lifted.

She toasted her teacup to the air and drank heartily.

Welcome, spring.

CHAPTER NINE

*T*he May sunshine was abundant, the air soft, and the summer bugs had not yet hatched. Longer days meant Cathryn could ride almost every evening after work. Occasionally there were others to ride with, especially if she and Henry were schooling in the arena. But he was already well schooled. She knew he preferred being out on the trails, and she indulged him.

Although thoughts of Jack sometimes whispered at the back of her mind, she'd done her best to bury that ember and move on. However, Quinn was a very small town, and the pool of datable men a mere puddle. Without meaning to be impertinent, she found none of them suitable. So on the advice of friends Cathryn signed up at a well-known internet dating site and was surprised at the number of matches, if she set her preferences beyond Quinn.

"It's like a part-time job," she explained to Lisa on the phone. "There are so many guys. Where does one begin?"

Lisa laughed. "At the beginning, of course. Maybe tighten up your requirements? Reduce your geographic range? Or focus on one state each week?"

Now it was Cathryn's turn to laugh. "Good ideas, but what a project. And I'm not sure—it just doesn't feel like a natural way to meet people."

"What are your options?"

Cathryn frowned. "Good point. Guess I have a new part-time job."

The next day during lunch she sat down, sandwich in hand, to scroll through the latest contenders. To her surprise, a cryptic message popped up from Lisa:

"We need to talk."

Cathryn immediately wrote back:

"What's up?"

Lisa replied:

"Jack's secretary called me for your contact information. I said I couldn't give it without your okay. So …?"

Cathryn was baffled. Didn't Jack already have her number from when she'd called his office about the horse fair? She typed back:

"Okay. Give him my cell, and this email. How curious after such a long time."

Lisa had a different opinion:

"How intriguing. I'll message you when I've sent it."

True to her word, Lisa confirmed when the information had been sent.

And true to form, there was no response from Jack.

The dazzling days of June were at hand and Jack's odd request still wreaked havoc with Cathryn's newfound serenity. Why would he stir the pot and then do nothing? Thinking of Austen's Edward Ferrars—whose reason for mixed signals and disappearances was a pivotal plot point in *Sense & Sensibility*—made Cathryn wonder what Jack's reason might be, if he had one. Or if a plot even existed in their rather empty story.

Then she caught herself. No! I'm not going there again. She would put him out of her mind, relying again on Emma's wisdom: 'I may have lost my heart, but not my self-control.'

A few days later Cathryn perched at her desk with a cup

of tea, which nearly sloshed into her saucer when she saw an email from Jack himself.

"How have you been? Riding much? Get to Fullerton often?"

Casual, non-committal, vague. Why is he so shootin' vague? She read it again and decided to respond in kind, letting his behavior be her guide.

Jack's vagueness brought to mind a phone call she'd had from a college boyfriend while the two were apart for the summer. At a lull in the phone conversation he had said, "What would you say if I asked you to marry me?"

She had paused, then said, "Well, are you asking me?"

"I don't know," he mumbled.

Apparently Never-Grow-Up-Land had many inhabitants.

Two days later another—chattier—email arrived from Jack:

"You and your horse okay after that storm? How close were those tornadoes? I've been playing matches around the region. Still looking for another polo pony. Let me know if you hear of a prospect; you know what I'm looking for. How often do you get down this way? Between matches and my ranch out west, I'm not often in town on weekends, but I'd like to set something up and show you how to play polo, like we talked about. Which upcoming weekends work for you?"

She let out a whoop—part joy and part relief. With tremendous effort she kept her sensibilities in check and waited a day before responding, once again in kind.

After a few more emails, the day and time were set and cell phone numbers exchanged. She would have a polo lesson. And she would ride with Jack. It was as beautiful as a dream.

Lost in that dream, she forgot to ask if it was a date or just recruiting for the polo team.

She forgot how she detested vagueness.

And Deb's comments completely slipped her mind.

CHAPTER TEN

*T*he long-awaited Saturday arrived; the day they would play polo. The sluggish sun rose late, bleeding into a brooding sky. 'Red sky at morning, sailors take warning.' This sultry weather usually produced thunderstorms—or tornadoes. Cathryn remembered Grandma Esther calling these 'the dog days.' But even threatening weather could not dull her enthusiasm for today's ride with Jack.

She and her sister had spent a busy week in Fullerton helping their parents move into an apartment after selling their home of forty-some years. So many memories. So much stuff! She was physically exhausted and every emotional nerve tingled. That was the only house she had lived in for more than five years. Ever. After lunch she departed for her polo lesson.

The polo field had used to be a cornfield and was located just across the road from Trinity Rock. Cathryn hadn't been out there in years. Young Cathryn had spent many sorrowful nights perched on the steep ridges that overlooked the cornfield, watching the moon rise over the winding river and aching for Trinity. Her dad had informed her that homes had been built on the ridge. She'd always meant to live there herself, on the riverbank at Trinity Rock.

Lost in thought, she nearly missed the sign to turn off the

highway. Truthfully, she was a little nervous about seeing Jack again. But it would be comforting to be near a place where she'd always felt such a sense of belonging. And to ride there —Trinity would be pleased. A smile lit her face as she turned off the oil road, oblivious to the thunderheads gathering in the northwest. A joyous warmth spread through her limbs as she made her way down the familiar gravel road that wound down to the river. Home. She was coming home.

After nosing her truck onto the path that led to the polo field on the north, she spied a horse trailer parked under some trees. Four horses were tied to it. The setting was picturesque—a lush valley and green field surrounded by ridges and trees, all laced together by the shining river. Shafts of sunlight broke through the clouds that stirred overhead.

As her truck made the curve Jack looked up and waved.

Cathryn parked and then made her way to where he stood. In her excitement she greeted him with an exuberant hug, forgetting they were practically strangers.

Startled, he drew back.

She blushed at her blunder.

He managed to put an arm around her in an awkward kind of side hug, and gave her a quizzical smile. He was dressed in jeans, an old T-shirt, a baseball hat, and well-worn cowboy boots. Nothing highbrow.

He immediately steered the conversation to the horses, introducing her to the geldings and sharing a story about each. His love for the horses was obvious; they were not just performers to him. In addition to being well cared for, the horses were calm and comfortable in his presence. Her respect for him grew, as a horseman and as a man.

"Well, now that you know each of the boys, which one—"

"Oh, Jack, I forgot my helmet. Do you have any extras?"

He looked dubious. "Just the one I use for matches. You can try it on. It's inside the trailer door."

She reached in for the helmet and put it on her head. It dropped down over her eyes to the tip of her nose. She looked out at him and laughed.

He chuckled. "We won't need helmets today anyway; we'll be keeping the ball on the ground."

"And if anything does happen, we have a doctor in the house," she quipped.

He colored and turned back to preparing the tack.

Her shoulders clenched at his puzzling response but she shook it off. Without a helmet she needed some way to keep her hair out of her eyes so she could look down to hit the ball. She trotted over to her truck and dug out her battered straw cowboy hat, pushed it into some semblance of a shape, and secured it on her head. She always kept a few spare hair bands on her gearshift so she braided the longer length of her hair to hold it out of the way.

Meanwhile, the air had grown heavy; so much so that it was an effort to breathe. She glanced up. The menacing clouds had stalled in the darkening sky. Then slowly they began to turn. Rotation was never a good sign. The hairs prickled on the back of her neck. Thunder rumbled above, echoing eerily off the water. Lightning crackled in the sky to the north, with several bolts making the lethal cloud-to-ground contact.

A shudder crept up her back and she glanced nervously toward the horse trailer. The horses were still calm, which reassured her. She took a deep breath and started back toward them. As she walked, she took in the scene—the land, the stormy sky, the horses, and Jack—to lock it in her memory, like a scene from a treasured movie. One she would take out and watch again and again.

Jack was showing her how to grip the mallet when the rain started. Just a few giant drops at first, but in minutes they were being pelted. He just kept talking while rain cascaded off the brim of his hat like a waterfall! She stared at him in disbelief. A loud clap of thunder struck close by and she jumped.

He peered up at the sky, suddenly aware, and laughed sheepishly. "Sorry. Here, hop in my truck." He opened the door for her and then got in on the driver's side himself, bringing the mallet so they could continue the lesson. Thunder boomed around them, but he kept up a steady stream of instruction.

She pursed her lips to hide her amusement.

In minutes the truck windows were steamed up. He looked slightly alarmed and turned the key to engage the defroster. A blast of music drowned out the thunder. With a flush, he quickly shut it off. It was classical music but she hadn't heard enough to recognize the piece. She was sure she didn't know any man who listened to classical music—in his truck—wearing cowboy boots. Her heart warmed.

It was a struggle to focus on the lesson. Sensations flooded her body and soul—the resonance of his voice, his warm scent, the relentless rain on the roof, and the explosive thunder around them. She watched his hands, long and strong, as he demonstrated the different grips. She yearned to touch those hands. This was a vivid daydream come to life.

Jack continued talking.

As the rain spattered noisily on his truck, she recalled a favorite John Sebastian song, heard one rainy day at the stables many years ago when she had first started riding lessons, paid for with her meager allowance. "You and Me and Rain on the Roof." Kismet.

The fierce storm moved through quickly, leaving a watery sun in its wake. They quit the truck and wiped down the wet saddles and the horses. Jack saddled a horse for her, then tacked up his own mount. As she stood next to the tall gelding she would ride, it was obvious her foot couldn't reach the stirrup to mount—it was at the height of her chin.

Jack cast his eyes around in concern. "I'm not sure I have anything you can stand on."

"Why don't you just give me a leg up?" She bent her left leg back at the knee and reached toward the saddle. "Just don't toss me too far. I don't want to land in a heap on the other side."

He lifted an eyebrow, leaned over to grasp her knee, and boosted her.

"Like a feather."

She smiled and settled easily into the saddle.

He eyed her with admiration, then adjusted her stirrups and checked the girth again. "Okay, does everything fit you?"

"Yes, it's perfect," she said, gathering the reins. "Thanks."

He grabbed two mallets and mounted his own horse, then tapped a ball toward the field. "Let's take a couple turns around the field first, so you can get used to your horse."

A light breeze was sweeping the clouds off to the south and the heaviness was gone from the air. The rain had released the rich smell of the soil.

Cathryn had used a double bridle before, but not with all four reins in one hand, so Jack rode up next to her and leaned in to help her with the finger positions and directional technique. Then he moved off and demonstrated different ways to attack the ball with the mallet.

She was fascinated. "Do you really do all this at a canter?"

He laughed. "You've never seen it played in real life? We're usually at full gallop! Come to our next match and see for yourself."

Another invitation? Better and better.

He turned his horse toward her. "Let's move the ball back and forth between us as we ride over the field at a walk. You try to hit the ball ahead toward the other end. If you miss it, I'll ride around behind and move it up."

Their back and forth actions became a kind of dance, each rider moving as one with their horse and each pair twining gracefully around the other. Cathryn was wholly engrossed in the rhythm of the movement, the smell of the horses, the creak of the saddles, and Jack's eyes seeking hers at every turn. It seemed they were floating in a timeless realm. She couldn't catch her breath, yet she hardly needed to breathe. Jack's eyes shone. She heard the melody of her own laughter and rejoiced at his responding lopsided grin.

Once she grasped the basic skills, their conversation grew livelier. In the end, there was more talking than polo playing. He asked about her kids, her work, her marriages, her sister.

She asked about his work, his ranches, his brothers, and his travels. Laughter sparkled between them, and she felt her face wreathed in smiles.

During their conversation, he offered no information about his romantic status—and she didn't ask. She couldn't bear to disturb this dream. Besides, it might look like she was fishing for a date. She cringed at that and so justified her avoidance of the hard questions. She would wait, to see if he spoke first.

To her surprise he did, in a way. Or was it just idle conversation? She couldn't be sure.

"Do you have to leave tonight?" he asked, hitting a ball her way.

Her eyes darted to his face.

"Uh, I mean, are you staying in town, or ... or driving back to Quinn?"

Her heart leapt. Was he thinking of such a possibility? She wished she could give him a different answer.

"I really have to go back tonight. I haven't made any other arrangements for my dogs. My neighbor Harry has been watching them but he's leaving later today to visit his daughter out of town." She sighed.

Jack made no comment. His face was turned away.

Was he disappointed? Or had that just been a casual question that he'd already forgotten?

Silence hung like a cloud over the sunny field.

Cathryn wasn't comfortable suggesting another time to get together. Had that even been what he was asking? She rummaged for a new topic to turn the conversation. At the funeral home, he'd told her about the house he was building. Her eyes swept the ridge.

"You built a house out here, right?" Several impressive homes topped the ridge that circled the field on the west and north. "Is one of those yours? Can we see it from here?"

He turned back to her, then pointed proudly to the large stone house at the far right.

She gasped. "It's just like Pemberley!" The words spilled out before she could stop them.

He cocked his head. "What's Pemberley?"

She blushed. "Oh, it's Mr. Darcy's home in *Pride & Prejudice*. Jane Austen. I'm a big fan of her novels and the films. You haven't read her?"

"No, I don't think so."

Cathryn was most curious to see his house. While she wasn't one to be impressed by money (other than the freedom and security it could bring), she longed to take in that hilltop view again—the one she knew so well.

"Are you living there yet?"

He just smiled. "Do you have time to come up now and see it?"

"Sure. My wrist is getting a little tired anyway," she said, resting her mallet across the front of her saddle.

They gave the horses another turn around the field on a loose rein, then dismounted near the trailer. She nuzzled her horse affectionately and he lowered his head.

"You went to a lot of work bringing them all up here from your place down by ... where was that?"

"By Sedgeway."

"Oh, yeah. That was really nice of you, Jack."

He flushed and turned to unsaddle the horses. She followed after him, currying and brushing. While they worked, he told her about his most recent polo match.

As they loaded the tack into the trailer she said, "My sister and I have been helping our folks move out of their house on Prairie Street; you know, in Valley View. They lived there forty-nine years. Can you imagine?"

"I've been to that house! One of your sister's basement parties."

They shared a laugh at those memories.

"How are your parents?" she asked.

He shook his head. "Neither of them is in very good health." He spoke with marked concern about his mother, who had recently been hospitalized.

Cathryn was touched by his candor on such short acquaintance.

But when he spoke of his father, there was a marked change. She was taken aback by his frown and the bitterness in his voice.

In an effort to lighten the mood, she said, "Well, I've heard your dad is quite the character."

His expression was stony, his voice strained. "No. No, he's greedy. And cruel."

She was speechless. Gone was his easy smile. Jack's face was tense and drawn. He busied himself with the grooming tools, securing them on the inside of the trailer door. Clearly there was a lot of water under that bridge, churning like the deadly whirlpools in the river.

"He's not a good person," he muttered. "Let's go up to the house now."

CHAPTER ELEVEN

"We can take my truck up the hill," Cathryn offered, noting Jack's was still hitched to his trailer. He had his back to her. His shoulders were stiff. She eyed him warily.

"I'll walk." His tone was glum and he wouldn't look at her.

She was at a loss. The only reply she could manage —"Oh"—was barely audible.

Then anger stirred in her at his self-indulgent moodiness. Whatever was causing him pain was not of her doing. She bristled as she stood by her truck. Perhaps she should leave.

He turned and eyed her, as if sizing her up, and then shrugged. "Sorry. Yes, of course I'll ride up with you." He looked a little embarrassed but offered no explanation.

They got in and she made for the road leading to his house. She left it to him to break the silence.

Her eyes darted toward Trinity Rock as they passed. It was now fenced in. Was there a gate? Did he know the owners? Might they let her see it?

As they wound their way up the ridge, he attempted to revive the conversation. "I built here, on the ridge, because Dad owns the polo field and I wanted to keep an eye on it. I'm the only one in the family who plays. I still have my place at Potter's Lake so I've been living there while I've designed and built River Run." He pointed to the wood and stone sign as she eased her truck up the curved driveway.

"River Run," she repeated. "I like it. It flows." She cackled to herself at her wordplay.

He didn't seem to notice.

"Not many people around here name their homes," she mused, "but I always have. Quite the English tradition, you know," she continued, looking over at him. He appeared a little more relaxed; at least he hadn't plastered himself against the pickup door as one boyfriend had their first time together in a vehicle. She smirked at the thought of anyone finding her scary.

"Most of our places are farms or ranches," Jack said. "I think it's more common to name those." He pointed to where she should park.

Cathryn had never known a nonfictional man who had named his home. The men she knew had named their cars or motorcycles, their guitars, or a precious body part. She wondered if Jack had ever done something similar and smiled to herself. He seemed so proper and reserved at times; a lingering reflection of that shy schoolboy?

They left the truck and she gazed at the structure before her. The imposing façade put her in mind that many of Austen's heroes were masters of manor homes or large estates —or about to buy or inherit one. This home, although somewhat smaller than those, could certainly stand among them with pride.

And how did Jack himself compare with those heroes? She didn't know him well enough to say. Among the men from her past only Bob could step forward as a hero. None of the others had owned much of anything. Not that a hero had to be wealthy or own a lot of things, but there was a level of integrity involved in the responsibility and commitment of ownership. The mismatch of herself and her past partners grew more apparent as she was in company with Jack.

River Run was impressive, built of timber and stone—real stone, not a surface layer or the artificial kind that was common. She was eager to see inside and quickly followed him onto the portico, where she couldn't resist touching the wall, solid under her hand. Stone would last forever. Well, forever in human terms. Jack had made a substantial and permanent choice. She looked again at the man beside her. In spite of his quirks, there was much to admire.

He unlocked the door and turned to welcome her.

She couldn't help but grin. At least I'm here with a proper invitation, unlike poor Lizzy at first seeing Pemberley in *Pride & Prejudice*.

Jack's cheerfulness returned full-force as they gained the entrance hall. He guided her through all three levels of the home. By his description of the challenges inherent in the craftwork, it was apparent he had seen to every detail himself, even though others did the actual labor. Stone and wood gave the place a timeless feeling that she marveled at, and esteemed. The home nestled organically into the hillside with the lowest level sunk into the ridge except for one side that opened to the east. The interior had a comfortable, country-manor style, decorated in earthy colors that she thought well-suited. He had chosen well.

But the house was massive. Almost like a castle. Four of her cottages would easily fit within its walls. Could anyone feel cozy in such a place?

Jack entertained her with anecdotes about the discovery of many unique items during his travels. It was obvious he'd enjoyed the entire process of designing and building. At one point, something about his enthusiasm tugged at her; it was very like the consuming passion some gay men had for their homes. She watched him describe with animation how he had stumbled upon and negotiated the purchase of one unusual light fixture, but could come to no conclusion on that head.

There were several ample bedrooms. One bedroom show-cased his collection of violins, under glass. Another displayed quilts and needlework. Several impressionist-style paintings graced the walls in another bedroom. She was asking him about one painting when they entered the master suite; the stunning view swept her words away.

Here was the very sight she had longed to see again. "Oh, how divine to wake to the sunrise over the river!" She hurried to the window, enraptured. They were up high enough for her eye to trace the river's glittering path through the trees.

She and Jack exchanged a look of mutual pleasure and he nodded at her appreciation.

"That's not all," he said. "Don't forget the sun*set* over the hills." He gestured toward a large high window on the west and grinned at her astonishment. The light there had taken on the golden hue of late afternoon.

Jack had seen to both the appearance *and* the function of the house. It was well done. He did not ask, but she approved. She liked it very much indeed. And was sure there were few who would not approve.

They were facing each other across the master bed when chimes sounded.

"The doorbell?"

He glanced out the window and his back stiffened. "Stay here while I handle this." His eyes caught hers; his imploring look made it more of a request than an order and she was content to comply.

As Jack moved toward the stairs, she glanced out the west window. A bright green SUV was parked next to her truck. Jack's booted feet clattered down the stairs. Curious, she tiptoed to the window but the massive entry overhang hid any view of the caller.

Making her way softly to the stairs, Cathryn paused at the landing, quieting her breath to better hear the voices below. She couldn't make out many words, but the rise and fall of a woman's shrill voice was easily discernible. Cathryn's brows knit together. Jack had no sisters. Surely Jeff's wife wouldn't talk to him in that tone, nor would a housekeeper. Only an emotional connection would give rise to such an outburst.

Her practical side prodded her—*ask the difficult question. Find out now.*

She knew that made sense, but she could not be sensible.

Feeling suddenly awkward at being in the master bedroom she considered joining Jack and the caller below, but was reluctant to intrude on whatever emotional exchange was happening between them. Still, her curiosity was piqued. Some women would march right down and confront the pair. But she wasn't like those women. She wasn't even clear about her own role with Jack. Besides, he had asked her to wait.

She quit her perch on the landing and slipped back to the master bedroom to enjoy the view once again. At the east window, she let her eyes follow the meandering river, her heart caressed by tender memories of Trinity.

But before long, the situation downstairs pierced through her nostalgia. Jack had been down there for some time. Her gut twisted. *Was* there someone else? She shuddered and hugged her arms to herself.

Although she felt comfortable so near to Trinity Rock, Cathryn wasn't sure how comfortable she felt in this particular house. Its massive size alone rendered it rather grand. By contrast, she herself had been downsizing and simplifying her own home and life. A life lived here would feel so ... large. Does one's life expand to fill one's space? She had read about people living 'large' in tiny places. Was she really simplifying? Or simply hiding?

But there was something else—something here that prevented a sense of ease, of comfort. She couldn't put her finger on it. She ran her hand over the top of the dresser. Not a speck of dust. This felt more like a hotel than a home— lovely to look at, but impersonal. Lifeless. Like a stage with no actors.

It dawned on her there was nothing alive in the house— no animals, not even any plants. Maybe he didn't live here yet? Was it just for polo guests? No, he had poured his heart and soul into the place, and said he wanted to keep an eye on the polo field, so he must intend to live here. The home's only personal connection to its owner was the small collection of family photos displayed in the lower level, with a few others in the library (the only room she thought entirely too small).

The homiest space was in that lower level, with its giant TV, stone fireplace, and his grandmother's well-worn table and chairs. There Cathryn felt a sense of love and family. Other than that, when she assessed River Run as a home, it came up empty.

Jack, where is your heart?

He had spoken of a ranch out west on the Moody River. Was that the place he truly loved? Then there was Sedgeway, where he kept his horses. And his place at Potter's Lake. Spread out among four houses—it could not be cozy being that scattered. Is he comfortable living like—

She jumped at the slamming of the entry door below.

Jack's boots tapped up the steps and she turned from the window as he entered the room. The light that had played in his eyes during the house tour was dimmed. He looked ill at ease. In a subdued voice he said, "I'm sorry about that," but offered no explanation about the visitor.

"Is everything okay?" she asked, risking being intrusive.

His eyes narrowed, then burned with the acrimony she'd heard when he'd spoken earlier of his father. Jack turned away, toward the west window.

If he were a closer friend, she would encourage him to talk, try to comfort him. But there was no understanding between them, not even of friendship. Further inquiry might invade his privacy or even assault his pride. His rigid demeanor told her to keep her distance.

The light had shifted in the room. Out the west window the sky now glowed with hues of rose and lavender. She would need to head back to Quinn soon. If only he would invite her to dinner. She didn't know him well enough to suggest it herself and was reluctant to do so after this episode with his visitor and his own moodiness.

His voice was dull when he broke the silence. "I suppose you need to get back to your dogs."

To my dogs?

He turned toward the door and she followed him wordlessly down the stairs and out the great entry doors. He avoided her eyes. Her pickup rumbled down the hill, carrying them back to the paddocks and the field, back to the scene of magical connection which now seemed to have occurred in some other place and time, and with a very different man.

He got out, closed the door to her truck, and stood stiffly just outside the passenger window. His face was grave while they exchanged perfunctory thank-yous.

This stilted interaction cut her deeply. Tears stung at her eyes. What a landslide of all the wonder that just an hour ago had borne her heavenward with joy.

He attempted a smile when he said, "It was nice of you to come give polo a try."

Out of habit, she maintained a neutral countenance and voice. "Well, it was fun, Jack."

She felt nothing. Numb. Where is *my* heart? If only I could fight with him, shake him, pound on his chest. Does he really have no idea how special this day was for me? How long-awaited? Had it not been special for him too? Or had she just imagined it because she wished it to be so? Her feelings were powerful but seemed far away, churning underwater somewhere beyond her reach. She could not summon them to action. Instead she clamped down on her grieving heart, respecting his need for distance—or was that her need?

"And I loved seeing your home," she continued in a voice that sounded strangely detached from herself. "It's a work of art. Really, Jack, it's splendid!" At least that was the truth.

His eyes softened a little and met hers.

She took a small chance and said, "I'd love to see a real polo game played. Is the season over?"

His neutral public persona returned. "Actually we're hoping to host a match here in two weeks, but it's not certain yet. I can let you know." His smile had warmed enough to hold a confusing hint of promise.

Twilight was descending and shadows began to fill the hidden spaces. He looked at the sky.

"It'll be dark by the time you're on the road." Thrusting his head into the pickup cab from the passenger side, he made an unexpected request. "Text me when you get home, so I know you made it safely?"

After all that had happened, she was puzzled by this, and not a little irritated. But if she was good at nothing else, she was good at being agreeable; skilled at the masquerade. "Sure. Ok."

A fleeting shadow passed over his face. She could not say what it expressed. He moved toward the horses and called out, "Don't be a stranger," then turned and left her with a wave of his hand.

Her eyes filled with tears as she mindlessly followed the winding road up and out of the river valley. This wasn't how it was supposed to turn out! Conflicting emotions beat at her senses. Hurt, sorrow, anger, disappointment—all battled to lead the attack on her fragile flicker of hope.

'Don't be a stranger'?

Excerpts from the day played and replayed in her mind during the dark drive back to Quinn. Every bone and muscle ached from such a physical week, and her heart was weary with the double trauma of saying a final farewell to her childhood home and the confusing interactions with Jack. With a frown she realized they had never gotten past a walk while on horseback. No delightful canter. We were too caught up in conversation, and each other—or so I thought. It felt like magic. And then it didn't.

It was nearly midnight when she opened her front door. She dropped her bags on the floor and flopped onto the sofa. Instantly the dogs piled on top of her, kissing her with delight. Elinor wound around her feet while Marianne nuzzled her hair from the back of the sofa. The louder she laughed the crazier the dogs acted. It's like I've been gone for months! She sighed, grateful for such unconditional love. A whirl of wagging and purring followed her as she fetched treats for each beloved creature. It was good to be home.

Whether at Barton Cottage or Pemberley, home was

about love and those who lived there. She didn't know how or if Jack fit into such a scheme. If she discounted the ending, today was the most fun she'd had with a man since ... Bob. Until Jack sullied it with his moodiness.

Then she remembered his request and grabbed her phone to text him of her safe arrival.

He responded instantly:

"Good, glad to hear it."

So he had been waiting. That buoyed her. Then, as an afterthought, she texted back:

"I just realized we didn't canter. Maybe next time?"

After a few minutes he replied:

"Yes, cantering is more fun."

She groaned. What did he mean? 'Yes' to a next time? Or literally 'yes' cantering is more fun? This man was a lot of work and she was too fagged to put forth any more effort tonight. But that little ember of hope in her heart still glowed. She wanted to see Jack again, even though he had not alluded to a future encounter. Her heart was trying to skip—blindfolded—over that missing piece.

Her practical side doubted another meeting would happen. Except ... she was quite sure she had not just imagined the mutual attraction that held her spellbound during their ride. No, there was some reality to that. There had to be. Certainly she knew the difference between a novel and reality. Didn't she?

She stiffened. This was like junior high again, but with no best friend to send to the potential boyfriend to ask him what he meant, or how he felt about her. And no common setting or activities or acquaintance to assure they would meet again. No, it would be up to her, or him, or fate.

Jack was the most bewildering man she'd ever met.

And so a weary Cathryn drifted into troubled sleep, walking endlessly through the rooms of his fine house.

CHAPTER TWELVE

*W*hat was that Grandma Esther used to say ... 'lucky at cards, unlucky at love'? Cathryn gathered her cards together, shuffled, and dealt herself another hand of Solitaire. Recently she had won at the game more times than not. As she placed an ace, her phone rang.

"Well, how did it go?" Lisa asked, her voice full of anticipation. "Tell me everything."

"How did it go? Lisa, I hardly know. It was marvelous fun while we were riding, even kinda romantic I thought. And he showed me his new house overlooking the polo field."

Lisa was envious; she'd heard about his new house, although Lisa and Jack no longer moved in the same circles.

"So, what have you heard from him?"

"Basically, nothing." Cathryn was aghast, hearing herself speak the truth aloud. "I'm not sure what to make of the whole event. He did have a visitor while he was showing me the house, but he didn't introduce me. He and I were viewing the master suite when she arrived, and he asked me to stay upstairs while he talked to her downstairs. Some woman with a bright green SUV who sounded more than a little angry. He just froze up after that."

"You know, he *had* been connected with a realtor who drives a bright green SUV; she even features it in her ads, like a mascot or something. But that was several years ago." After a thoughtful silence Lisa asked, "What do you think about calling him?"

Cathryn sighed. "Oh, Lisa, I don't think I'm the calling-a-guy type."

"Me either. I get it. I'm glad I'm not out there. But I'll tell you if I hear anything useful. I wish it would work out for you two. I think you'd be great together."

"Thanks. What I need is something to shed some light on his hot and cold behavior. Or explain why he never married." She frowned. "What's wrong with me? I should just give up on him. But I don't want to. Not yet. He seems so nice, until he gets all moody. And he's so blasted ... evasive. Yeah, that's the word. Like trying to grab hold of fog."

Lisa commiserated, but neither of them came up with any explanations or solutions.

Cathryn kept busy. A ride in the countryside on Henry or a long walk with her dogs usually cleared her head for a while, but thoughts of Jack persisted like a dark undercurrent. How had Austen's Elinor borne such frustration with Edward? Cathryn reread *Sense & Sensibility* and watched both recent adaptations again to see if there was some nugget of wisdom she'd missed.

If we could just connect somehow.

She sent him a short friendly email, inviting him to stop in Quinn sometime on the way to his ranch, to meet her horse and go for a ride.

His answer, after two days:

"Thanks, that sounds like fun."

She seethed with frustration. She'd been out of the dating game a long time but was it up to her to pin him down with a place and a time? That just felt ... well ... pushy. Especially when she didn't know if their polo ride had even been a date. With no one to ask, and no Austen-like standard of manners to guide her, she found herself at sixes and sevens.

That possible season-end polo match Jack had talked of was only a few days off. Would he invite her? Was it canceled? A haze of doubt began to dampen her little ember of hope. She made excuses for Jack; all kinds of excuses. He was busy. He had to run two homes, plus a farm and a ranch. He had a demanding professional practice. Maybe his mother got sick again. Maybe ... maybe next time I should check the footing on the other side of a fence before I throw my heart over it.

What was he about anyway? Was he an awkward but well-meaning guy, like Austen's Edward Ferrars? A self-serving flirt like Frank Churchill in *Emma*? Or a corrupt cad like Henry Crawford in *Mansfield Park*? Could a good horseman be a cad? Hmm ... Willoughby, the scoundrel in *Sense & Sensibility,* had been described as a bold rider ... which was not necessarily the same as a good horseman. Nothing answered.

Cathryn brainstormed every possible reason why Jack might not have pursued her. Did he think her below his sphere? Maybe she wasn't 'handsome enough to tempt him'? Her whole one-sided entanglement with Jack was rife with contradictions. And she was devoting far too much energy to sorting it out.

But she couldn't believe she'd been wrong about the strong attraction between them, especially while they were riding. No, she was sure there had been an attraction, a connection on both sides.

≈

After another restless night, she woke early. While preparing a pot of tea, her phone rang.

Gwen!

"I'm calling with an invitation, Cathryn. My niece has recovered from her knee surgery and is back to full duty. So my time is much more my own again and I'm ready for company. How soon can you get away?"

"How's the week after next? I'll check with work."

Gwen then described her new job at a Granite City bookstore and told Cathryn about her volunteer work at the local food pantry.

"Already deep into Granite City community life, aren't you?"

"Of course. It's the best way to meet people." Gwen had always been a joiner and a doer in her quiet, matter-of-fact way.

Cathryn was a little envious. She found it difficult to feel part of a group or a community, unless it involved kids. She was almost always comfortable with kids. Adults had agendas, and she often could not sort out appearances, character, and motivations. Kids rarely had agendas—and if they did, those agendas were usually quite transparent.

Plans for the Wyoming trip gave a welcome new focus to her chaotic energy. Her gloomy mood lifted. She was heading for the peaks herself and could honestly declare, 'What are men to rocks and mountains!'

Saturday Cathryn woke to a drenching rain. She and Deb had planned to ride but a late summer storm had stalled over the prairie, forcing the women to rendezvous at the coffee shop instead. As Cathryn opened the door to Brews the rich aroma of coffee teased her senses. She ducked in and threw back her hood. After hanging her dripping coat on the stand by the door, she made her way to the table where Deb was seated. They hadn't talked since before her polo ride with Jack. There was much to say and Cathryn related the whole tale.

Deb listened with interest to the polo lesson and to details about the house, but expressed impatience with Jack's moody behavior.

"Well, to my way of thinking, a man is either in or out, if you know what I mean," she quipped. "Personally, I don't have the patience for games. I do sympathize with you, wanting a man who rides. Bill used to ride. But like a lot of men, he now prefers a four-wheeler to a four-legger. Once in a while I can talk him into a trail ride at dawn. And I do hear that decent men are scarce. Especially beyond a certain age."

She gave Cathryn a stern look. "If this guy won't step up, why not just move on? There's other men out there. Gotta be. And you only need one, right? Life's too short. Unless you're into that kind of drama?"

Cathryn shook her head. "No. Definitely not into drama."

There wasn't much else to say about Jack. It was easier to summon excitement when she told Deb about her upcoming trip to Granite City.

"Maybe you'll find a real cowboy up there." Deb chuckled. "Hey, my nephew Josh works for a big outfit just outside Granite City. Does your friend ride?"

"I'm not sure."

How is it I don't know if Gwen rides?

"Let me give you Josh's number. They run horses; in fact, I think they breed. Owner's a rich and powerful man. Guess it's quite the spread. Josh and his wife Jessie live in a cabin on the ranch. They'd help you find a place to ride." Then she stared off, her eyes glowing. "Oh, wouldn't it be fun to ride in *those* hills. Well, except for the grizzlies and the mountain lions," she allowed, with a wry face.

Cathryn was sure Deb could probably manage even grizzlies and mountain lions with aplomb.

CHAPTER THIRTEEN

*C*athryn had traveled the road through Granite City
years ago. When returning home for her first
wedding, to Steve, they'd followed a snowplow over the
mountain pass—in June. As a daughter of the prairie, she was
weather-wise and prepared for anything, but on this trip she
hoped for nothing out of the ordinary.

Most of her journey to Gwen's new home passed through
territory with a desolate kind of beauty that ranged from
boring to inspiring. It was no-man's land. Literally, it was in
the middle of nowhere; long narrow stretches of road with no
buildings in sight. Ranches were large here; thousands of
acres large. Not a place you'd run into anyone without planning to. Jack's ranch was out here somewhere, on the Moody
River. She chuckled to herself—it was a fitting place for
Nowhere Man to live.

The parched landscape was withered in want of autumn
rains. Although the calendar showed September, the day was
hot enough that the road ahead glistened in a watery mirage.
Not one to enjoy driving, Cathryn didn't mind it as much on
these roads less traveled where her thoughts and attention
could wander at will.

On her last visit—more than thirty years ago—Granite
City had been the real deal, an authentic cow town. From

Gwen's description it had now morphed into more of a Holly-wood cow town, similar to the fate that had befallen Jackson Hole and Deadwood—progress. Why did they have to pave paradise?

A lone tumbleweed rolled across the road, unimpeded on its erratic journey across the high plains. It called her focus back to driving for a moment but soon her thoughts drifted to a previous trip west when she'd left Fullerton behind. Her car had made it to California but then broke down in Berke-ley. She slept in it with her dog until her parents wired her money for repairs. Ah, the days of peace, love, and flower power—followed by those magical few months with Bob: days at the college or at one of the wild northern beaches; evenings playing music and taking long walks. He, like Deb, always had his camera with him. Waking in his arms, she had basked in the glow of good company, and bloomed with the honest affection of a true friend. It was everything she'd dreamed of—and everything she was afraid to lose.

A hawk swooped low overhead, yanking her attention back to the road. The landscape had changed now. Here were forlorn ridges and foothills, with mountains marching in a disordered fashion in the distance. Scrubby cedars huddled in small groups on the rocky plateaus.

Disconcerted, she flicked on the radio. Only one station came in. Neil Young was singing "Harvest." She knew all the words. His plaintive voice still reached into the depths of her soul. She hadn't been able to take all Bob had to give. She didn't know how to fuse—in the sun or anywhere else. Did she know now? Her brow knit. Maybe she had more in common with Nowhere Man than she cared to admit. She stroked the end of the braid hanging over her shoulder.

Several miles later she crested a hill, then found herself winding down through barren plateaus to a hole-in-the-wall town. Cedar Gulch, the sign said. She eased her truck into a parking spot near a little diner. When she opened her truck door a blast of scorching air hit her body but she shook it off, stretched, and walked down the block to loosen her bunched muscles. Car rides seemed longer nowadays, but she was willing to pay that price for a change of scene and the possibility of adventure—or a new perspective.

It was early for supper so the diner wasn't busy, and it looked clean. The old sign in the window had drawings of blue icicles advertising "Air Conditioned," from back in the day when most places weren't. She seated herself at a table by a window and checked her phone. Only two bars. A gum-chewing waitress breezed by, dropping off water and a menu, and Cathryn considered her choices.

After placing her order, she leaned back and surveyed the room. The low drone of multiple conversations filled the air. It was the typical mix of diner customers—mostly men wearing jeans or work pants, tees or western shirts, and boots. Several cowboy hats along with seed- or equipment-labeled baseball hats hung on a rack near the door. A few men ate alone at the counter. Others sat at tables, in groups of two or three. A rowdy table of five was enjoying pie, coffee, and a game of cards. At the corner opposite her own, three women —looking like a mother and daughters—talked and laughed in a familiar way. In the back corner a man and a young woman sat across from each other. His back was to Cathryn and his dark hair, laced with silver, spilled nearly to his shoulders. Not the usual look around these parts. The girl's face was lively and her brown hair was pulled into a simple ponytail.

Just then the waitress returned with the meal so Cathryn set to work on her grilled cheese and coleslaw.

The early diners began to file out and the waitress swished by, slapping a ticket on the table. Cathryn was reaching for her purse when her eye caught a movement that was somehow familiar. She looked up just in time to lock eyes with the long-haired man—and froze.

Jack flashed her a grin.

She looked away, discomfited. As he paid his bill, she watched him sidelong. He looked at her again but she couldn't interpret his expression. It wasn't a smile. Then he ducked out the door, his arm around Miss Ponytail.

Cathryn was stunned, but couldn't bring herself to look away. The girl gave Jack an affectionate hug before getting into her car. But instead of walking off, he turned back toward the diner.

As she fumbled in her purse for her wallet, a pair of lean blue-jeaned legs approached, then stopped in front of her table. Her breath caught in her throat. She looked up and to her astonishment, Jack's face was flushed and he looked most uncomfortable.

"Ah, it *is* you Cathryn. Hello. Can I ... do you mind ... if I join you?"

A riot of feelings surged through her. She nodded weakly, doing her best to compose her countenance. She decided to adopt a friendly yet disinterested attitude. Jack eased into the seat opposite her. While grappling with her own chaotic feelings, she found it equally difficult to conceal her surprise at his uneasiness.

He looked down for a moment, as if to gather his thoughts. Or pray. Then his eyes met hers again.

She leaned back and held her breath.

"I never expected to see you *here*, of all places," he began. "And I *am* happy to see you." He searched her face and compressed his lips. "I hope you're happier to see me than, well, than your face suggests? Although I realize I've been a rather ... unsteady friend. Am I intruding ...?"

A remonstrance of "Badly done!" nearly escaped her lips. But that Austenesque remark would not change his ways so she reined it in. Instead, she gave him what she hoped was an enigmatic smile.

"Your intrusion is not unwelcome, but you *are* an unsteady friend," she said, a smile twitching on her lips. "What are you doing out here anyway?" she charged with mock seriousness.

He lifted a brow. "We're only ten miles from my ranch. On the Moody River. I told you about it before, right?"

She had not forgotten. But the odds of running into him in this vast expanse of prairie ... well, it was just so unlikely. Scrambling to find a conversational foothold, she fixed her eyes on the clouds gathering in the sky. At last she looked back at him, still a little breathless. "So tell me about your ranch, Jack. Does it have a name?"

His brow smoothed at this reprieve and he eagerly picked up the conversation. "It's called Cedarstone Ranch." He proceeded to tell her how and when he had acquired the place.

"However do you manage a ranch out here while your job is more than halfway across the state? I suppose you have a foreman?"

"Yeah, my cousin lives in the main house with his wife. I stay in the cabin when I'm out here. But I'm curious—what are *you* doing out here? Are you by yourself?" His eyes zipped about the room.

Her mouth curved at one corner. "I'm on my way to see a friend in Granite City," she replied, deliberately ambiguous. "I was planning to stay in Hay Springs tonight and then drive the rest of the way tomorrow. Hay Springs isn't too far from here, is it?"

"It's about ninety miles past my place." He gave her a long look. "Would you ... could I try to be a more steady friend by inviting you to stay at Cedarstone instead of a motel?"

Her jaw fell open.

"On whatever terms you wish," he reassured her, with a crooked grin. "I'd love to show you the ranch, and I think the gathering clouds will make for a great sunset from the porch. How about it?"

Her mind raced. This was unexpected. She didn't trust her instincts with unexpected. She hesitated, fingering her phone. "I wouldn't want to impose on your plans for the evening," she hedged. "Were you meeting that young lady later?"

"Jaimie?" He looked genuinely surprised. "No, no, she's ... well, it's kinda complicated, but no, she isn't a date or anything like that, not at all." He threw his head back and laughed. "My humble plan was to sit on the porch with a beer and watch the sunset. Having your company and conversation would be a great improvement on that. But ... oh, were you meeting someone in Hay Springs?"

"No," she replied, a little too quickly, then squirmed. "And it looks like a storm's brewing." She glanced at him. Did he recall the storm at the beginning of their polo ride?

He looked at the sky thoughtfully and then back at her. "We seem to draw storms, don't we?"

Then he gave her an irresistible smile and planted his palms on the table. "So how about it—to the ranch?"

CHAPTER FOURTEEN

*C*athryn drove behind Jack's pickup, relieved to be alone with her thoughts about the night ahead. What should she anticipate? What should she be on guard against? How much should she reveal? She frowned. Too many 'shoulds.' As she took a long uphill curve she questioned the need for them. She never felt a need for 'shoulds' or even much preparation when she talked with kids.

Maybe this was an opportunity fallen into her lap—a unique chance to get some answers from Jack. Like who was the girl at the diner? Who was the angry woman at River Run? Why didn't Jack explain it that day? Why had he withdrawn since their polo ride? Had their ride been a date? Was he involved with someone?

Then she laughed out loud. Good work, Cathryn, if you can uncover all that in one evening!—just as Elinor had admonished Marianne at their first interaction with Willoughby in *Sense & Sensibility*. Although, on reflection, it certainly wouldn't hurt for her to adopt more of Marianne's forthrightness and be a little less cautious Elinor for one night. Maybe this was also an opportunity to experiment. Yes! Tonight she would abandon defense in favor of offense. At this point she had nothing to lose—and perhaps some peace of mind to gain.

The gravel road snaked its way up and around a few hills, then crossed over an old iron bridge. The clouds continued to gather ominously. It *would* be much better to ride out a storm with a friend than be alone in some motel room. Soon Jack turned into a lane marked by a row of tall cedars on each side. The overhead sign confirmed their arrival at Cedarstone Ranch. The cedar part was obvious. She wondered what the 'stone' part was about, then realized it was probably for Jack's name. After parking her truck next to Jack's she got out.

The air was still and the Moody River gurgled in the gulch nearby. The storm had stalled and Cathryn was grateful for the remaining daylight so she could get her bearings. In the country there were few man-made signs, and the landmarks she usually trusted could look very different coming from another direction, or in the dark. She looked around carefully.

What, am I plotting my flight from a gothic villain? A nervous laugh escaped her and she reminded herself this wasn't *Udolpho*.

The main house faced east toward the road, with pastures rolling away to the north. The barn was on the north of the farmyard, with paddocks and gates on three sides. She noted a dozen or so contented horses munching hay from several piles on the ground, with one pile to spare. More piles than horses—a sign of a knowledgeable horseman. Compliments to Jack, or to his foreman. Two small cabins sat to the west of the farmyard. Beyond them, down a bit of winding path, a larger cabin looked out over the gulch. The mix of hills, trees, and prairie in this setting was particularly scenic. Taller mountains rose in the distance, their peaks now obscured by dramatic thunderheads.

Jack carried her larger bag toward the big cabin while she shouldered her tote and purse. "Those cabins are for extra hands when we need them, and sometimes for hunters," he explained, gesturing toward the two identical structures as they walked by. "This one ahead is my retreat. You work with kids—you might call it my 'happy place'." He turned to her with a half smile. "Or as close to that as I can get." They both knew the meaning of that phrase: when you couldn't be at your 'happy place' for real, you took it with you in your head and heart. She had helped lots of kids find their 'happy place' to use as a soothing, if temporary, retreat from chaotic or troubled lives.

Jack and Cathryn entered through a screen door and dropped her things in the bedroom then made their way through the little kitchen and another screen door onto the porch—complete with glider. She settled herself on it immediately, delighted with the comfort and the view of the river.

"This is lovely, Jack. It sure beats any motel." She smiled quickly to hide her sudden awareness of the cozy intimacy suggested by the setting, and maybe by her words.

"So what's your pleasure?"

She spun her head toward him.

His eyes crinkled with amusement. "I mean, what would you like to drink? Water, wine, a beer?"

She shrugged, hoping to appear calm and detached. "Whatever you're having."

He opened two beers and joined her on the glider, handing her a bottle.

She took a few swallows, then steeled herself to commence with her plan. She must be bold. Schooling her expression into nonchalance, she asked, "So who was your dining companion?"

Jack looked down at his beer and hesitated.

She quailed. I knew it. Too pushy.

But remembering she had nothing to lose, with a deep breath she stumbled on. "Is she someone you're seeing? We didn't really talk about our personal situations last time, so I was just ... wondering." It was a struggle to mask her discomfort but she was determined to check out the far side of this fence before she attempted any more jumps.

He gave her a puzzled look. "No, you've got the wrong idea there. Actually Jaimie's kind of like a daughter to me. Just turned twenty-one."

"Oh, is she a step-daughter?" Cathryn hoped her manner was casual and friendly. She was trying for casual and friendly.

Jack gave her an earnest look and took a deep breath. "It's complicated. She *thinks* she's my daughter. And for now, I would like it to stay that way. For *her* sake."

At Cathryn's look of confusion, he said, "I trust you'll keep that confidential?"

It made no sense, but it was typical Jack. She stared out at the river, at a loss for words, then mumbled, "Sure. Your secret is safe with me."

He paused for a few swallows of beer before taking up the conversation again. "And no, I'm not dating anyone. It's been awhile since I have. In my position—and I don't mean to sound arrogant—but sometimes it's like being stalked, like I'm some kind of prize. I mostly just ... keep to myself," he ended lamely, taking another drink.

Cathryn sat in silence, but her mind was sparking with questions. But she decided to let him talk.

"Maybe this sounds strange, but I feel comfortable around you, Cathryn. You're easy to talk to. I haven't felt that way in a long time with a woman, or really with anyone except maybe my brothers. I'm sorry I can't explain more right now, about Jaimie and all, but it would hurt people I care about. It's complicated." He frowned, and was quiet again.

She peeled at the label on her bottle, unsure how to respond. This wasn't going quite the way she had planned.

Jack spoke again. "I'm sure you're wondering about, well, how I've acted since that day on the polo field."

She glanced up, startled that he'd read her thoughts.

"You see, I had my reasons for avoiding you, although avoiding you is *not* what I wanted to do." He sought her eyes.

There it was; that longing she'd seen before. She turned his words over in her mind but all his statements just gave rise to more questions.

The wind stirred. The storm was becoming active again and the clouds were drawing nearer the cabin.

"And no, I'm not gay," he said, shaking his head. "I get that a lot, I guess because I've never married."

He took a long, slow drink of his beer. "I've often envied my brothers their happy marriages and families. We each pursued different careers and interests, but somehow they managed to get a good woman and a family wound into their lives. I think I got lost somehow, somewhere."

The porch screens rattled. The wind was now gusting in earnest. Her skin prickled.

"But what about you, Cathryn? We talked a little about your marriages, but what about ... do you have any present ... involvements? Has there been anyone, uh, special since your last divorce?"

Before she could answer, the sky flashed. A bolt of lightning struck the ground across the gully and a dead tree exploded in flames. The crack of thunder was deafening and shook the cabin. She jumped, instinctively reaching for Jack's arm. Flames raced along the tinder-dry ground on both sides of the burning tree.

He frowned and set his beer down. "This isn't good. With this wind, and the river so low, it won't take long for that fire to spread."

Then he looked at her with alarm. "The horses! My cousins are gone for the week. It's just you and me. Let's go!" They dashed through the cabin and out the door toward the barn.

Lightning flashed all around. The sharp smell of smoke stung Cathryn's nostrils. Worried horses circled the paddock, ears flicking, nostrils flaring.

"We gotta get them out into the big pastures," he shouted over the wind and thunder. "I'll get the east gate. Can you turn those geldings out to the north? Careful they don't trample you." Horses, being prey animals, needed to run from danger. If they couldn't, they would hurt themselves and anyone else in their panic to flee.

Lightning and metal gates were a dangerous combination, but Cathryn chucked her fear for the sake of the horses.

Thunder rumbled non-stop, with an occasional sharp crack. Nimbly she scaled the fence then edged along the outside of the paddock to the far side of the gate. The sky lit up and flashed again. The agitated horses circled faster and faster. The constant flicker in the sky gave enough light to see the workings of the latch and she was able to swing the gate free. The geldings burst through into the open pasture, racing to the north. She secured the gate in an open position.

Smoke billowed into the farmyard. The air was thick. She tried to retrace her steps. Her eyes burned and it was hard to see. Or breathe.

"Jack!" She couldn't see him in the haze. "Jack?" Her voice was drowned out by another crack of thunder and she covered her ears while the ground lurched beneath her. Which way was the cabin? Another clap of thunder shook the ground, almost throwing her off balance.

Suddenly Jack appeared through the smoke, racing toward her. Just as he reached her, the sky opened and a wall of rain drenched them, nearly knocking them down.

"Thank God!" he shouted. "This'll quench any blaze." He scooped her up and whirled her round and round, laughing as torrents of rain poured from the troubled sky. Lightning flashed and the roll of thunder was still loud overhead as he set her down.

She looked at him in amazement and began to laugh herself.

He pulled her close and she buried her face in his chest. The rain drove hard against them. His mouth was near her ear. "We may attract storms, but we're pretty lucky, aren't we." Then he pulled back, took her hand, and turned toward the cabin.

"Come on, let's get into dry clothes."

CHAPTER FIFTEEN

*H*olding a cup of hot tea, Cathryn joined Jack on the glider again, accepting the warmth of a blanket big enough to encompass them both. They sat side by side, wrapped in silence. The ragged clouds hurried off to the southeast, unveiling the stars. The air was fresh and the night hushed in the aftermath of the storm.

He stole a glance at her, cleared his throat, and then quietly asked, "Are you warm enough?"

She smiled. "Yes, thank you."

"So ... shall we pick up where we left off?" His tone was tentative.

Her eyes widened as she looked at him. "Your mind is keener than mine. After all that just happened, I don't remember what we were talking about."

He looked at her closely. "Not keener; but your answer is something I really ... well, remember? I asked if there's been anyone special since your divorce because I'm ... ah, just wondering if I'm ... keeping you from other plans." His eyes narrowed and he took a drink of tea. "And trying to learn ..." he trailed off, looking to the west.

Cathryn was quite sure she understood the meaning of his convoluted words. But again, these were just words. This evening was not a planned encounter, this was a fluke—not anything he'd made an effort about, not anything he'd committed to.

Austen's words echoed. 'Let his behavior be your guide.' Just how did one do that? Jack's present behavior seemed sincere. But so had Frank Churchill's flirtatious behavior toward Emma; and Captain Wentworth's indulgence of Louisa Musgrove in *Persuasion*. Even Henry Crawford had seemed sincere about Fanny in *Mansfield Park* at one point.

Oh, Miss Austen, how am I to know, when his behavior contradicts itself?

Cathryn really didn't think Jack was a scoundrel, and knit her brows as she debated with herself. There was nothing for it but to meet what she hoped was his honesty with her own. At least they'd both know where they stood. Maybe. Anyway, what was at stake here? Not much.

She pushed her doubts aside and let her words flow. "I'm not sure what to say, Jack. I know you, a little, but not enough to know what's going on here, or if you're honorable—you know, if you mean what you say, if you do what you say. You've been so vague in some of our encounters, but candid in others. I can't make out your character. I don't know what to think. I only know how I feel. Which still leaves me uncertain of how to act." She sighed. "Does that make any sense?"

He leaned forward, his elbows on his knees. "Can I share something with you? Something I think I've figured out?" He looked toward the river. "It's my belief that we who are honest have a hard time detecting dishonesty in others. It's how we end up being burned. Once we're burned, we start to mistrust others, and eventually even ourselves." He looked over at her. "What you're saying makes a lot of sense to me."

He sat back and pushed the glider to and fro with his right leg. "And you're absolutely right about my vagueness. But I don't know how else ... geez, in a way I'm still being burned. But even at this point, it would hurt me more to put a stop to my situation, because of the others who would then suffer." He frowned. "I wish I could explain it to you. And I get that it's unrealistic of me to expect you to just trust me."

She looked closely at him, still trying to determine his intent—and gauge his sincerity.

"It's complicated." He held up his hand to quell her protest. "I know, I've said that several times tonight." He laughed, a mournful little laugh. "I *did* try to avoid you. I told myself it wasn't fair to drag someone into this quagmire; especially someone I found myself starting to ... care about."

He looked sincere as he spoke. But so had Wickham and Willoughby at first, two of Austen's most duplicitous scoundrels. Cathryn was not yet convinced.

Jack gulped his tepid tea and continued. "That day we played polo, I told myself it was just a friendly invitation, and I was simply getting to know you as a fellow horse person. And that was true, to a point. But I also convinced myself that the only heart at risk was my own. After our ride, and your emails, I realized maybe that wasn't true?"

She met his gaze. It would be useless to dissemble now.

"Then I didn't know *what* to do, so I did nothing." He drained his cup.

For a few minutes they sat in silence. The stars winked across the deepening sky. Cathryn felt like the whole world was on its jolly way somewhere while the two of them were stuck, each sinking alone in their own private quagmire, as he had called it. Maybe this was the adult version of the 'quicksand' and 'hot lava' of children's play. Only this wasn't play. The silence grew uncomfortable, but she couldn't find words for her jumbled feelings.

"So, how about it?"

She gave him a puzzled look. "How about what?"

"Now *you're* being vague," he accused, but there was a twinkle in his eyes. "You haven't told me yet if you're involved with someone. Is there someone special in Granite City?"

Cathryn heard him with astonishment. "You're right. I haven't answered you. I *am* going to visit someone special. My friend Gwen." She flashed him a grin. "She recently moved to Granite City from Quinn, after her husband died. She and I worked together for years."

A small smile played across his face.

She took that as a sign to continue. "I've had some losses that I've ... maybe not recovered from. And I've made some poor choices along the way. Obviously, with two failed marriages ... but those are over and not relevant. Since my last divorce, I haven't met anyone even marginally interesting until I ran into you that day at the funeral home. I wanted to know you better but, well ... I'm not one to push my way in."

He nodded, then chuckled. "Well, I'm glad I'm at least marginally interesting."

She saw the amusement in his eyes. It reassured her. She went on before she lost her courage. "My instincts tell me you're a good person. Much of that is based on you as a horseman. Horses know."

He nodded again.

"Even Lisa couldn't tell me much about you as far as relationships. I didn't know if you were involved with someone, or gay, or what. You gave some pretty mixed signals that day we rode. And, well, I was scared to ask, because it wasn't really my business. I wasn't sure if our ride was a date, or recruiting for the team, or ..." She stopped and took a sip of tea before speaking again, then said—almost to herself —"Maybe I didn't ask because I was afraid you were taken and ... I wanted someone to ... dream about?" The last part came out in a broken whisper.

Jack snugged the blanket over her shoulder and pulled her closer. "And here I thought you didn't ask because you weren't interested in me."

She looked at him with genuine surprise. "Really?"

He laughed. "You've given off a lot of your own mixed signals, you know. I wasn't sure how far to push either, especially being still somewhat, uh, constrained myself. When I saw you at the diner today ... well, I took that as a sign."

The glider creaked back and forth, filling the silence as they pondered their mutual confessions. It had not occurred to Cathryn that she might give mixed signals herself. On reflection it made sense; she *was* often in a quandary about her feelings in the moment. It took her a little time to process things. Or overthink things?

Here, for the first time, she was hearing another view of a relationship—calmly, intelligently, and directly expressed. No hollering, swearing, name-calling, or violence. She could examine both sides and actually found it intriguing—and enlightening. Lizzy's comment after reading Darcy's letter in *Pride & Prejudice* now took on a personal meaning—'Until this moment, I never knew myself.'

Jack continued. "So as someone who is marginally interesting, and slightly scary, and very vague—but an honest horseman—how about this? We make some kind of pact to explore this ... friendship, step by step." He looked around. "What can we swear by?"

Cathryn glanced out at the sky. "Star light, star bright ..."

He looked at the night sky and then at her. His eyes were kind and inviting. Slowly he reached for her face, touching her cheek. He was so close that his breath warmed her skin. Tilting her chin up, he gently kissed her. A flood of warmth rushed through her body and she instinctively kissed him in return. He was strange and familiar, exciting yet comforting, all at once. When they drew apart, she nestled her head into the crook of his neck, taking pleasure in the scent of him. She drifted into sleep, lulled by the rhythm of his breathing, the gurgling of the river, and the creak of the glider.

A short time later, she woke. Her neck was stiff; she tried to move without disturbing him.

His eyes opened. "What?" he whispered.

"As cozy as this is, after driving all day I just can't sleep sitting up all night."

He rose and stepped out of the blanket, wrapped the rest of it around her, and picked her up. She leaned in, letting his strength support her. He carried her to the screen door, then stopped abruptly. "You're still as light as a feather, but I only have two arms." He nodded toward the door with a playful smile.

Laughing, she worked one arm out of the blanket and

opened the door. With a few more steps they were in the bedroom. Her heart drummed in her chest as he set her on her feet and unwrapped the blanket.

"Can we continue the coziness here?" Jack asked, his voice a ragged whisper in the dark. "Or shall I sleep on the sofa?"

She touched his arm and murmured, "Sleep here." The storm had dissolved some of her reserve. She removed her jeans and heard him do the same. She turned toward the bed but was stopped by his gentle touch on her shoulders. He removed the band holding her braid. Slowly he unraveled the plaits, spilling the tendrils onto her shoulders. Then he bent and pulled back the covers. She climbed in and he eased in behind her, wrapping her in his arms. Once again she was comforted by his steady breathing, and a deep sleep soon engulfed her.

CHAPTER SIXTEEN

The twitter of birds roused Cathryn and she opened her eyes to a pale gray light. The warm, solid body next to her rekindled her memory of the night before. She and Jack had shared a bed. Although they had merely slept on the same surface, she felt a ribbon of connection that was new: a sense of knowing, and of being known. An old song by the Monkees, "Sometime in the Morning," played through her drowsy senses. The two of them were close as the summer air. As she glanced at him, he opened his eyes.

"I'm hungry," he declared with a smile and a stretch. "Did you sleep well? Want something to eat before we ride?"

"Ride?" Her head was spinning at the staccato of questions.

"Nothing like a ride at sunrise. I hope you can function without caffeine, I only have decaf—but I have both coffee and tea." He sat up and reached for his jeans.

"Perfect. I don't do caffeine." She raised herself up on one elbow. "Does this window face east?"

"Of course," he said. "Actually this cabin was my first design-and-build project. I designed River Run kinda like this, but on a larger scale. Sunrise. Sunset." He nodded in each direction.

"Swiftly flow the ..." She gasped. She had said it out loud.

Jack looked at her with amusement as he buttoned his jeans. "'Fiddler on the Roof', right?"

"Yes." The smile on her lips broadened. "I'm a quoter. I quote books, movies, songs ... things remind me of other things, like some kind of mystical web. Most people don't recognize the quotes, or even realize I do it." She tossed him a grin of acknowledgement as she sat up and moved to the edge of the bed.

He pulled on a tee shirt. "I like that idea. It's like everything is connected." He paused, as if pondering something in his head. "The older I get, the more I believe that." He handed her jeans over and moved toward the kitchen.

"So can I give you a horseback tour of the ranch before you go?" he said over his shoulder. She heard him pop bread into the toaster and clatter about making coffee. "Will some toast and honey do for now? We can have a big ranch breakfast after our ride. I'm really a good cook. You do have time to stay for that, right?"

She smiled at his boyish energy. Tempered with the substance and power of a man, it was a heady combination. A slight thrill moved through her body at the awareness that she was really here with him. She donned her jeans, rebraided her hair and, after a quick check in the mirror, joined him in the kitchen. Jack pulled a chair out for her at the little pine table by the window, then poured two steaming mugs of coffee and sat down.

"Gwen expects me later today, but my schedule is my own. So, yes, I can stay for a bit. "

After their toast and coffee he led the way out the door. "Hopefully the horses will be back in the paddock." As they approached the barn, several eager faces hung over the fence.

"Good, they're here. I thought we might ride double?"

The intimate nature of that idea flustered her at first, but why not? She and Jack had shared a glider, a kiss, and a bed. She hadn't ridden double in a long, long time. Not since junior high when she learned to jump from a friend who'd brought his mare to town and they jumped hay bales riding double in a western saddle.

"Sure, double," she replied.

The herd dynamics, with horses jostling about in excitement at feeding time, brought Henry to her mind. He was likely just as eager for his fresh hay this morning too.

Jack opened the gate and put a halter on a big bay gelding, then brought him out to tack up.

"Hey, since they're all up here, could you close the pasture gates again? On both sides? We'll have a little more peace on our ride if they don't all follow us," he said, brush in one hand, saddle pad in the other.

Cathryn climbed lightly over the metal panel and managed the gates with ease. While perched atop the last panel a sudden puff of wind ruffled her hair and caressed the land—the fresh breeze that signaled dawn. She raised her head to sniff. Sunbeams broke the horizon in the east and the prairie welcomed a new day.

Jack finished tacking up the bay, then forked several flakes of hay over the fence to the others. "That'll keep 'em busy," he remarked. Then he offered a big handful to the horse they would ride and swung up into the saddle.

"Can you mount from the gate?"

"I'm an old hand at that," she replied, climbing up a few rungs as he edged the horse close. She grasped Jack's arm and slipped lightly behind the saddle.

"This is Ben. He's a real teddy bear. He was my polo buddy for years, but has gotten a little old for that now, huh Ben. Are you ready, Cathryn?"

She placed her hands tentatively on Jack's sides, delighting in the sound of him speaking her name.

"Yes. Let's ride."

They moved quietly out the lane and then turned north, shortly entering the far pasture through another gate. Trotting through the wet meadow, the fragrance from last night's rain filled her senses. Then they began to climb. Slowly Ben picked his way around the rocky areas until they reached the top of the ridge.

"Oh, Jack, this is breathtaking! You're so blessed to have this, as I'm sure you know. Land—room to stretch out and breathe—is important to me. I just couldn't live in an apartment."

"Me either. I'd feel hemmed in."

Cathryn admired the colors of sunrise as the morning mists lifted and disappeared. The serenity of the unfolding day seemed a world away from last night's stormy chaos.

They rode on in companionable silence for some time, their bodies moving in unison with each other and the horse. Cathryn drank in the tonic of beauty around them.

"This is nice, Jack. Riding with you. And you ... you seem so relaxed again, like on our polo ride. And like when you were showing me your house until ... until your visitor arrived," she said, her heart in her throat. Interrupting the peaceful beauty of the moment went against all her instincts but this was likely her only chance to see the other side of this fence.

His back stiffened under her hands, but he made no reply.

She started to panic, but locked it down. Gritting her teeth, she asked, "What was that all about? Who is she? If I'm not being too nosy." She gave his sides a playful squeeze.

He remained silent for several more paces.

If her hands hadn't been on Jack, she would have wrung them in remorse. I've been too forward, too persistent. I've ruined this beautiful morning; ruined everything.

"Jack, I'm sorry. It really is none of my—"

"No. Don't apologize. It *is* your business," he said emphatically. "Well, it affects you, or you and me, if we were to be ... uh ... more important to each other."

After a huge sigh, he continued. "Blaire is someone I was involved with more than twenty years ago." There was a tinge of disgust in his voice when he said Blaire's name. "And I *don't* think it's nosy of you. It's arrogant of me to not explain. After all, you were there and I'm sure heard some of what she said, or at least her tone of voice. How could you not? That voice *does* carry. I wish I could tell you more, but I just can't say much right now." He sounded cross.

Cathryn's brow furrowed. With a gulp she asked, "Are you still involved? Do you still care for her?" In a way, she didn't want to know. But she *had* to know, to protect her own heart.

"No, I don't ... care for her, that is. But we *are* still involved, though not romantically, at least not on my side. My heart is free; but other parts of my life, well, they aren't—not yet." He stopped Ben and let him nibble at a patch of fireweed.

Once again, Jack's answers had only given rise to more questions. What did 'involved' mean, if not romantic? And why was Blaire so angry?

After a few minutes of thoughtful silence, Jack urged Ben on.

"What are you looking for, Cathryn? Friendship? A relationship? Do you see yourself getting married again?"

She drew a quick breath. Thrown by such a serious, commitment-like question from Jack, she stalled to regroup. "Isn't that odd? By this age, I figured those questions would be long settled for me. Maybe that's why I'm floundering a bit. Things in my life have not turned out as I expected; not at all," she mused, half to herself.

He twisted around to look at her.

She felt rather exposed, but continued to express her rambling thoughts out loud. "Sure, I'd like someone in my life to care about, and who cares about me; someone who gets me and enjoys me; someone to laugh with, to talk with, to listen to. All the usual things. Oh, and he should be a good horseman, if at all possible." A soft laugh escaped her lips. "But beyond that?" She sighed. As they moved on, the breeze brushed Jack's hair against her cheek and she closed her eyes. "I guess no one has inspired me to think beyond that."

To herself she added, 'No one until you, Jack.' She leaned in a little closer, struggling to contain an overwhelming desire to bury her face in his hair and wrap her arms around him, tight. She was relieved he couldn't see her face; she knew it would betray her feelings for him: besotted. Most definitely besotted. And not a little terrified.

They stopped at the edge of the ridge and sat quietly, looking out over the gulch.

Prompted by the beauty before her, Cathryn recited softly: 'Love is not love which alters when it alteration finds, or bends with the remover to remove: O no! It is an ever-fixèd mark. That looks on tempests and is never shaken ...'

"Shakespeare?"

"Sonnet 116. *That's* what I'm looking for, I guess."

"You never found that in either of your marriages?"

She hesitated. Two failed marriages—what a sad reflection on her life. No matter. She had chosen to be honest and would keep to that path.

"No, not really. I did know it once, early on in California. With a guy named Bob. But that much happiness scared me, and I bailed. Instead, I chose someone I knew I didn't really love. So that if I lost him, it wouldn't hurt so much." She shook her head. "Sounds crazy, doesn't it?"

A realization unexpectedly struck her. "I think after I lost Trinity, I just couldn't risk that kind of loss again. I wasn't sure I could survive it."

She told Jack the story of Trinity, and how she had named her place on the river—by River Run—after her horse.

"And this Bob—where is he now?"

"When I realized he was the one I began a serious search, but all I found was his obituary." Her voice trailed off in a hoarse whisper.

He squeezed her hand in sympathy. "What a loss. Two big losses. I'm so sorry."

She brushed her face against the back of his shoulder. Leaning against him, she tried to absorb some of his warmth and strength. The water murmured, the birds chattered, and Ben chewed at the fireweed, swishing his tail at flies.

After a while she asked, "How about you? What are you looking for, Jack?"

He turned again in the saddle. "I think I'm just now realizing I've been missing something."

The warm look they shared filled her heart. As he turned forward to bring Ben's head up, she wrapped her arms more closely around Jack, feeling profoundly content in the moment, and fully aware of being so. Hang the future. She would soak this in now.

Jack directed Ben down a steep path toward the river, then they followed the riverbank for some time. Coming around a sharp bend, an enormous outcropping of granite filled their view, with a scrubby cedar somehow surviving in a fissure of the massive stone.

Jack made a gallant sweep with his arm. "Miss McNeil, I give you Cedarstone."

She caught her breath. Here was *his* special place. And he was sharing it with her. It touched her heart and she looked at him with new understanding ... a fondness ... maybe even— no—no it was too soon to go there. She must stay here, in this moment.

"It's amazing, Jack! Survival, perseverance ... isn't nature incredible?"

He turned toward her again and nodded. He didn't quite meet her eyes but she could see the pleased expression on his face and felt they both knew the significance of what they'd now shared.

Silently they rode on. The Moody River was shallow this time of year, even after last night's storm, and they crossed it at several points.

Cathryn dared to forge on, in a gentle voice. "Can you tell me more about the girl?"

"Jaimie? She goes to college out here."

"Is she related to ... ?"

"Yes, Blaire is her mom. And Jaimie believes I'm her dad. I *do* care for her like a daughter, I guess. I've pretty much raised her."

"Do you have other kids?"

"Nope."

"Never had a relationship serious enough?"

He pulled Ben to a stop and looked off into the distance toward the mountains. Some minutes passed before he spoke. "Once I did. For a while."

After a deep breath he continued. "Ellen and I were planning our wedding, after being together for a couple of years. I was finishing my residency back east. She had just found out ... well, she was on her way to tell me when ..." He sighed. "A drunk driver was going the wrong way. Hit her head on. Her car went over an embankment. Found out about the baby later, from the OB. No survivors," he mumbled, and slumped in the saddle.

"Oh, Jack, how awful!" Instinctively she wrapped her arms around him and he grasped her hands with his free hand.

At length, he took another breath and straightened in the saddle, squared his shoulders, and urged Ben on.

"Blaire was kind of a rebound thing when I moved back here. I was trapped before I realized it. She was hunting for an up-and-coming professional with money. Lots of money. Blaire was definitely into up-and-coming and money. Now she thinks that through my status and wealth she's part of some social hierarchy that's important—to her. None of that ever mattered to me. I chose my work because it's fascinating and challenging, and I can help kids. You know, how that doctor helped my brother years ago. But it was and is all about money and status for Blaire. Never about me as a person. I was just some kind of trophy. It only lasted a few months."

A memory of Jack's brother in a wheelchair and then later in leg braces flashed through her mind.

After a time he continued. "It's made me wary. I hate being stalked for my money, or for my so-called social position. And it happens a lot. I even suspected you at first, at the funeral home, when you asked about my work. Now my only connection with Blaire is Jaimie. After Blaire, I just gave up and mostly kept to myself. Oh, I dated here and there. Nothing serious. And then you showed up."

He turned his head to her with a half smile. "Seeing you at

the funeral home was kind of an awakening—of a part of me I thought had died with Ellen. Talking to you about our childhoods, our love of horses and the land—it just feels so comfortable, so nice."

Cathryn remembered those feelings—of sharing, of knowing, of comfort. She'd known them with Bob. It surprised her that Jack felt comfortable with her; she would not have guessed it. As they rode on, she considered the possibility of receiving those very things from Jack. Her chest tightened. With *receiving* came the risk of *losing*. Her head could accept that but, much as she longed for a partner, the possibility of such a loss was still terrifying, at a gut-wrenching level.

Did Jack feel that way too?

Back when she had parted with Bob (by choosing Steve instead), she hadn't really admitted the loss. She had always believed there would be more time, or even another chance. Even when faced with Bob's obituary, she had just scrambled on, refusing to acknowledge the shock or mourn the loss— fearful she would drown in the flood. She'd never found that kind of joy again—or allowed it to find her.

The couple rode in reflective silence for a time. The fragrance of the woods, the smell of the horse and of the leather and of Jack all created memorable sensations for Cathryn that were heady, but frightening.

As they zigzagged their way up and out of the gulch she found the courage to ask another question.

"I was wondering about your house, Jack, about River Run. Are you living there?"

"When I showed it to you, I hadn't moved in yet. Actually, I was so used to living next to my brother and his family that the move was harder than I expected. I'd really gotten used to their company."

"It's a beautiful house, and in a good way—not pretentious—but it seemed, well, lonely. It reminded me of Jack T. Colton and his plan to sail around the world all alone, in *Romancing the Stone.*" Jack remained silent, so she continued. "There was nothing living. No plants, no pets. I love my cottage; it's little, and definitely lived in, but even with my cats and dogs, I still get lonely there sometimes. Do you get lonely at River Run?"

He gave her a sidelong look. "I guess so. But it doesn't seem practical to have living things when I travel between four places, plus being on the road for polo. But, yeah, you might be onto something."

Then he chuckled. "No wonder you work so well with kids. You're full of curiosity and candor, just like a child. And I mean that in a good way. You're easy to talk to. I feel like you understand." He reached back and patted her thigh.

They began to negotiate the most difficult part of the path up and out of the gulch, and she leaned forward with Jack until they gained the ridge top. Heading back across the north pasture, urged on by a rising breeze, Ben carried them at an easy lope until the hoof-carved path turned south. They trotted until they reached the woods, then slowed to a walk. After winding among the trees, they emerged near the large cabin.

Ben ambled toward the barn where his buddies were still munching hay. Jack reined him in, then lifted his own leg over the horse's neck and slid to the ground. Turning to help Cathryn down he lowered her slowly and carefully, their eyes confirming a new, unspoken awareness of each other. He grazed her lips with a tender kiss as he set her on the ground. Then it was back to tending horses.

Once they moved indoors, Jack threw himself into cooking. Cathryn was impressed at how skilled he was in the kitchen, unlike previous men in her life. Another pot of coffee was set to brew. He finessed sausages and cheese omelets 'run through the garden' while she made toast and poured juice. The smells were enticing; they had worked up appetites. He refilled her cup before he sat down, and they lingered over his culinary creations, reluctant for this encounter to end.

Jack insisted on doing kitchen duty, so Cathryn freshened up and gathered her things to make ready for her departure.

Fetching a map from his pickup, Jack spread it out on the table, pointing out the road back to the highway and determining the distance to Granite City. She liked the way he cared about her safety and comfort. It was a rather new experience. She had always been the responsible one in her relationships with men.

But there was a contradiction here: if he really cared, why no explanation before now? What if this chance meeting hadn't happened? Yes, he had claimed complications, but there was still much to clarify. If Jaimie wasn't even his child, and was obviously now a young woman, what hold could Blaire have on him? It made no sense. That hold was certainly an obstacle for Cathryn and Jack to pursue a relationship.

She contemplated that possibility: a relationship with Jack. If she let his behavior be her guide, after today she would think he might be falling in love with her. She was definitely attracted to him, and even felt close to him—a great change in less than twenty-four hours. But she was still too skittish to call it love. Her practical side reminded her she was looking for someone she could count on, someone who could be wholly there. His secrets, and his 'non-romantic' involvement with Blaire surely precluded that.

"The cell signal out here isn't very steady," he warned, bringing her attention back to what he was saying. "If I don't get back to you, this is the number for the land line at the main house. If I don't answer you can leave a message there." He wrote it on the map. "Please call or text me when you get to your friend's place?"

With her new understanding of this request, she was happy to oblige.

He set her bags in her truck and looked at her intently, taking both her hands in his. "This time I'm not going to do nothing."

He stopped a minute, as if considering something, but then shook his head. "I don't head back to Fullerton for seven days. How long will you be at your friend's? If the timing works, can I convince you to stay here again on your way back?" His expression appeared earnest.

She calculated on her fingers. "Let's see, this is Wednesday, and I'll be driving back from Gwen's on Monday, so it seems like good timing, doesn't it? I'll let you know." She was cautious about making promises because she liked to keep her word. What if she changed her mind about him after visiting Gwen?

He gazed at her fondly and then pressed her against the truck. His face was close to hers, his eyes penetrating deep into her being. "I hope you still want to dream about me," he said, with a tender catch in his voice. He leaned in and kissed her.

His warmth enveloped her. She ached at the thought of leaving him. And panicked a little at her growing desire for him, fearing an avalanche of feelings. She decided to focus instead on the mountain adventures ahead and drew back, trembling a little. She had a lot to think about. Like fusing. And ever fixèd marks.

Jack opened the driver's door and she climbed in. He closed her door and once he pounded on the hood she started the engine.

Driving out the lane, she caught his wave in her rearview mirror and wondered when, or if, she would see him again.

CHAPTER SEVENTEEN

*T*he road rushed under her wheels as Cathryn sped west. Her mind, however, dawdled as she reflected on all Jack had shared—and puzzled over what he hadn't. Blaire and Jaimie seemed at the crux of something. What kind of hold could Blaire have on him? More importantly, why did he allow it?

After a time, and to her own surprise, she wearied of the whole Jack situation. In spite of the tenderness they had shared, he'd still not committed to anything more than 'exploring' a friendship. Not much of a commitment. To prevent his issues from clouding her visit with Gwen, she decided to set Jack and his secrets aside for now and give herself a needed break and a fresh start.

When she arrived in Granite City she pulled over to text Gwen for directions to the house. That reminded her to text Jack of her safe arrival. While awaiting replies, Cathryn surveyed her surroundings. The town nestled charmingly into the foothills, backed by the peaks of the Rockies. The downtown area, called Old Town, was plainly visible from where she was parked. Main Street was narrow and the shop signs quaint; the view was altogether picturesque. Like an English village with mountains. Like Derbyshire. Only people probably didn't wear cowboy hats in Derbyshire.

Gwen had made a major life change by moving here. Sitting in this new location herself, the magnitude of that change hit Cathryn hard, but in a good way. She was eager to explore Gwen's new world, and inspired to make some changes in her own life as well. She was ready for new ideas. Dragging around her past—prior relationships, unresolved feelings, old fears—suddenly seemed like so much cumbersome baggage. She was ready to be rid of it. Here, for this week anyway, she would let all that go and see what happened. She longed for adventure.

A text came in from Gwen with the needed directions and soon Cathryn was in the driveway of an older cedar home with a broad deck and a splendid view of the mountains. Gwen was outside to greet her.

"Gwen, it's wonderful to see you again." Cathryn gave her a hug and took a close look at her friend. "Everything's different here, isn't it?"

Gwen's eyes shone. "And that's *exactly* what I wanted." Gwen's enigmatic blend of intensity and serenity was rare—and engaging—for those mindful enough to perceive it.

The women settled on the deck to enjoy iced tea and talk about what to do during Cathryn's visit.

"There *is* something I thought you might especially enjoy," Gwen said. "A nearby ranch is hosting a polo match on Saturday, with a dance after. Interested?"

"I had no idea people played polo up here in cowboy country."

"Well, remember Granite City is more like 'Granite Hollywood' now. Anyway, the host is Warren Sterling, owner of the Lazy S Ranch. Everyone just calls him Sterling. Big hat and *lots* of cattle," she said with a hearty laugh.

Cathryn laughed too, remembering how they used to joke about their former supervisor—a spoiled rich boy with no integrity—with the old saying 'big hat, no cattle.'

"The polo thing sounds fun. Say, Gwen, do you ride? My friend Deb has a nephew who works at a spread up here somewhere. She thought he could hook us up with some kind of horse activity, like a trail ride, if you're up for it."

"Oh, I've ridden some; I'd do a trail ride. Now tell me, who is Deb?"

Gwen and Deb had never met, which seemed odd now that Cathryn thought about it, but those two did move in very different circles, and circles were tight in small towns like Quinn. Cathryn explained a little about her friendship with Deb and their horse activities. Gwen listened with interest but without comment. For a moment her face had a pensive expression, but that vanished so quickly Cathryn thought she might have imagined it.

Clearing away the tea things, Gwen asked, "So dinner in town okay for tonight? If we leave a little early we can check out some of the shops. You can see for yourself how 'Hollywood' Granite City has become since you were here last."

After Cathryn freshened up, the women headed downtown. Some of the changes she saw were positive, such as dining choices beyond steak and buffalo burgers. But the town itself seemed rather high-profile, almost self-conscious —like it was trying too hard. Gone was the sleepy little cow town she remembered from years ago. Feeling a little nostalgic, she reminded herself that life is like riding—it's more about the ride than the destination.

They explored some shops, then Gwen chose a pub for dinner. Cathryn was itching to tell her about her experience at Jack's ranch, and had started talking about the diner when a waitress brought them each a glass of beer. She pointed to a man at the bar. "They're from him."

Gwen turned to see who it was, and Cathryn's eyes followed.

The man smiled and nodded his head.

Gwen's countenance softened. As she waved the man over, the women exchanged glances and Gwen whispered, "He's one of my new friends that I especially want you to meet." He walked over and stood comfortably close to Gwen.

"Cathryn, this is Adam Monroe, foreman at the Lazy S—

Sterling's ranch, the one hosting the polo match. Adam, this is my friend and former coworker Cathryn McNeil. She's a therapist with a gift for working with children. She's also a horsewoman."

Cathryn reached out to shake hands and looked into a pair of deep blue eyes framed by graying brown hair.

"Welcome to Wyoming, Cathryn." Adam pulled up a chair. "I'll only stay a few minutes. I know you two want to catch up, and I've got a lot to do to get ready for Saturday."

He and Gwen looked at each other. The smiles they exchanged looked warmer than mere friendship. Cathryn observed it with curiosity, then said, "So, about the polo match. I've never seen one in person, have you Gwen?"

"Actually, I've been to two since I moved here. This group is part of the circuit in the region."

Recalling her own desire to ride, Cathryn said, "My friend's nephew works at a ranch around here, maybe you've heard of him—I have his last name in my purse—Josh and his wife Jessie?" she said, reaching around her chair.

"Josh!" exclaimed Adam. "He works with me at the Lazy S. He's our farrier, and of course does a whole lot more than trim and shoe horses. He has a way with them. Good guy. Yeah, he's been with us almost seven years now."

"I haven't had a chance to call him yet. His aunt—my friend Deb—thought he might be able to connect us with a trail ride or something."

"Well, Sunday afternoon would be good for a ride, after all the excitement from Saturday has wound down. You go ahead and call him, but I'll be talking to him later today too. Say, I'd like to get in on the fun, if you ladies don't mind me joining you on the trail?" He winked at Gwen and received a warm smile in return. "We can go over the details tomorrow."

As an afterthought, Cathryn asked, "Adam, which polo team is coming here?"

"The club from Fullerton."

Cathryn gave a little gasp. Jack hadn't mentioned this.

Gwen glanced over at her.

Adam continued, "They're always a fun bunch. Not nearly so serious as the Boulder club." After a fond look at Gwen, he stood to leave. "See you ladies tomorrow then." He gave Gwen's shoulder a squeeze and headed out the door.

Why hadn't Jack told her?

Gwen's eyes followed Adam to the door.

With a laugh Cathryn gave Gwen a shrewd look. "I can see we have a *lot* to catch up on."

Thursday they toured some local landmarks, met Josh and Jessie for lunch, visited the bookstore where Gwen now worked, and then joined a couple of her coworkers for dinner. Cathryn hadn't gotten around to bringing up Jack again. She found herself reluctant to dampen the joyful spirit of Gwen's new life, and didn't wish to bog down her own fresh start. This visit was about new possibilities.

Friday night presented an interesting new possibility in the form of Warren Sterling.

Gwen had suggested the foursome for dinner. The women were shown to a table with a spectacular mountain view. The men were already seated, enjoying cocktails.

Sterling stood to pull out her chair and Cathryn caught her breath. He definitely didn't look the way she'd expected. Something about his appearance and bearing bespoke a certain elegance, although he was friendly enough when they were introduced. 'Common' even, as Grandma Esther used to say of those in high places who were affable and kind to those beneath them in status.

"Just call me Sterling," he said, taking her hand in both of his. "Everyone does." His smile was warm. Silver hair, just long enough to flatter, set off his face in an attractive way. There was an air of merriment about him, as though he found much of life amusing. He looked far more the gentleman and far less the cowboy than Cathryn had anticipated. His manners were impeccable, even slightly formal, but this was

balanced by a quick sense of humor evidenced in the anecdotes he shared over dinner. The staff treated him with
special courtesy and he honored them with that same respect,
and not an ounce of haughtiness.

Sterling sat next to Cathryn during the meal. His physical
presence was powerful. She found herself not only enjoying
his attention but seeking it—delighted when his gaze found
hers, charmed at his consideration of everyone's pleasure,
feeling a rush when he touched her arm to make a point. He
regaled them with fascinating historical tales about Granite
City, with Adam chiming in. Both had lived in the area all
their lives and had a depth of knowledge to share.

Unlike most of Cathryn's other dates and companions,
Sterling seemed truly interested in *her* and made particular
efforts to draw her out. He asked thoughtful questions about
her work, her family, her childhood in Fullerton, and her
present life in Quinn. Over dinner he probably learned more
about her than some with years of acquaintance could claim
to know.

It was delightful to have someone so interested in herself.
Is this how it could be with a companion who was a true
match? She had rarely been more agreeably engaged. A glow
that she could not credit merely to the wine kindled within
her. Was he particularly attracted to her, or was he this
charming with everyone? He was so skilled at making each
person feel important that she couldn't tell. He was an amal-
gamation of all the fine gentlemen in her favorite Austen
books. If one were to design the perfect hero ...

They were hours at dinner. No one seemed keen for the
evening to end. When the wine and brandy glasses were
empty again Adam suggested a moonlit walk down Main
Street and they set out. It was a fine night. The moon was
nearly full and so bright the stars were diminished in its glow.

Cathryn had worn a light jacket but still shivered in the
mountain air. Sterling, perceptive of the slightest nuance,
gallantly draped his sport jacket around her shoulders. It
smelled of brandy and cedar. And Sterling.

The men accompanied the women to Gwen's car with promises to see them at the polo match the next day.

Cathryn was flushed from the heady evening of wine and stimulating company. Gwen looked to be in a dreamy state as she drove in the moonlight. Cathryn chuckled. We are not so unlike young ladies in one of Austen's novels, basking in pleasant thoughts after a gratifying assembly. And tomorrow night after the polo match there would be a 'ball,' western style. Something fascinating was sure to happen at a ball.

As she reviewed the interactions of the evening she noted that despite hours of conversation she knew little about Sterling himself. He had entertained them royally but shared next to nothing personal. How had he done that? *Sense & Sensibility's* Mrs. Jennings had nothing on this guy; he was marvelously good at 'winkling'—the old English term for wrangling information out of people. Admitting her own vanity had been flattered by his attention, she felt a little sheepish at having discovered so little about him—she, whose career as a therapist depended on such skills.

Tomorrow he would be busy playing host. Still, she was determined to make what she could of it and try to learn more about Sterling, the man.

Thoughts of tomorrow stirred up feelings about Jack. This was *his* polo club coming to Granite City. Was he too busy at the ranch to come up here? Even so, he knew she wanted to see a match. Why had he not mentioned it?

She was mulling this over when Gwen turned into the driveway. It wasn't quite eleven o'clock but neither of them seemed inclined to talk. They agreed they were looking forward to tomorrow and said goodnight.

～

It was late Saturday morning when Gwen and Cathryn departed for the Lazy S. The polo match would begin at two o'clock, with a light luncheon before and a dinner and dance afterward. Quite the event. Once they were on the highway, Gwen became more talkative.

"I really enjoyed dinner last night—the food *and* the company." She looked directly at Cathryn. "What did you think of Sterling?"

"Well, he was totally *not* what I expected. Much more sophisticated than I'd imagined in a rancher. He was kind. And entertaining. But in spite of all the interesting conversation, he remains kind of an enigma. Do you know him well?"

Gwen laughed. "Enigma is a good description. And no, I don't know him very well yet; to me he's just Adam's boss, and someone who puts on social events and is a 'big hat' in the community. He seems nice enough, and he's very generous, but I've always been with Adam when he's around. I've never talked with him one on one."

Cathryn fell quiet. Sterling was every woman's dream—handsome, clever, and rich—with an air of the Quality about him, in the best sense. But she wasn't sure how comfortable she felt around him. Was it because he was a finer gentleman than the men she was used to? Perhaps. Nevertheless, her mixed feelings surprised her. Not knowing exactly what to do with these feelings at the moment, she changed the subject and cautiously mentioned Jack.

"Is this the same guy you talked to me about before? The polo player from the funeral home who hadn't called? Then finally called, and you played polo, and then didn't call again?"

It sounded ridiculous when put in such a way.

"The very one," Cathryn admitted. Briefly she described their run-in at the diner in Cedar Gulch, and the time she spent unexpectedly at his ranch. She didn't tell Gwen everything Jack had confided, but enough to get some feedback.

"Well, he's sure not a fast mover, is he? What do you think is going on there?" Gwen looked directly at Cathryn again. Gwen was almost always very direct.

Cathryn made no effort to hide her doubts and confusion. "He's made no effort to follow up, even after our unexpected encounters before. Yet he invited me to the ranch and was very kind, and ... well, affectionate. But he still can't—or won't—explain his inscrutable connection with that woman. Am I just mired in a lost cause?"

"You know me. I'm all about right now and being forthcoming. But you and I are very different, Cathryn. You tend to be intuitive, and quite cautious, am I right? Focusing on the other person while sharing little about yourself?" Gwen possessed a gift for seeing to the bottom of a situation. "Maybe acting the therapist in a non-therapeutic relationship?" Her voice was kind but always held an air of authority.

Cathryn was taken aback by that idea. All she could say was, "I don't know."

Gwen thought for a minute and then continued. "But if things were good when you talked frankly, it could be a promising path. I wonder what his reasons are to conceal things though? That would make me uneasy. The whole thing is puzzling. You're far more patient than I would be."

Gwen turned the car onto a gravel road. "I'd say 'hear his words, but listen to his actions'," she said, nodding her head with conviction.

Cathryn smiled at this unintentional reiteration of Emma's advice.

Good advice was timeless. Like Austen.

They made another turn and entered the ranch lane.

CHAPTER EIGHTEEN

*A*s they drove past the main house and its broad welcoming porch, Gwen waved to Sterling. He smiled and waved back. Sterling, the enigma. Cathryn wondered what his story was. And where Gwen's story was going.

In her few days here, Cathryn had noticed a difference in Gwen. This wasn't surprising, given all the changes she'd made. But she seemed much more relaxed now, and more sociable. Had the negative energy of working at the agency just drained her before? Or were there other forces at work? Cathryn stole a glance at her friend, pleased at the thought of Gwen enjoying a new love.

Maybe it really could happen. Love. Even after the bloom of youth was long gone.

The day was bright and sunny with just a touch of crispness in the air, befitting mid-September. Gwen parked the car and they made their way to the horse barn where Josh would be working. People wandered about the grounds, the women arrayed in everything from fancy dresses and elaborate hats to blue jeans, tee shirts, and ponytails.

They entered the barn and made their way down the center aisle, admiring some of the stalled horses. At the far end, Jessie was assisting Josh with a horse. He greeted them in a friendly way, but with three horses in queue for his attention before the match, he and Jessie couldn't stop to visit. So Gwen and Cathryn moved on to the big tent for the luncheon. They got in line, filled their plates, and found seats next to a couple that Gwen knew from church.

As Cathryn returned from another trip to the buffet for seconds of a particularly delicious coleslaw, a breeze whipped her napkin to the ground. While balancing her plate and leaning to retrieve it, a pair of tall polished boots stopped in front of her, and a hand swooped down to recover the napkin. When she straightened to thank the owner of the boots, her jaw dropped and her knees weakened.

Jack stood before her, his eyes alight with pleasure.

"Surprise! I didn't say anything before because I wasn't sure I'd be able to be here unencumbered. And I'm not, actually, but ... oh, Jaimie's here too. I'd really like her to meet you. She rides with us, you know." He was bursting with energy. "Can I join you for lunch?" His plate held only a few morsels of food. At her inquisitive look, he said, "I don't eat much before I play."

When they reached the table, Gwen looked up. Her eyes twinkled when Cathryn announced, "Look who I found on the buffet line." She introduced Jack and he squeezed in next to her on the bench. Although he joined in the general conversation, his eyes kept returning to her.

Soon another team member, Dan Fielding, stopped at the table to claim Jack for the match. Fielding's friendly and agreeable nature immediately confirmed Cathryn's initial phone impression of him from back in February—he was the personification of Mr. Bingley in *Pride & Prejudice*. His cheerful attitude and captivating smile engaged everyone.

Jack rose. "Time to saddle up. I hope we provide an entertaining afternoon for you all. Good weather, a good field, and good company." He looked pointedly at Cathryn, who immediately blushed. Bending close he whispered, "Might you honor me with a kiss for luck?"

She kissed him lightly on the cheek, then watched as the two polo players strode off together.

"Well, this is an interesting turn of events," Gwen said with a wicked smile as they rose and made for the field.

Cathryn looked at her dubiously. "This is exactly why I find him so confusing. You saw how friendly he was, right?"

Gwen laughed. "Friendly? He was looking at friendly in the rear view mirror. Smitten is more like it."

And what did he mean by 'unencumbered'? Surely he wouldn't consider Jaimie an encumbrance. Then a vision of a bright green SUV formed in Cathryn's mind. Was *she* here?

Adam approached, carrying lawn chairs, and helped them choose a good spot for viewing the match. Neither he nor Gwen made any attempt to hide their mutual affection, although there was nothing untoward.

Activity on the field then demanded Cathryn's attention. Riders mounted. Horses danced about with excitement. The teams lined up for the opening throw-in. As host, Sterling did the honors with fitting flamboyance. So handsome. So captivating. Does he not play polo?

Cathryn had learned a few polo terms from Jack and had done some research on her own after her lesson with him, but Adam's narration during the match was still helpful. Jack's team had first possession and the action was heated, but the first chukker ended with no score for either side.

Ponies were changed and play was on again. Fielding led the charge this time, using a ride-off to divert the player with the ball as Jaimie swooped in for the possession. A fast pass scored a point for Jack's team.

Cathryn was amazed at the speed and agility shown by the horses, and equally appreciated the skill of the riders in maintaining their seats while concentrating on the ball in play. She was engrossed in the game and jumped at an unexpected hand on her shoulder.

"Sorry Cathryn, didn't mean to startle you. How is your view from here?" Sterling leaned over her shoulder to catch her eye.

She could have identified him by scent alone.

"The view is great, thank you. Adam got us set up. This is

my first polo match." Sterling knelt beside her chair, so she asked, "Do you play?"

"I did in years past. Too intense for me now with this old injury ..." He patted his hip.

"It's too intense for any sensible person," Gwen remarked.

Adam chuckled.

"How is it that you host matches here, and built this field?" Cathryn asked. "I thought this was cowboy country."

Sterling looked at her with a satirical eye, as if considering how much to say, and then flashed her a genial smile.

"I played with the Boulder team years ago and have stayed in touch with some of them. When Granite City was ready for a team of its own, I simply nurtured it along. I figured 'if I built it, they would come,' and I'd get to see more matches without having to travel."

She had to laugh at his quote and their eyes locked in amusement. She didn't meet many fellow quoters.

His eyes searched her face. "What about you? You're a horsewoman. Ever play polo? You grew up in Fullerton; maybe you know some of these players."

"Well, it so happens I went to school with one of the guys on the team. Jack Stone. We ran into each other a while back, and he was kind enough to give me a polo lesson. In slow motion, that is. I think it's a sport to begin when one is younger. Much younger."

She tried to laugh casually, but felt exposed under Sterling's unwavering gaze. What is he about? She felt her cheeks coloring again, and adjusted herself in her chair. Eventually—to her relief—he stood.

The men remained with them until halftime and Cathryn observed Gwen and Adam's interaction. It struck her that this new Gwen was very like an evolved Marianne from *Sense & Sensibility*, which Cathryn found most intriguing. Like Marianne, Gwen was not one to hide her feelings or opinions but—unlike Marianne—Gwen's expression of those feelings was tempered by the wisdom of age and experience. A tantalizing combination any evolved man would appreciate, which Adam obviously did.

At halftime, the four of them joined the traditional divot stomp, with Sterling taking Cathryn's hand and leading her onto the field. It was flattering to be singled out in such a way and the curious glances of others courted her vanity again.

When they returned to the sidelines Sterling announced, "Ladies, I regret that duty calls. We have a good turnout today so there's a lot to do. I am *especially* pleased you've joined us today, Cathryn. Such charming company is always welcome, and not often found." He nodded to the women and was off, Adam at his side.

The match resumed and Cathryn became absorbed in watching Jack. She admired his unity with his horse. He was rather bold with the ball and a good strategist. Jaimie was a light and catty rider, and seemed to be in the right place at just the right time. On several of the plays, father and daughter were in sync—it was obvious they'd played together a great deal. The teams were well matched so the competition was keen, yet there was lots of laughter from both sides and none of the snooty intensity Cathryn had assumed was part of polo. The score bounced back and forth, with loud moans and roars of laughter at fouls called on both teams. With some intense blocking by Jack in the last chukker, the ball was freed; Fielding deftly turned it and swept down the field for a dramatic winning score.

Refreshments were offered after the match, along with entertainment by two fiddlers. The crowd—larger than Cathryn had anticipated—was a curious mix of the hoity-toity types she figured would follow the circuit, along with ranchers, common folk, and general horse lovers. Cathryn was fascinated by such scope, and she and Gwen enjoyed sharing observations and opinions.

Cathryn took special notice of Sterling as he mingled with his guests and was impressed by his confidence and quiet sense of power. What would life be like, partnered with such a man?

"Here you are." Adam had found them again.

Cathryn understood Gwen's attraction to Adam. He was quiet and steady, with a gleam of mirth in his eyes. Other locals joined them, and the air was filled with lively conversation about the match, the food, local events, and the weather. People interacted with Adam and Gwen as if they were an established couple. Soon Josh and Jessie joined them too, off-duty for the present.

While Cathryn was scanning the crowd for Jack and Jaimie, Sterling joined her group. As he visited with the others he kept one eye on her. He was smooth, no common cowboy. She admired how he navigated the growing cluster of people with finesse, drawing everyone into the conversation. Her own ability to feel comfortable in a group started and ended with kids. She wished she didn't find adults so daunting, and envied him his skill.

Soon Sterling had maneuvered himself next to her and began making quiet side remarks that only she could hear, leaning in and touching her arm or her shoulder. Although still everything a gentleman, something about his presence now felt imperious, almost possessive. The hair on the back of her neck stirred, but when she glanced up, his expression remained innocuous, and a complete denial of the undercurrent she sensed.

Her chest tightened. This was no longer flattering. Rather, she felt more like a mouse cornered by a handsome but hungry cat. Under the smooth surface was he 'your typical rich man used to having his own way'? She shuddered.

Although she ignored his asides and tried to redirect him back into the group conversation, he would have none of it and smiled at her unsuccessful attempts. What did he want from her? What was he trying to do? How far would he go to get his way?

"Come. I must show you my newest stud. As a horse person, you'll appreciate the traits I'm breeding for."

But she saw through his attempt to get her alone. She struggled to concoct a logical protest but he was quick.

Taking her elbow, he began to propel her away from the group and toward the barn. Her back stiffened and her breathing grew quick and shallow. She didn't want to appear peevish, and glanced about for an escape. Her effort to signal Gwen failed; she and Adam were immersed in conversation, their heads bent together. Panic rose in Cathryn's chest. Sterling tossed her a smile—a smug acknowledgment of his power.

Then Jessie seemed to pick up her signal.

"Hey, Sterling, can Josh and I tag along?"

Cathryn thanked her with a pronounced nod.

Jessie smiled agreeably and the four of them made for the breeding buildings.

The stud was handsome and the barn a facility any horse lover would envy. After they'd admired a few of the mares and learned more about the selected bloodlines, Jessie reminded them it was time to finalize evening preparations.

"And do you have a companion for dinner, my dear?" Sterling looked Cathryn up and down in a rakish manner, grinning his approval. He was still in possession of her elbow.

She demurred. "Thank you, but I'm Gwen's guest and will sit with her."

"I see," he said in a quiet voice, a bemused expression dancing in his eyes.

"I like to take good care of my friends *and* my guests. I value good company. I fancy myself the host of happiness."

His manner and countenance remained maddeningly benign. He was toying with her, like a cat with its prey.

She hoped Jessie could see what was happening. Josh seemed oblivious.

The four began the walk back. Although uncomfortably aware that Sterling's eye was still on her, he had let go her elbow. She avoided his gaze and deliberately infused some confidence into her walk, to 'bring up her life' like she did when dealing with a too-dominant horse. This dominant side of Sterling had caught her off-guard.

They rounded the corner of the last barn and there—

straight ahead—shone a bright green SUV, cozily parked next to Jack's truck. And there also were Jack, Jaimie, and a smart-looking brunette she guessed must be Blaire. Jack and Jaimie were cleaning tack while Blaire reigned from a lawn chair, occupied with her phone.

Jack jerked in sudden awareness of the approaching group. His body stiffened, and he dropped a bridle he was holding.

Cathryn frowned. This was a wretched beginning. Where was that friendly Jack from the luncheon?

Sterling looked curiously at Cathryn and took hold of her elbow again. He presumptuously cleared his throat to announce their presence.

Blaire lifted a piercing eye. "Taking good care of your guests, I see," she remarked with a curl of her lip.

Sterling made a slight bow. "You know I always do. I'm showing this *very* special guest around my humble home."

Blaire gave an audible sniff.

"Cathryn, have you made the acquaintance of *Miss* Blaire Burgess? And her daughter Jaimie? I believe they're here with Jack." There was an impudent twinkle in Sterling's eye.

Jack grimaced at him, but stepped forward with Jaimie. He might have been attempting a smile, but his face just appeared oddly skewed.

"Cathryn, this is Jaimie. I told you about her at lunch."

Blaire righted herself rigidly in her chair.

Josh snorted.

"Jaimie, this is Cathryn McNeil; we grew up in the same neighborhood in Fullerton. She was in Uncle Joe's class in school."

Jaimie appeared uncomfortable, and Cathryn instinctively moved to lessen the tension for the girl, who seemed younger than twenty-one.

"Hi, Jaimie. Today was my first polo match. You did some great riding." She hoped her friendly chatter would lessen Jaimie's anxiety and divert the daggers Blaire's eyes were shooting at everyone.

Sterling continued to smile insipidly, but Cathryn detected amusement in his eyes.

After casting a worried glance at Blaire, Jaimie offered a tentative smile.

Cathryn reached out to shake her hand.

Blaire was now *intensely* busy with her phone, but she continued to watch them all surreptitiously.

"Well, the dinner hour approaches," Sterling announced, "and I must escort my beautiful guest back to her group, which unfortunately does not include me," he said, looking straight at Cathryn.

She glanced at him and saw a hint of a smirk. It reminded her very much of Mr. Tilney's teasing in *Northanger Abbey*, except for the undercurrent of power she felt Sterling subtly wielding.

He lifted an eyebrow at her and said, "I'm looking forward to more of *your* company later this evening, my dear."

Jack looked on with a frown, shifting uneasily from foot to foot but saying nothing.

Jaimie still looked uncertain. The poor girl was caught in multiple crossfires.

Josh was trying to stifle his laughter, encouraged by Jessie's nudge in his ribs.

"Oh, by the way ... nice match, Stone." Sterling tossed the comment over his shoulder as he moved his hand to the small of Cathryn's back and led the party away.

"Thanks," Jack mumbled, then stomped off to the horse trailer.

Cathryn felt possessed against her will but could think of no course of action that wouldn't look ridiculous.

Something is going on here, and I seem to be the only one not in the loop. She hoped Jessie could enlighten her. While they walked, Cathryn brooded about Blaire's presence, and wished Sterling would take his hand off her back.

When they reached the dinner tent, Sterling relinquished his control and turned to face her. "I'll make it a point to see you later this evening," he promised, with a smile so dazzling that her eyes smarted. "Please be kind enough to save me a dance?"

She nodded and he was off. His retreat left her shaky.

Josh and Jessie waved as they walked off to attend to their duties. Josh was hooting with laughter.

Cathryn was left to ponder the baffling interactions she'd just witnessed and felt. At least she hadn't been alone with Sterling. His presence left her feeling on edge and vulnerable but she could not put her finger on exactly what had changed from the other night at dinner.

How could someone like Adam work for a man like Sterling? It didn't make sense.

Jack's hot and cold behavior didn't make sense.

Sterling's presumptions didn't make sense.

Where was Gwen?

CHAPTER NINETEEN

When she spotted her friend alone, sipping a fruity drink at the edge of the canopy, Cathryn hurried over. "Oh good, there you are," she said, attempting to sound nonchalant.

Gwen eyed her with suspicion. "What's with you?"

"Me? Oh, I'm fine. Shall we go freshen up?" The words spilled out of her mouth more quickly than she intended.

"Sure, we can do that, but your 'fine' doesn't fool me. You spend far too much time in your head. Why is it you were beaming at lunch and you're brooding now? It really is okay to share with your friends, you know."

Cathryn looked down and fidgeted with her ring. "I guess I'm not used to doing that. I don't want to burden others, or bore them ..."

Gwen stared at her.

"Okay, okay ... did you see Sterling kind of herd me away, supposedly to go look at his stud?"

Gwen thought for a minute. "No, I just noticed you two had left with Josh and Jessie. I didn't see any herding."

Cathryn smiled. "Your eyes were engaged elsewhere."

Gwen blushed, just a little.

"Anyway, Jessie saved me from being alone with Sterling. He makes me uneasy. What's up with him?"

"Before we get into that," Gwen said, "what else happened? I don't think some guy coming on to you would make you look like your world has fallen apart."

Cathryn was aghast. Am I that transparent? She tried to put her thoughts in order but the words just tumbled out.

"Well, on our way back from the breeding barns we saw Jack and his daughter, with the woman who is her mother, a smart-looking brunette named Blaire. You know, the woman with the bright green SUV, the angry woman I heard that day at his house. Oh, Gwen, Jack wouldn't even look at me. Then Sterling sort of demanded introductions be made."

Gwen chuckled. "I can see Sterling doing that."

"The tension was palpable. Blaire was hateful, and everyone was uncomfortable. Except Sterling. And Josh—he kept laughing. Sterling seemed to find it all quite amusing too, but I don't know why. He was still making me nervous, it was like he was trying to control me. He kept hold of my elbow. Jack ignored Blaire. Sterling was the only one who talked to her. Jack certainly didn't stand up to her. She clearly rules Jack and Jaimie with ... I don't know ... an iron claw. Dagger eyes. Why does he let her? And this, after he said he wanted to 'explore a friendship' with me. What does that even mean? And he was so more-than-friendly at lunch. I don't get it. Should I just give up on him?"

Gwen was quick with a reply. "Why would you give up when you don't even know what's going on? This was one incident, from only your perspective. You have questions. Let's walk over there and see if we can get some answers." She looked intensely at Cathryn. "Brave enough?" she teased.

Cathryn swallowed hard. Gwen was right. Instead of stewing about it, she should just cut to the chase. What's the worst that could happen by asking a few questions? It hadn't turned out so bad at Jack's ranch. She was, after all, committed to creating a new and expanded life for herself, like Gwen had done. No time like the present—and in the company of a helpful expert.

"Okay. I'll approach this Jack thing like I do my riding—

whole-hearted, body and soul. It's not like I have anything to lose at this point anyway," she said with a rueful smile.

Gwen laughed. "I'll be your backup. I'm curious to meet this Blaire. Let's find Jack and see what's up. We can figure out the Sterling thing later. One situation at a time."

"That makes sense. But what will I say to Jack?" Cathryn importuned as they walked toward the trailer area. "I don't want to seem all possessive and bitchy."

"Cathryn," exclaimed Gwen, "you are *way* the other side of possessive ... and of bitchy. You know, there's also such a thing as being so distant and so self-contained that he wonders if you care about him at all."

Cathryn started. That echoed Jack's comment at his cabin, the one about mixed messages and why he thought she hadn't asked about his social life. Where was the sweet spot between too transparent and too self-contained? Somewhere between too vulnerable and too self-protective, she suspected.

"Wouldn't it be helpful to know what role the girl's mother plays in Jack's life? If they're really not done with each other, it's better to know than to waste any more time. What do you *want* to say to him?"

"Hmmm ... well, I want to know what he's about concerning me, but I don't really know how to ask that, and I can't in front of others. No, that's something I'd have to ask him when we're alone. Hey, maybe Jack and Jaime, and even Blaire, could join you and me and Adam for dinner. Is Adam free to eat with us?"

"Yes, he's planning to sit with us. And that sounds like a reasonable plan." Gwen nodded as she played with the idea. "Yes, yes ... just a nice, friendly invitation. Then see what hits the proverbial fan."

They both laughed. Maybe this wouldn't be so bad after all. Cathryn squared her shoulders.

As they approached the horse trailers near the barn, they saw Jack, Blaire, and Jaimie sitting in lawn chairs. Jack and Jaimie were still in their polo clothes, sitting close together and talking. The approach of Gwen and Cathryn appeared to have caught Jack's eye. It was uncanny how he always seemed as aware of Cathryn's presence as she was of his.

She took a deep breath, summoned what she hoped was a friendly smile, and said, "Hi again, Jack."

"Cathryn, good to see you. And, is it Gwen?" He looked a little nervous, but was coping much better than just a short time ago.

The mother and daughter turned toward the new arrivals.

"Blaire, Jaimie, you've met Cathryn, and this is her friend Gwen, who recently moved here to Granite City."

Blaire stirred in her chair but made no motion to get up, and said nothing to acknowledge the introduction.

"You two used to work together, am I right?" He seemed more at ease with a neutral third party present.

But weren't Josh and Jessie and Sterling neutral? Maybe not. She recalled Josh's laughter and Sterling's amusement.

Jack motioned to Jaimie, who came forward to shake hands with Gwen. Blaire continued to feign haughty indifference. Cathryn noted a suppressed grin playing about Gwen's mouth as she eyed Blaire, who was doing a poor job of concealing her anger with a brittle smile.

Jaimie still looked uncomfortable, so Cathryn jumped in to help her feel at ease. "You are quite the polo player, Jaimie. How long have you been with the team?"

"About three years now," Jaimie said, warming a bit. "Dad and I used to practice in the field all the time, way before I was officially on the team. We did lots of horse things together. I just love horses." She produced a hesitant smile.

"I know exactly what you mean," Cathryn said with conviction. "Everyone thought I was just a horse-crazy girl that would outgrow that stage, but I never did, and I never will. Horses are in my blood. I'd like to tell you about my wonderful old gelding Henry sometime, maybe over dinner? Would you all like to sit with us tonight?"

Blaire jerked upright and glared at Jack, then glowered at Cathryn.

Jaimie looked anxiously at Jack.

Gwen broke through the awkwardness. "I know Adam would like to catch up with you, Jack. He says he knows one of your brothers?"

"Yeah, my older brother Joe. He ranches not far from here. Joe and Adam were good friends with Dan Fielding's dad Larry, who was one of the founders of this Wyoming team. Larry's gone now," he said in a quiet tone.

Blaire's shrill voice cut in. "Jack, you know we're sitting with the Bruenings and the Stewarts at dinner. You'll have to do your catching up on your own time." She drilled him with an insistent look.

Turning to Gwen and Cathryn with a saccharin smile she said, "Some other time, ladies. So *nice* to meet you." Then she stood, as if to dismiss them.

There was nothing nice about Blaire. Cathryn glanced at Jack but he was staring at his boots. She longed to ask him why he didn't confront Blaire. Or at least dismiss her attempts at control. Just now, he was a bit of a disappointment—and not much of a hero.

Cathryn turned to Jaimie. "Okay, some other time then. It was wonderful to meet you and see you play; you're a great rider." She gave the girl a warm smile, brimming with friendly regard mixed with sympathy.

Jaimie returned a grateful smile and said in a small voice, "I'd like that."

"A pleasure to meet you all," Gwen offered with a twinkle in her eye.

Cathryn and Gwen walked off, leaving Jack still staring at his boots. Once away, Gwen pressed her hand over her mouth to stifle a laugh.

Cathryn glanced over at her. "You were right, Gwen. It does feel better to take action. I don't know how much we learned about Jack's situation, but now I feel like the burden is on *him*. I'm relieved. If he wants to explore a friendship or a relationship with me, he'll need to make the next move. But I wonder why he doesn't just stand up to Blaire?"

Gwen smiled broadly. "Fascinating dynamics. Wish I could have filmed it for a training session. And you're right, Blaire has some kind of hold over him," she mused, "but I don't think it has anything to do with affection."

Cathryn looked at her friend with appreciation, glad to have a wingman again. Gwen's input helped keep a more realistic perspective, and prevented Cathryn from getting her perceptions, wishes, and feelings all tangled together.

Gwen linked her arm with Cathryn's. "I hope he didn't stare too many holes in those boots."

Cathryn threw her head back and laughed.

The large tent area was set up for dinner. Adam had secured a table for their group, which did not include Jack or Jaimie or Blaire; but it was nice to feel part of the friendly bunch Adam had gathered.

Once dinner wound down, Sterling made a little speech about the history of the matches held at the Lazy S. He was a captivating speaker, to be sure, and got several laughs from the crowd. He was in his element and, oddly enough, Cathryn was finding him attractive again, in spite of her earlier unease in his presence. Nor was it difficult to compare Jack's seeming lack of fortitude unfavorably against Sterling's appearance of mastery and ease.

After that last episode with Jack, Cathryn had no desire to look for him or his entourage in the crowd. She didn't see him at all until Fielding was announced as the MVP of the match and came up to receive the traveling award: a cracked polo ball mounted on a setting of crazily-bent horseshoes. He accepted with a good-natured flourish and a dramatic bow, garnering massive applause.

Cathryn followed his progress back to his table and saw Jaimie beaming at him as he sat down next to her.

In that moment, Jack must have felt Cathryn's gaze and, finding her eyes, smiled at her with a nod. Knowing the ball was now his to play and, best of all, knowing *he* knew that, Cathryn was able to return a generous smile.

A spirit of warmth flowed through her now that she was finally free from trying to predict or control what happened next. Odd how one small action could untangle so many knots. Simply confronting an issue and then letting it go had ironically given her a stronger sense of being in control. The day was full of conundrums.

With a contented smile, she rose and made her way to the dessert table. The fragrance of apple cobbler tempted her. As she reached for a plate someone bumped her arm. She turned and found herself face to face with Blaire, whose outthrust chin propped up cold eyes that glittered as she looked down her aquiline nose.

In an icy voice, Blaire cautioned Cathryn in no uncertain terms. "Back away from Jack, honey. You are *way* out of your league and messing with business that doesn't involve you. Go back to your little town of Quinn and find someone at your own level, or you will deeply regret it," she hissed through clenched teeth.

Cathryn arched her brow at the mention of Quinn but did not reply.

"Yes, I've done a little investigating. Like I said, you're out of your league. If you know what's good for you, you'll cut off the revival of this pathetic little friendship before someone gets hurt." Her stony eyes threatened unnamed evil.

Cathryn had been intimidated by the likes of Blaire before; high-society types who seemed to have the perfect looks and the perfect life, but were usually saddled with a severely flawed character.

Then a switch flipped inside Cathryn. She recalled Lizzy's declaration from *Pride & Prejudice*: 'My courage always rises with every attempt to intimidate me ...' The famous words bolstered her determination to turn this high-society encounter into a horse of a different color. She knew how she must act.

Composing her countenance into one of unexpected

sympathy, she turned to Blaire and addressed her in a measured voice. "Why Blaire, how kind of you to take such an interest in me, and even go to the trouble of researching me. I'm impressed. I'm sorry to say I couldn't be bothered to research you. Just not interested. I already know you're ill mannered and ignorant. And Blaire, be advised that I've dealt with your kind before. Surely you know I have extensive clinical experience treating sociopathic patients ... you know, the kind of people who threaten others?"

Blaire's eyebrows flew up.

"Oh, did you miss that in your research? Pity."

Looking steadily into Blaire's astonished face, Cathryn made her final sally. "Let me share something that might save you some time and effort, Blaire. It's simple, really. My decisions in life are based on what will lead to my own happiness, or bring happiness to those I care about. I am in no way influenced by someone so wholly unconnected to me as you are. Your opinions and advice have *no* bearing on me."

Cathryn picked up a dish of apple cobbler, took an appreciative sniff, and gave Blaire a final look.

"I think we're done here."

With a pert smile, she walked off, unaware she left a dumbfounded Blaire gaping after her.

CHAPTER TWENTY

*C*athryn was grateful that guests were not formally announced as she and Gwen entered the party room where the polo dance was to be held. She had enough on her mind without trying to make a dazzling entrance.

Dozens of people milled about, greeting each other and gathering in small clusters. The bar at the south end was already crowded. Cathryn and Gwen found seats on their own—no obliging Mr. Tilney was there as in *Northanger Abbey* to assist them or to comment on their attire.

A gigantic fireplace dominated the north end of the room, with sofas and comfortable chairs adjacent. Other chairs and benches were scattered in groups along the walls, leaving plenty of space in the middle for dancing. Musicians tuned their instruments. The room itself had walls of heavy milled lumber. Three sets of French doors opened onto a patio area that overlooked a broad valley to the west. The intensifying colors of the approaching sunset cast a dramatic glow on the scene. Large windows to the east framed the darkening sky on that side of the room. Obviously, great thought had gone into the planning of this space.

With surprise, she recognized the similarities to Jack's cabin, and to River Run. Which place was built first? She wondered what kind of relationship existed between Jack and Sterling. They did not seem on friendly terms.

Adam joined the two women, beer bottle in hand, and stood next to Gwen, their shoulders touching. Gwen's new romance and indeed her new life had happened so quickly. Maybe there was something to be said for being direct—even blunt—about expressing oneself.

Cathryn wandered further into her own thoughts. Her brow furrowed as she considered Jack and the evening ahead. Would he be at Blaire's side? Would he even be here? The night might yield some deeper knowledge of him. Then again, it might yield nothing.

While Gwen and Adam talked quietly together, Cathryn surveyed the crowd and found her eye drawn to Sterling. He shone as a host, mingling with group after group. He was almost as baffling as Jack. She could find no clarity regarding her feelings about either of them. Her river of emotions was muddy indeed.

Just then Jaimie entered with Dan Fielding, her face aglow. The two had eyes only for each other. Young love. Did Jack approve the match? Cathryn didn't know Fielding's profession or social status. Jack didn't value social status anyway. She guessed he approved. Sensing a lull in the conversation next to her, she remarked, "Don't they look happy?"

Adam and Gwen followed her gaze.

Adam looked pleased. "I believe they are. Fielding has taken over his late father's fencing and equipment business. It was quite a successful venture and I think he'll be able to build on that. He's a good guy, friendly attitude, people really like him. He and Jaimie are both horse people. But I'm not so sure her mother approves. He doesn't have that social standing Blaire likes."

They watched the couple talking with some of the other younger members of both teams.

"Social standing doesn't tell much about a person," Gwen observed.

"I agree," Cathryn chimed in. "Character is far more

important. But sometimes true character is difficult to determine." She was speculating about Jack. And Sterling.

Adam and Gwen gave her a speaking look and she blushed, thinking they were reading her mind. Then she heard a familiar voice behind her shoulder.

"Can this character get you ladies something to drink?"

Her face flooded with color. How long had he been standing there?

"I see Adam's already working on a brew. I'm heading over to get one myself." Jack's smile was easy and relaxed.

Such a chameleon. So unpredictable. And surrounded by drama. Her misgivings surfaced again. How could anyone have a relationship with someone as changeable as Jack?

"I'll have what Adam's drinking," Gwen replied.

"And for you?" Jack looked at Cathryn.

Jolted out of her reverie and unprepared for his sudden friendliness, she could only mumble, "Uh, I don't know. What do they have?"

"Shall we go have a look?"

"Ok." She didn't know what else to say, and was trying to figure out where she wanted this interaction to go. She had assumed the dance would be like the dinner, with Jack being Blaire's companion, and had prepared for *that*. Not *this*. Now what? Throw my heart over the fence ... into the quagmire? She was growing impatient with Jack and his quagmire.

"Won't your 'companion' be a little upset about you escorting me?" she asked with an arched brow.

"My companion? Ah, well, I've had a little talk with that person who, by the way, is *not* my companion, and I hope the rest of the evening will be more enjoyable than dinner was." He looked sidelong at Cathryn.

Had her exchange with Blaire influenced this new arrangement? And where was Blaire anyway?

As the two of them crossed the room, Jack nodded at several acquaintances.

Cathryn now comprehended that all her predicting and preparing had been for naught. No one could foretell what might happen, or what others might do. Maybe life was like riding. As long as you have a strong seat in the saddle you can pretty much manage whatever happens. That metaphor made her smile.

Seeing that smile, Jack touched her shoulder.

His hand was warm and she trembled, just a little.

They got their drinks and were making their way back to Gwen and Adam when Sterling waved them over to the small group surrounding him. He introduced them both but focused his attention on Cathryn.

"So, my dear, are you enjoying your evening thus far?" He looked at her with a mischievous grin.

She squirmed beneath his gaze. Trying to brush him off, she gave him a brusque, "Of course," then added, "Do you often have dinners and dances after a match?"

Sterling smiled knowingly at her attempt to redirect him but let others answer her question while he continued to watch her, his eyes alight with unexplainable mirth.

Color forced its way into her cheeks again. She hoped no one noticed.

Convinced Sterling was aware of what he was doing, she decided his intent was to disarm her. But to what purpose? She had to admit he was good at this. Very good.

After some general remarks from others about the party, Sterling said, "I must apologize for my behavior earlier today, Cathryn. I wasn't aware that you were spoken for."

Cathryn muffled a gasp. Astounded at this brazen remark —made so publicly—she struggled to regain her composure. Somehow she managed a cool, detached reply.

"That's no wonder, as I'm *not* spoken for, as you call it. Such an antiquated notion ..."

"Really? Am I mistaken? I was sure I had observed something between you and a mutual acquaintance." It was both a tease and a challenge. He took a drink from his glass, but his eyes never left hers. His manner was as smooth as Wickham's in *Pride & Prejudice*.

Jack stood by—rigid, mute, useless.

Apparently she would have to fend for herself.

In what she hoped was a casual, friendly voice she replied, "I can't imagine who you mean?"

Sterling looked at Jack, then back at her with a crafty expression.

Glancing at Jack herself, she feigned surprise. "Oh, Jack and I are friends from school. We both grew up in Fullerton. But I'm actually visiting my friend Gwen, who moved here a few months ago." She looked at the others, silently imploring someone to take the conversation in a different direction.

But Sterling kept control and continued. "Ah, yes. My foreman, Adam, is quite taken with her. Seems a charming woman, although I'm always a little wary around those in the psychology field," he joked, evoking chuckles all around.

At that, Jack found his voice. "Then you may wish to be on guard around Cathryn. She works in that field, although I believe your area of expertise is with children, right?" He turned to her and held her eyes.

Surprised at his sudden support, she managed to say, "Yes; well, it was. Because of changes in agency policies, with which I disagreed, I am now working in the legal field."

Several faces smiled at that.

"There's another profession one usually wants to measure their words around," quipped one man in the group, and they all laughed.

Just then Blaire approached the gathering and skillfully wended her way toward Sterling. Her eyes smoldered at Jack.

"What a lively group we have here," she said in a syrupy voice. "Warren certainly knows how to throw a party, don't you, dear," she said, taking hold of Sterling's arm.

Cathryn was astonished at this familiarity.

Sterling basked in the false admiration. Cathryn was sure female attention was commonplace for him with his good looks, his self-assurance, and his wealth. But what ties could he possibly have with Blaire?

"Well, these drinks aren't getting any colder," remarked Jack. "Better be on our way. Good to see you all again."

"Yes, nice to meet you," Cathryn added and turned to follow Jack. She felt betrayed by him, confused by Sterling, and was sure Blaire's eyes were drilling holes into her retreating back. Something was going on and she had best get to the bottom of it before she drowned in her ignorance. When they returned to Gwen and Adam, the women exchanged a meaningful look.

"Will you guys watch our drinks while we freshen up?" Gwen asked.

Cathryn was thankful for the chance to gather her thoughts and said so to Gwen as they walked away.

"Fascinating interaction in Sterling's little group," Gwen remarked. "What do you know about this Blaire?"

"Not much," Cathryn admitted. "Just that's she's a realtor in Fullerton, and a determined social climber. And Jaimie's mother, of course."

Gwen cast a glance in Blaire's direction. "She seems on intimate terms with Sterling too, although I haven't seen her before. But I'm fairly new. It might not hurt to find out a little more. Something about her puts me on alert ..."

Cathryn nodded, then voiced her own concern. "I just don't get her connection with either of them, and why she has such control over Jack." She frowned. " 'Something fishy this way comes'... or whatever the saying is," she said, with an uneasy laugh.

"Wicked. Shakespeare," Gwen replied. "Adam doesn't say much about her, other than she's been around this group for several years. But Adam's not one to gossip or pay attention to the grapevine. I wonder who would know more about her?" she mused.

In *Emma* Frank Churchill had extolled the blessing of a female correspondent when one wanted news.

"Another woman," Cathryn said. "Maybe Jessie? She's way younger than us but she's been around here for a while. She might know something."

Gwen nodded.

As they left the ladies room, Cathryn scanned the crowd and saw Jessie tending bar. "Guess I'll have to catch her later."

Although still bewildered by Sterling's remark and irritated by Jack's flimsy and delayed support, Cathryn saw Gwen was clearly eager to get back to Adam.

The band had begun playing and before Cathryn could sit down Jack asked, with peculiar gallantry, "Will you do me the honor of dancing with me?" and offered his hand.

She looked at him with guarded amusement. "If I didn't know better, I might think you've been reading Jane Austen."

He lifted an eyebrow and, with a winsome look, led her to the dance floor. Here was the charming Jack again, and she was in his arms.

The band was playing "My Girl." Cathryn was transported back to the warm May night of the ninth grade dance. She'd worn the dotted Swiss dress she'd sewn for the occasion. She'd made many such dresses through the years, back when girls and women wore 'occasion' dresses. She still had several of them as keepsakes, and the sight of each dress and the feel of the fabric carried special memories. Tonight she wore the batik dress she'd made a few years ago—the same one she'd worn at the funeral home when she met Jack. Only tonight her hair was not confined in a braid. And tonight she wasn't a ninth grader.

She looked up. Jack danced well, which was no surprise for a fine horseman. But her feathers were still ruffled at his lack of response to Sterling's provocative comment. Her forbearance was wearing thin. After all, she was building a new life, and for the romantic part she wanted a man she could count on. She could not be content with ambushes of delight, and swings from intimacy to abandonment. She didn't want to be toyed with. He had no right ... who did he think he was to change on her again? Her mind was a vortex of gathering anger—she would get to the bottom of this once and for all.

"Why does Sterling think I'm spoken for?" she demanded.

At the same moment, Jack blurted, "What's the deal with you and Sterling?"

They glared at each other.

"Why do you care what Sterling thinks?" he asked, suspicion in his voice.

"Sterling?" she said with disbelief.

They stared at each other again.

"Ok, you start," she conceded, in a clipped voice.

He looked over her shoulder momentarily, then back into her eyes. "I saw Sterling hit on you, twice; earlier today, and again a few minutes ago." He was scowling but his voice held a note of pain.

"What if he did? I didn't see you staking any claim, public or otherwise," she reproached. "Why does he think I'm spoken for? Just walking across a room with a man wouldn't make people say that. What are you telling people?"

His mouth dropped open but he didn't speak. He didn't have a chance.

Her fire was lit and she continued to rail at him. "And let's talk about Blaire," she said, sounding more defensive than she intended. "She was all possessive of you earlier today, and again at dinner. At your ranch you said you wanted to explore a friendship with *me*, and it seemed like maybe more. How can you do that when *she's* your constant companion? Then when she's chummy with Sterling, you're friendly with me again. What's that about? Why is she calling all the shots?"

Jack gawked at her.

Strong feelings drove a slew of suppressed words out her mouth from their hiding place in her heart. "You're all frank and honest with me, but only when we're alone. Or maybe only when it suits you? But earlier, in front of Sterling and the whole group ... well, you left me dangling out there. Some friend. And when Blaire or Jaimie are around, you won't even look me in the eye. Obviously Blaire has some kind of hold on you," she accused.

"But I ..."

Her eyes flashed. "Yes, you admitted to some kind of

constraint there, but really Jack, what am I to think? I'm not looking for an affair or an intrigue. I don't want to be someone's backup flirtation, or part of a big drama. I'm only interested in the real deal, plain and simple. You know, like an honest horse. And I have to say I'm surprised, because this ... this flimsiness of character doesn't quite fit with the man I thought you were."

Both stiffened, but neither let the other go. Their bodies and minds worked vigorously at odds until the slow dance ended and Jack stalked off.

Alone and fuming, Cathryn remembered Mr. Tilney's remarks from *Northanger Abbey* on the similarity of dancing and matrimony. How surprisingly pertinent. 'Fidelity and complaisance are the principal duties of both ... And it is the duty (of each) to give the other no cause for wishing that he or she had bestowed themselves elsewhere ... .'

Did Jack wish he had 'bestowed himself' elsewhere?

Did she?

Cathryn stared blindly at the blur of dancers until she saw Adam and Gwen heading out the doors to the patio. She rose and started in that direction, but was stopped by a strong hand on her shoulder and a velvety voice in her ear.

"Can one that is spoken for still dance with others?"

She whirled around to see Warren Sterling smiling and offering his hand. Her shoulders stiffened. She gave him a civil smile but inwardly she cringed. Dozens of women would gladly take her place, but having no reasonable excuse she accepted his hand as a country waltz began—"The Tennessee Waltz," to be exact. She remembered listening to it on Grandma Esther's old 78 rpm record player. Her mother had taught her and her sister how to waltz to this song. She had never danced to it with a man.

Sterling led her onto the floor.

She looked up at his pleasant expression, not sure whether to relax in his arms or be on guard. So she chose to discover more about him, and maybe uncover something useful about Blaire too.

Before she found any words to say, he opened with, "I know you're living in Quinn now. Do you think you'll remain there in the future?"

Surprised at the polite neutrality of his question, she gave him a brief reply and then quickly turned the conversation around to forward her agenda. She could make small talk while doing some investigating.

"And what about you? Are you content living here?" To her surprise, he was forthcoming.

"As you know, I inherited the Lazy S," he replied matter-of-factly. "My grandfather settled this spread originally. My father built it up into what it is now, and I'm humbly trying to at least maintain it, along with my other businesses. Except for college in Colorado, I've always lived here. My main interest is the breeding program."

"I don't know much about quarter horse pedigrees, but your stud is handsome and seems to have a good temperament, which one doesn't always see in a stud." She paused. "Do you ride at all since your injury?"

"Rarely. If I ride, I pay dearly afterward," he said with a grim smile. "Have you always been interested in horses?"

"Always." Horses. She relaxed and told him about her beloved Henry and how he could no longer jump fences.

He nodded thoughtfully. "It's a pity we usually outlive them." His eyes misted over. "I've had a few that were heartbreaking to lose."

This was not *at all* the Sterling she had expected. Gone was the smooth veneer. She felt like she was talking to a real person—a kind, caring person.

He must have seen her puzzled look. "Surprised?" he asked. "I'm not really the smooth rich guy of my public persona," he admitted, "nor the ladies' man of my reputation." He chuckled, then looked long at her, but this time she didn't feel uncomfortable.

He said, "I like Jack. He's an honest guy and a good horseman. I've known him for years, although we've never been really close; I'm not sure why. Still, I'd like to see him extricate himself from the situation he's in with Blaire. I don't know exactly what it's about; she's dropped some hints but I'd never interfere in his business. I do know she has her claws in deep," he said, with a look of dismay.

"How do you know Blaire?"

"Oh, she's my ex-wife." He laughed at Cathryn's shocked expression. "Yes, it's pretty obvious why she's an ex, isn't it. That's one conniving woman. We were only together two years when she started cheating on me. I've made my peace with her. Maybe Jack feels awkward because she left me for him. She thought he might climb higher into the social stratosphere than I could. It doesn't matter to me; it wasn't a marriage I wanted to stay in." He frowned. "Or maybe Jack wishes I'd warned him about her. Anyway, my money gives me the upper hand with her now, although it may not appear so in public. Trust me, I know some of Jack's misery."

Cathryn turned all this over in her mind.

"Sterling, why did you refer to me as spoken for? Why would you say that?"

He pursed his lips and gave her a penetrating look. "You and Jack seemed more than just old school chums, if my instincts are still good in such matters. I wanted to be sure of your character before I got honest with you. Jack's been pursued by several gold-diggers; I've seen it over the years. He's a good guy; a nice guy who's been through a lot. I like to keep an eye out for my friends, and help where I can."

Looking into his eyes as they moved across the floor, Cathryn saw genuine concern.

"Plus, I wanted to challenge ol' Jack to step up," he added with a sparkle in his eye. "I have a feeling you're worth it."

Color poured into her face. How wrong she had been! About Sterling. And about so much more.

She cringed. Her imagination had been wildly out of control. Mixed messages and wrong conclusions had muddied her perceptions and narrowed her perspective until she had imprisoned herself in a gothic novel of her own making!

Perhaps it *was* possible to read too many novels.

It was time to take this story in a different direction.

Her eyes returned to Sterling's face when he spoke again.

"If there's any way I can be useful to the two of you, just let me know. Even if it's to get Blaire out of your way for a few hours." He laughed and twirled her around. "Which is not an easy or pleasant task."

She was delighted. And much relieved.

"And what about you?" Cathryn asked, after another breathless twirl. "Is there a lady love in your life?"

"Yes," he confided as they walked to the sidelines. "But we keep it very low key. She lives in Colorado, and I visit often. She's staying there for now—her mother is terminally ill—but eventually she will join me here at the ranch." His features smoothed with pleasure. "I trust you'll keep that to yourself. Adam is the only one who knows."

"Of course."

"Good," he said, assuming mock earnestness. "That way you won't destroy my local status as a ladies' man. Thinking *I'm* available keeps the gold-diggers busy and the townspeople supplied with gossip. I must do my public duty." He gave her a smirk and kissed her hand with a flourish. She laughed as he moved off to resume his obligations as host.

Perhaps there was a Mr. Tilney at this ball after all.

Cathryn's world had just shifted again. Like when she'd first crossed the Golden Gate Bridge and gone through the rainbow tunnel with Bob. And she felt oddly serene—something she had experienced rarely since then; and when she did it was mostly in the company of children or animals.

In her work with children she had sometimes utilized eastern concepts and practices, and had taught yoga to kids with behavioral challenges. She knew the benefits of 'beginner's mind,' that state of openness, eagerness, and lack of preconception that children often possess. In the beginner's mind there are many possibilities, while in the expert's mind there are only a few. Had her own beginner's mind been hidden under her cloak of self-protection?

Protection was an illusion. She knew that. The ability to

feel things was either open or shut—to the good and the bad alike. She knew that too. She just hadn't applied this knowledge to herself. Or perhaps she'd lost its truth amongst the swirling plots of all the novels she'd read.

The radiant colors of the sunset beckoned and she walked through the French doors and onto the patio, where she took in a great breath of the mountain air. She found a secluded spot at the far side and stood staring out at the valley. In her conversation with Sterling she had found an internal foothold, a position of balance and strength long sought. She gazed up at the vast sky overhead and felt Bob smile. The people and sounds around her blurred as she floated amongst the stars. Peace filled her soul.

After a time, she sensed a presence behind her and turned. Jack stood there.

In a quiet voice he said, "Sorry for that outburst. I don't know where we're at, or what I'm doing, but I'd really like to just ... be here with you right now." He put a hand on her shoulder. "If you'll have me."

Suddenly the dance, and Blaire, and all the unanswered questions didn't matter. She was already standing on firm ground. She leaned her back into Jack. His arms surrounded her with a warmth not unlike the sunset colors that filled the sky. Her heart was full. They were together. The noise and the people around them melted away.

Sometime later, Cathryn noticed folks gathering around the fire pit. When she spotted Gwen and Adam, she nodded to Jack and they walked over hand in hand. The logs snapped and crackled merrily.

Cathryn hadn't seen Blaire again and wondered if Sterling had diverted her. She saw Sterling saying goodbye to small groups as they departed.

Jack followed her gaze but said nothing. He looked a little glum.

Does he wonder about my feelings for Sterling? Deciding to let that lie, she asked, "Where are Jaimie and Dan?"

"I think the younger ones went to town to hit the hot spots," Jack replied.

"It's getting kinda late," Gwen observed. "What time are we riding tomorrow?"

"I thought we could head out after lunch, if that works for everyone?" Adam glanced around for agreement.

Jack looked at Cathryn, bewildered. "What ride?"

"Join us," Adam said. "Most of us have our own mounts, and Josh has picked out a couple of sure-footed trail horses for Gwen and Cathryn. You got a trail horse with you, Jack?"

"Two of mine are good on the trail. Say, I bet Jaimie and Fielding would like to join us. Would that be okay? Jaimie hasn't done much trail riding; she'd love it."

The plan was set to meet at the main barn at one o'clock and the two couples wandered off, slowly making their separate ways back to Gwen's car.

Cathryn and Jack stopped to watch the moon rise over the open field to the east. It was as if all the land slumbered in hushed darkness, although she knew many night creatures were on the prowl.

"The moon is waxing," he observed. "This will be the Harvest Moon—or you can call it the Corn Moon, or the Barley Moon. I'm guessing two nights till it's full. What do you think?"

"I've never heard of the Corn Moon or the Barley Moon. But I love the moonlight." She sighed. "It illuminates, but ever so softly. Tolkien tells some lovely tales about the rising and setting of the moon and sun. They're pulled into place by horses, you know." She flashed Jack a grin, then asked, "How do you know which moon is the Harvest Moon?"

"Whichever full moon is closest to the equinox."

"I always wondered that," she murmured, her head tipped back, taking in the stars and the night air.

"Are you okay with me coming on the ride tomorrow, Cathryn? You didn't really invite me."

She looked at him with surprise. "Of course. You just weren't at *our* dinner table tonight when we talked about it. I believe you were with a different companion." She gave him a teasing look.

He grimaced.

"We had talked about doing a trail ride on Sunday but I hadn't heard any firm plans. You see, Josh is the nephew of my friend Deb, back in Quinn. When she learned I was coming here, she asked him to set up a ride for Gwen and me, before I even left. Before I knew about Gwen and Adam ... or this ranch ... or you." She looked over at him again.

Stepping closer, he put his arm around her and they continued to stare at the night sky.

"Do you and Jaimie sleep in the horse trailer?" Cathryn asked, her eyes fixed on the moon.

"Yeah, usually. Sometimes we tent camp."

"Mmm ... I can't see your companion sleeping in a tent, or in a horse trailer. Where does she stay?" She knew she was badgering him. It felt a bit wicked, but she indulged herself.

Jack winced at her use of the word 'companion' again.

"Blaire usually stays at the finest hotel around or with one of her high-class friends. I have no idea where she's gone tonight. I don't keep track of her." A little irritation had crept into his voice.

"No worries," Cathryn said breezily. "It must be nice for you and Jaimie. I never got to do much with my dad. He was always working." She looked at Jack. "Jaimie's a lucky girl."

"Yeah," he said, a trifle wistful. "We used to have some real good times together. We still do, but her focus has moved beyond me now. In case you hadn't noticed, she only has eyes for Fielding."

"I *had* noticed. And do you approve of her choice?"

"Sure. But I don't think her mother does. Fielding's not high enough in society's ranks for Blaire's taste."

"And you don't share Blaire's taste for the importance of society's ranks?" she asked archly.

"You know I don't." He sighed. "I know ... I'm a doctor, and have a certain amount of wealth, and I play polo, but in all these years I've really never outgrown my roots in Valley

View. I like stuff that's real. You know ... family, friends, the land. And honest horses."

The significance of his last comment was not lost on her.

"Me too, Jack," she said, taking his hand in both of hers.

Over by the parked cars a light flashed as a door was opened. She saw Gwen get in.

"Hey, that's my ride back to town."

"I'll walk you over." Silently they made their way across the moonlit field. He opened the car door.

"So you'll ride tomorrow Jack?"

"Yes, count me in." Taking hold of her shoulders, he bent to kiss her.

She was momentarily engulfed by warmth, then opened her eyes and touched his cheek with affection.

"Sweet dreams, Jack."

"Until tomorrow then."

CHAPTER TWENTY-ONE

*M*orning dawned soft and gray. Mists wound playfully about the mountain peaks while Cathryn and Gwen enjoyed an egg bake with muffins, and lingered over tea. There was much to discuss.

"How long have you and Adam been seeing each other? You haven't been here all that long. How did you meet?"

Gwen poured more tea for each of them.

"One of the ladies I work with—you met Rachel—is Adam's cousin. Soon after I moved here, she had a barbecue to celebrate Jim's and her golden anniversary. She introduced me to Adam and he and I fell easily into conversation. We found we had a lot in common, in our personal history. He lost his wife to cancer six years ago. They had no children. We were both rather alone in the world."

Cathryn nodded, trying to comprehend that level of aloneness. Her own children and grandchildren had always filled a big portion of her life. Even though they didn't live close by, they were always 'out there' and visited often.

"We're both used to living in an adult world and having things pretty much our own way." She chuckled. "Luckily, our ways are mostly in agreement. We enjoyed each other's company, and things just moved from there, more rapidly than I might have imagined."

Gwen glanced out the window with misty eyes, then turned back, her face flushed. "Cathryn, he asked me to marry him!"

"Oh, Gwen! When did he propose?"

"The day before you arrived. He took me on this lovely picnic ... I admit I was hoping he'd ask, but hadn't expected it this soon."

"And Sterling is okay with you living there too? Of course, Jessie lives there, doesn't she. Adam probably has his own cabin, right?"

"Yes, he has a nice two-bedroom place, a little set off from the others. After all, he's been foreman there for years. And Sterling is a real sweetheart." She held up her hand. "I know he gives the impression of being a ladies' man, but he's really not. He's a kind man with good principles."

Cathryn was relieved at this confirmation of her own amended opinion of Sterling and just nodded.

"So ... what did you say to Adam?"

"I said yes! Oh, Cathryn, I never thought I could be this excited, especially at my age. I didn't expect to find someone again, not someone I could commit to. I'm so blessed."

Cathryn darted around the table to give her friend a hug. "I'm so happy for you, for *both* of you."

Drawing apart, tearful, they burst into laughter.

"Truly, tears of joy," Cathryn said, wiping her eyes. "You two will have a wonderful life together, I just know it."

"We don't want to announce anything yet so keep it a secret. Sterling is the only one who knows."

Cathryn was certain others might guess the reason for Gwen's radiance.

~

The women arrived at the ranch in high spirits, eager to explore the outdoors on horseback. Gwen would ride a gray mare, and Adam handed Cathryn the reins to a buckskin gelding. "This is Bud. He's sure-footed and you won't find a smarter guy on the trail."

She stroked the gelding's neck and looked into his soft eye. He dropped his head under her gentle touch.

Cantle packs filled with nuts, jerky, and dried fruit were already attached to the saddles; bottle holders were slung on saddle horns, with containers of water, or water and a beer for some. The sky was washed with the pale blue of early autumn. A few fluffy clouds drifted gently on the breeze. The day was perfect for riding.

Riders began mounting their horses. Adam and Gwen, Josh and Jessie, Josh's uncle Mike, Jaimie and Fielding, Jack and—*no!* Jack and Blaire?

Jack led his horse up beside Cathryn. "Yeah, kinda weird huh? But she *is* Jaimie's mom, what could I say? You need a leg up?"

Cathryn's face froze into neutrality, a well-practiced expression for her. "Yeah, sure." She tried not to sound as testy as she felt, but why should she hide her frustration? It wouldn't be proper to read a peal over him in front of all these people, but Blaire's company was less welcome than Lucy Steele's was in *Sense & Sensibility*.

Blaire had probably been one of those rich horse show kids with an expensive pushbutton horse that won all the ribbons.

"Does Blaire ride a lot?"

Jack laughed. "No, hardly ever—says it's too smelly and dirty. I think we have *you* to thank for her joining us today." He grinned at Cathryn then grasped her knee, boosting her into the saddle.

"Me?" Cathryn said with a huff as she settled into the saddle.

"She hasn't been able to intimidate you, or even figure you out. She can be like a dog with a bone." He squeezed Cathryn's thigh then turned to mount his own horse.

Cathryn was determined to enjoy the day despite this unwanted development. But here was the same question again: Why did Jack put up with Blaire? Jaimie wasn't a small child.

Was I mistaken last night, about Jack?

Adam looked around the group. "Ok, everyone ready? For those who might not know," he glanced at Blaire, "here are some rules of the trail. Everyone goes the same pace; no one takes off running. Don't rush up behind another horse, and don't pass another horse unless you get the okay from the riders ahead. I'll be in the lead. Josh and Jessie will bring up the rear; they'll watch for any problems. We're taking a scenic route out to Wilbur's Pond." He shot Gwen a quick smile.

A private joke? A secret? Maybe it was where he'd proposed. Cathryn grinned.

"We'll make some stops along the way, and there's a meadow to do some loping. Then we'll take a different way back. Us natives will point out special sites and share some local stories. Turn your phones to vibrate. Oh, and watch out for snakes."

"Snakes?" Blaire looked a little shaken.

Cathryn had noticed Adam's pistol, and Josh had a rifle in the scabbard on his saddle.

Adam shook his head. "Just stay with the group and you'll be fine."

Blaire did not look reassured.

Josh snickered.

"Ladies and gentlemen, let's ride," Adam announced and led the way.

The group set off at a walk. The riders turned their horses down the ranch lane, then crossed the oil road onto gravel. They moved along in small groups of two or three, chattering and laughing.

Cathryn focused on getting the feel of her horse. Bud's nice little jog trot was easy to sit and she settled deep into the saddle with a contented sigh. She always felt at home in the saddle. Jack was somewhere behind her, with Blaire; but she put that image out of her mind to enjoy *this* horse and *this* trail on *this* day. Beginner's mind.

Soon Adam left the gravel and led them onto a path through some tall grass and into a grove of aspens. The chatter died away. In the filtered sunlight, the hush of the woods was soothing and the smell was rich. Cathryn drew in a deep breath: a heady draught of horse, leather, soil, and trees. The breeze ruffled the leaves around them. She gazed into the dappled light of the woods and wondered what kind of wildlife lived there.

As the way narrowed and began to climb, the riders fell into single file. At a bend in the path she turned to see Jack riding along in contentment and Blaire scowling behind him. She could feel Blaire aiming hateful eyes at the back of her head, but Cathryn refused to let any negative energy intrude. This was beautiful land and she meant to enjoy it.

After some rocky outcroppings, the aspens gave way to scrubby evergreens. The horses' feet had been padding quietly in the woods, but now gravel crunched under their hooves as the trail continued upward. It wasn't long until they reached the summit where the path opened onto a broad plateau with breathtaking views in every direction. Phones were passed around as riders posed for each other against the stunning backdrop.

Cathryn was taking pictures of Adam and Gwen when Jack rode up. "How about one of us against those western peaks?" he suggested, handing his phone to Adam.

Gwen reached for Cathryn's phone with a raised brow.

Jack drew his horse in next to Cathryn's for a few pictures. She found it easy to smile.

"Now one of me and Gwen please," Cathryn said, and Jack obliged.

"Jack," wheedled Blaire, "come here for some *family* pictures." Her voice dripped with false sentiment. She made a good deal of commotion but no one paid much attention. Jack was extraordinarily patient—for Jaimie's sake? A young lady of Jaimie's age would certainly be aware no love was lost between her mother and Jack, and Cathryn wondered again why he maintained the charade.

"Enjoy a drink now before we ride on." Adam raised his bottle for a long draw then pointed down the westward path. "Wilbur's Pond is just beyond that patch of pines."

Jaimie piped up. "Adam, why is it called Wilbur's Pond? Who is Wilbur?"

Adam leaned on his saddle horn and warmed to his story. "Well, you see, Wilbur was an old mountain man who worked for Sterling's grandfather, the one who homesteaded here and established the Lazy S. According to the tale, Wilbur didn't care much for cabins or people, preferring his horse, the cattle, and his mangy dog. Old Sterling could convince him to hole up in the far cabin—the one I live in now—during the worst of winter, but the rest of the time he lived in a shallow cave at the north end of the pond. They say he lived off fish and rabbits and berries. They also say Old Sterling's wife could temp him in with her potato salad or her blackberry pie. Wilbur's buried alongside his dog near a big tooth maple, just east of the creek that feeds the pond." With that, Adam turned his horse and they began the descent toward the pinewoods.

The horses picked their way along and Cathryn admired Bud's sure-footedness. Her confidence in him allowed her to enjoy the incredible view. A broad valley spread out below, turning hazy to the distant south; the taller mountains rose in the west. She could make out the two-lane oil road to the north. Clouds were gathering in the northwest but with no wind driving them she guessed they wouldn't move in any time soon.

The patch of pines they were approaching hid most of the pond, and soon they entered the cool, fragrant cathedral of trees. The trail was wide enough for two horses to walk abreast and Jack rode up to join her.

"Beautiful, isn't it?" he said, gazing high into the treetops. Small birds twittered above as the horses moved almost silently on the mossy, needle-strewn path.

"It's heavenly," she breathed. The surroundings had mellowed her anger for the present. She no longer wished to glare at him. "You know, this reminds me of the redwoods in California. When I'm there, I always feel like I'm in God's greatest church. And," she eyed him mischievously, "I always hope I'll meet up with an ent."

"Treebeard or Quickbeam?"

"You've read the books!"

He nodded, his eyes twinkling.

"In those coastal forests it's often foggy and misty; it feels like you've entered a magical realm. Have you been to the redwoods, Jack?"

"No. San Francisco, yes, but never north or south of there."

"Muir Woods is just north of the Golden Gate. I used to live on Mount Tamalpais, which overlooks Muir Woods. I would hike down there with my dogs back then. Before that, I lived way up north, in Ferndale. They call it a Victorian village, nestled between the redwoods and the sea." She sighed at the memories. "Between San Francisco and Ferndale you travel through some majestic redwood forests. I can't even describe or explain them. You have to experience them, feel their timeless grandeur, and realize our own smallness in the big scheme of things." Her voice had a reverent tone.

"Then I won't rest until I've seen them."

Blaire's brittle voice broke in. "That should be our next *family* vacation, Jack."

"I agree!" he exclaimed with uncharacteristic enthusiasm.

Cathryn turned to see Blaire's look of surprise, and guessed her own face showed the same.

"And I think we should bring Cathryn with us, as our guide." His tone was serious, but Cathryn saw the gleam in his eye and tried to hide her smile.

"*Hrumph.*"

Blaire urged her horse past them, nearly running Cathryn and Bud into a tree. "Think you have it all figured out, don't you; well, you just wait." And away she flopped on her poor horse, elbows flapping like chicken wings.

Jack and Cathryn smothered their laughter. Blaire was

insufferable. Cathryn felt sorry for the horse having to endure the discomfort of an awkward and uncaring rider.

The trees thinned out as the pinewoods opened onto a large meadow. The group—most of the group—was surprised to see a pickup parked at the north end of the pond. A long table was draped with a white cloth. Several stems of red zinnias stood in tall narrow vases that sparkled in the sun. Sterling, framed by the mountains behind, held a lavish bouquet of daisies tied with a long red ribbon.

Jack and Cathryn exchanged a puzzled look but when she looked over at Adam and Gwen, their happy smiles gave away the secret.

"Dismount and tie your horses to the picket line, then gather round," Sterling directed the bewildered riders. "I need Cathryn and Mike up here with me please," he added. Mike reached into the pickup and pulled out a guitar and then joined Cathryn and Sterling. The riders gathered together and Mike began to play. Cathryn recognized the song by the opening chords: 'Slow dancing ...'

Gwen tucked her arm into Adam's as they walked toward Sterling.

Cathryn's eyes welled with tears. This was so unexpected.

"Dearly beloved," Sterling began, with a broad smile, "as a duly ordained matrimonial official—designated by a website somewhere in cyberspace—I gather you all here to witness the marriage of two minds, two hearts, and ... (flicking his eyebrows), two bodies in holy matrimony."

Gwen and Adam stood before him, facing each other, their hands joined. A hawk cried out above.

Cathryn glanced around. Fielding's arms were wrapped around Jaimie, who was all smiles. Josh and Jessie were holding hands and whispering. Jack stood rigid, next to a scowling Blaire, who clutched pathetically at his arm. His eyes held Cathryn's and were filled with such warmth ... she caught her breath and turned back to the ceremony.

There, by the deep blue water of Wilbur's Pond, Sterling

intoned, "I now pronounce you husband and wife. Adam, you may kiss your lovely bride."

Cheering and clapping echoed off the water and many hugs were exchanged. Champagne corks popped and the large sheet cake was cut. Happiness brightened the faces of all but two of the party: Blaire stuck like a burr to a frowning Jack who—try as he might—could not detach her. Cathryn wondered again when he would take a stand—if ever—and what could keep him so miserably bound.

Adam now motioned them all in closer. "Okay, folks, time to ride the return loop, which I hereby christen the Honeymoon Trail; and I'm definitely ready to begin our honeymoon." He embraced Gwen and gave her another kiss, garnering a round of hearty applause.

Meanwhile, Sterling and Mike had finished loading the pickup.

"See you all back at the ranch," Sterling said. "And you'd better make good time. There's weather comin' at us." He gestured to the northwest.

Cathryn was staring at the clouds, surprised at how quickly they had been set in motion, when Jack appeared at her side, somehow free for a moment.

He took her hands in both of his. "That was nice, wasn't it? They look happy."

"Oh, I think they are. It's a good match. Two people who love each other—with no impediments."

"Yeah, some people are lucky that way."

"I don't know, Jack ... some people believe we make our own luck." She turned toward Bud and bent her knee for a leg up. Wordlessly, Jack obliged. She looked down at him from her perch on the saddle. "What do *you* believe?"

He stared at her in silence, his face a kaleidoscope of emotions, then looked at the clouds and frowned. "Storms can roll in pretty quick up here," he muttered. "Stay close." With a thoughtful expression on his face he walked over and mounted his own horse.

The wind had changed. The riders followed Adam along

the north edge of the pines. The clouds were still far to the northwest but, if she listened hard, Cathryn could hear the faint roll of thunder echoing off the peaks. If you could hear thunder, then lightning could strike you. She shuddered and urged Bud on. The group passed the pines at a gentle lope and, since everyone seemed in control of their horses, they continued the lope across the open meadow. At the base of a rocky ledge they gathered up again.

"We're taking these switchbacks at a trot," Adam said, "to get over the highest part before that lightning gets closer." He squinted at the sky. "I think we're okay so far."

As they began to climb, the horses grew uneasy; ears and tails twitched. They were probably sensing the storm, and not happy to be climbing a narrow path with no way to escape. Cathryn hoped none of them spooked. Keeping them together would help the horses cope, but if one spooked, the others would likely join in. She sat deep in her saddle to communicate calmness and strength to Bud. There was no chatter as the riders and their mounts maneuvered the back and forth trail across the face of the ridge.

Just as the party neared the summit, Blaire cried out, "Jack, ride beside me. This is all just too much."

His reply was terse. "Blaire, we have to go single file; just keep quiet and follow along."

"I will not!" she shrieked, causing her horse to jump, which almost jolted her out of the saddle. "How dare you blow me off!"

Cathryn was behind Blaire and Jack, watching this drama unfold. She had a bad feeling, and stopped Bud in order to avoid the fray, holding her hand up to signal those behind her. The horses, already nervous at being perched on a ledge, pawed and shifted uneasily at the scuffle in front of them.

Blaire, now in full diva mode, angrily kicked her horse. Frightened, the poor thing scrambled and bolted, racing past Adam and Gwen, who had gained the crest of the ridge. Fielding and Jack were instantly in motion.

Cathryn's ear caught a noise above her and she looked up. Stones! Loose stones were tumbling down, right at them.

"Back up!" she cried to those behind her, as she cued Bud to back.

"Rockslide!" Josh hollered.

The horses danced in fear as boulders and stones filled the path in front of them, slicing the riders into two groups. Dust billowed over the rocks. Riders covered their noses and mouths. Horses snorted and shook their heads.

Josh took charge. "We gotta go back. Turn around. Easy; real easy."

Cathryn sat deep and gently urged Bud to turn. Once they'd made it around she saw Jaimie frozen in place, her horse's ears and tail twitching.

"Jaimie. Look at me. Sit deep and breathe. Your horse is counting on you." When she had Jaimie's eye she said, "Now turn him gently."

Jaimie took a deep breath.

Cathryn nodded at her. Slowly and carefully, Jaimie managed to get her horse turned on the narrow path. Poor Jaimie. Riding on the open trail was far different than riding on a contained field or in an arena.

Thunder rolled overhead, blocking out any voices that might be heard from the other side.

"I know a shortcut off this ridge," Josh said. "It's steep. But we'll be less exposed. When I turn off, follow me." As they rode, he rotated his head slowly from side to side, scoping out everything from the rocky ledge above them to the wooded area below. The three women solemnly followed Josh in single file with Cathryn bringing up the rear. She hoped it wasn't far to the shortcut.

A few minutes later the hair on the back of her neck prickled. Bud twitched his ears and tensed underneath her. A few small stones broke loose from above. She peered up at the ledge. Mountain goats wouldn't make horses nervous. Bears weren't usually up this high.

Then she spied them—large paw prints in the dust, just

above the trail they were on. Her heart froze. She hardly dared to breathe.

"Josh?"

He turned to look at her. She tipped her head toward the tracks and he followed her direction. His eyes widened, then he gave a grim nod.

She nodded back and said nothing more, but kept watch above and behind them.

Bud's ears continued to twitch. How long until we're off this blasted ledge? Thunder rolled and echoed. The minutes seemed like hours. It was as if the mountain itself was holding its breath before the plunge.

At last Josh spoke. "Here we are. Give your horse plenty of rein when you jump the creek bed. Don't crowd together." He urged his horse down a steep drop, then horse and rider leapt over the creek and onto a path that veered into the trees. They each waited for their turn to maneuver off the ledge. It took Jaimie a while to work up her courage; finally her horse bucked over the creek bed. Luckily her seat was strong and she stayed in the saddle.

Cathryn took a last look up at the ledge just before her turn. Out of the corner of her eye she caught the quick motion of ... a long tail? She couldn't be sure. She leaned forward and gave Bud his head and he sailed over the creek bed and onto the path below.

Under cover now, the four rode through a stand of hardwoods that still had most of their leaves. Rain spattered higher up, but the path was mostly dry. Cathryn kept watch behind her but knew it was unlikely she'd see anything until it was too late. The big cats were clever and wary. Bud's now-calmer demeanor was reassuring, but his right ear still twitched; he was listening behind him. Cathryn kept one ear on the trail behind too, but hoped they'd left that danger back at the rocky ledge.

The timber began to thin out as they followed a gully downward. Light rain sprinkled on her hands and arms with the promise of more to come.

Jaimie turned around in her saddle, her face pinched with worry. Before she even spoke, Cathryn attempted to soothe her.

"We'll be back at the ranch soon, Jaimie. It's up ahead there, see? On the left. Don't worry about the others, they're in good hands."

"I hope so. Oh, why does my mom always ruin things with all her drama?" The girl slumped in her saddle.

"Let's put that aside for now, Jaimie. Focus on the trail. We can talk more once we're back at the ranch, if you like. I'm a pretty good listener."

"Okay. Yeah, I'd like that." Taking a deep breath, she straightened her back and set her shoulders.

Cathryn sympathized. How awful it must be to have a mother like Blaire. No wonder Jaimie and Jack were so close. She wondered who clung more to whom?

Josh stopped the group and turned his head toward them. "There's a wash off this gully that runs east of the ranch. It lies low so we're taking it to avoid lightning. Not enough rain to worry about flooding. Yet." He scanned the sky. His face appeared calm, but there'd been caution in his voice.

They rode on, picking their way along the gully until Josh turned his horse north. The wash was broad and flat. "The footing is nice and sandy here. Let's lope, but keep it easy. Don't let 'em race for home. "

As they loped easily along Cathryn couldn't help but wonder what had happened to the other riders. Where were they? With a grimace, she prayed no one—human or horse—had been hurt trying to diffuse the needless peril Blaire had created with her tantrum. The multiple dangers of the storm, the big cat, the rockslide, and Blaire's reckless behavior didn't bode well for them all getting out unscathed.

Cathryn especially pitied Blaire's horse. She detested people who took out their own pain on helpless animals. People who hurt animals—or kids—brought out her usually-dormant warrior streak. Were it up to her, she would have made Blaire return to the ranch on foot. Alone. In the rain.

The four reached the end of the wash and turned back west. Soon they trotted into the yard and dismounted.

A pickup engine roared to life.

"Take care of him?" Josh said to Jessie, handing her his reins. He grabbed his rifle out of the scabbard, then turned and walked toward the lane.

"Be careful. I love you," Jessie hollered.

He waved as he walked off.

Someone in the other party must have phoned Sterling. That was a hopeful sign. Wasn't it? The truck rolled up, Josh climbed in, and they blasted down the lane.

The women led the horses into the barn, their thoughts on the fate of those they'd left on the mountain.

CHAPTER TWENTY-TWO

After the tack had been dried off and put up, and the horses given fresh hay, Cathryn and Jaime followed Jessie to her cabin.

"Tea?" she offered.

The others nodded.

After borrowing dry tee shirts and applying a hair dryer to their jeans, the three women settled into the cozy living room, sipping a warm drink. A friendly cat wound himself around their legs, not sure whose lap to honor. Jessie kept vigil at the window from the arm of a big recliner.

Jaimie fidgeted in her seat. "Where are they, Jessie?"

Jessie studied the girl a moment, glanced at Cathryn, then flung her legs over the arm and sank into the depths of the chair. Her voice was calm and matter-of-fact. "Oh, they're probably riding some low-lying paths—you know, to avoid lightning. It hasn't rained much so no worries about flash floods yet; none of this ground lies that low anyway. The clouds are still moving in, but I don't see a lot of rain coming out of them."

Aiming to get Jaimie's mind distracted, Cathryn asked, "How long have you lived here, Jessie?"

"I grew up on a ranch about forty miles west. Been here with Josh for the past two ... no, it will be three years this

Thanksgiving. He's from around here too—as you know, his family ranches nearby." She gave Cathryn a curious look.

Jessie had tapped the ball back.

"Jaimie, my good friend near Quinn, where I live—her name is Deb—is Josh's aunt. She and her husband ranch near me and I ride with her often. She gave me Josh's info when she learned I was coming up here to see my friend Gwen. I didn't know Gwen had any connection with this ranch, or with Josh. And I didn't know Jack did either." She smiled to herself. "It's all been kinda surprising. Like an English village." She doubted they would get her Austen reference. There was no reaction, but she was gratified nonetheless to see Jaimie drawn into the new topic and listening aptly.

Cathryn kept the thread going. "I'm overjoyed for Gwen. That was one of the happiest weddings I've ever been to. And so spontaneous! They'll do very well together."

"I agree," said Jessie. "I don't know Gwen real well yet, but Adam is one of the good guys. He's kind and smart, and you can count on him. Like my Josh." She nodded and took a sip of tea.

'You can count on him.' The words struck Cathryn.

Jaimie was quiet for a moment, then looked at Cathryn again. "So you and my dad went to school together?"

Cathryn was pleased she'd remembered. "Yes, although I knew his brother Joe better because he was in my class. Jack is a few years younger, if I remember right. Jack and I ran into each other by chance a few times over the past year and discovered our mutual interest in horses. One day he brought his horses up to the polo field in Fullerton, and showed me how to play. It was fun, but I must tell you we played at a walk. Your speed yesterday was astounding."

A smile crept across Jaimie's face. She looked at Cathryn, blinked, then asked, "Are you and my dad ... dating?"

Cathryn pursed her lips. "Well, I'm not really sure. We're just getting to know each other. I'm not even certain what his relationship status is—"

"Oh, he and my mom aren't dating," Jaimie said. "In fact,"

she said with a puzzled look, "they've never gotten along, ever since I can remember. I don't understand why they still hang out, except maybe because of me, which is dumb cuz I can see Dad on my own now. And actually, I do. It's not like I'm a little kid anymore." She wrinkled her brow.

"It's a challenge for everyone in that kind of situation—parents *and* kids—to find a spot that's ... comfortable for everyone," Cathryn acknowledged.

Unexpectedly Jaimie's eyes filled with tears. "And now they're *all* out there—the three most important people in my life—out on the trail, in that storm, and we don't know what happened with Mom and her horse ..."

Jessie glanced at Cathryn with raised brows and mouthed, "What is happening?"

In a calm voice Cathryn said, "Jaimie, your dad and Dan are expert horsemen, as are Adam and Mike. And your dad's even a doctor. He could handle anything that came up, I'm sure of it."

"Plus, no one knows this country better than Adam," Jessie added.

"And now Sterling and Josh are headed—" but before Cathryn could finish, the sound of hooves in the yard prompted them all to hop up and peer out the window. Josh jumped off the paint gelding Blaire had been riding and headed toward them through a now-steady rain.

Jessie shot to the door.

From the window, the riders looked wet but otherwise unharmed. Only there was no Blaire.

"Where—?" Jaimie started, but Josh interrupted her as he stepped in the door, water dripping off him from every possible angle.

"Jaimie, your mom's on her way to the hospital. Sterling's driving her." He held up his hand at Jaimie's gasp. "Nothing serious. She's just a little banged up. Her knee hurts pretty bad though. Fielding will drive you into town. You two can be with her till they get it figured out." He stared at Jaimie, as if expecting a practical and immediate response.

Jaimie nodded, but remained rooted to the floor.

Josh frowned. "So get what you need from your trailer in case you stay over. Fielding's getting his stuff and his pickup. The rest of us will see to the horses and gear. Gwen will join you ladies." He looked at Jessie. "She'll need dry clothes."

Jessie was in motion before he finished speaking, and Josh made for the barn. Cathryn noted the two of them worked well as a team, especially for such a young couple. With some people it all seemed so easy and natural.

Then the new bride entered the cabin.

"They say rain on your wedding day is good luck," Cathryn quipped.

Gwen laughed. "I don't know about that. But it was an adventure. Anyway, we all got back safe and sound, mostly."

Jessie was trying to usher Jaimie toward the door. "Here, wear my jacket to your trailer. It's raining hard."

Jaimie just stared at the door so Cathryn stepped in to assist. "Come on, Jaimie. I'll go with and help you get your stuff together. Jessie, can I borrow this jacket?"

"Sure. You get her to Dan. Gwen, there's dry clothes on the bed and I'll fix some tea for you."

Cathryn threw on what must have been one of Josh's jackets; it was huge on her, but she zipped it up. It had a nice big hood that she drew tight and tied. Then she pulled up Jaimie's hood and tied it, as she might for a child.

"Okay, Jaimie, let's go." She took the girl by the arm. "You'll feel better once you see your dad and Dan."

Jaimie gave her a feeble smile at the mention of the familiar names, and they headed out the door. Rain gusted across the yard. They clung together as they made their way to Jack's trailer. Thunder echoed across the sky.

Once in the familiar surroundings of the trailer, Jaimie rallied a little. She gathered a few things for her backpack and pulled on her own rain poncho.

"Anything your mom would want? Where's her stuff?"

"She wasn't bunking here, she was staying in town with a friend. But here's her purse."

"Good. That oughta do it. You or Dan can fetch whatever else she needs from her friend once you get to town."

Tears welled in Jaimie's eyes again. "She's so ... I don't understand her. Dad and I get along pretty well most of the time, but Mom has always been ... I don't know ... all about herself. Full of drama. I never could count on her. Why'd she even come on the ride? She hates riding, and hates horses."

Not as much as she hates me, Cathryn thought, but kept her own counsel.

"She's so mean to Dad. And to you. Why you? Seems like she hates everybody, even me," she wailed as tears rolled down her cheeks. "I'm so sorry she caused all this."

Cathryn took Jaimie by the shoulders and looked her in the eye. "Jaimie, I get that it's hard for you to see all that, but it does no good to dwell on it. We can't fix other people's problems, only our own. I'm sure your mother loves you, in her way. It's unfortunate, but some people are simply not very good at showing their love. You are *not* responsible for her behavior. We all understand that. It will get sorted, somehow. Your dad will be here soon."

With a twinge of sadness, Cathryn remembered what Jack had said before the ride, about why Blaire had come. It had *not* been for her daughter's company. Parents who hurt or neglected their children brought out the healer in Cathryn— after she calmed her inner warrior that was provoked in a child's defense. It had helped, a little, when she learned to see those parents as hurt children themselves, which they almost always were.

As she gave Jaimie a comforting hug, the door opened. Jack stepped in, followed by Dan Fielding.

"Well, we got the horses all—"

Jaimie turned to Jack and burst into tears.

He exchanged a look with Cathryn and took Jaimie into his arms.

"Aw, it's been quite a day, hasn't it? Dan can tell you the whole story on the way to town. Hearing what actually happened will help, I promise." His voice was composed and comforting. "Your mom's injury is nothing serious, you'll see. It will be okay." He gave her a hug and a kiss on the forehead and turned her over to Fielding, who took her hand and got Jaimie and her things situated in his truck. In a moment they were off to town.

"Will it really be okay, Jack?" She eyed him closely, then realized her question could be taken in different ways.

"I think so," he said, opening the little clothes closet. "Blaire did something to her knee, and in general got banged up. She'll be sore but basically it's all good. I need some dry clothes. Then we can go back to Josh's and swap stories. And you, are you all right? I figured with Josh and Jessie as guides, you'd be fine, but this *is* wild country. No place for drama queens like Blaire." There was irritation in his voice. He turned and changed clothes.

Flustered, Cathryn stared out the window.

It was odd how sometimes she and Jack felt like old friends, yet at other times he acted like she was a stranger, or even a danger. The puzzle wasn't solved by any means, but she could let it lie for now.

She shrugged. Maybe I won't even be involved long enough to need any answers.

Jack pulled on his rain poncho, then stood in front of Cathryn. He drew up her hood and placed his hands on her shoulders.

"Thanks for being there for Jaimie."

"I'm happy to help."

"Ready?"

She tied her hood closed, took his arm, and they headed out into the watery blast.

~

The remaining riders—minus Mike, who had other business to tend to—gathered at last in Josh and Jessie's living room. She had stoked up the little red wood stove. Soon all were warm and dry, sipping hot tea or coffee.

Jessie folded her legs beneath her. "Okay, last thing I saw before the rockslide was Blaire kicking her horse until he spooked and bolted, with you and Fielding taking off after her. Fill us in, Jack."

Jack set down his mug of coffee and picked up the tale. "Luckily, Blaire was on a sensible horse. He didn't go far. Once he was off the ledge, he stopped and was sort of slowly spinning. I think he knew we were coming and was actually waiting for us. But Blaire was furious: at the horse, of course; and at all of us."

"Fielding got hold of her horse and had things under control, but then Blaire got off in a huff and started stomping off in those ridiculous shoes. Not watching where she was going—too busy yelling at us. Lost her balance and slid on some loose stones, fell and tumbled a bit; banged her knee pretty hard when she landed."

"These two (he indicated Adam and Gwen) and Mike caught up with us then, and we managed to get her back in the saddle. Like I said, that's one decent horse. We warned her to sit still—no more shenanigans—or she'd be on her own feet the rest of the way back. Adam slipped a spare halter on her horse and I ponied her horse back to the road, listening to Blaire gripe and moan all the way."

"When we came out of the trees Sterling and Josh were parked on the road. We got her into Sterling's truck and they headed to the hospital."

He turned to Adam and Gwen. "Sorry your Honeymoon Trail was not very ... romantic."

They laughed.

With a warm look at Adam, Gwen said, "Actually, all the drama added its own twist to an unforgettable day."

"And the honeymoon is just beginning." Adam smirked, and got a laugh from the group.

Jack looked at Josh and Jessie and then over at Cathryn, who had claimed the rocking chair. "So how did it go with you guys? That rockslide sure stirred things up, on top of what Blaire did. How was your return ride?"

"We definitely had less drama," said Jessie with a grin.

"Seemed like it, yes," Josh said, suddenly and uncharacteristically serious, "but actually we had a close call." He glanced sidelong at Cathryn. "It wasn't just the storm that made the horses skittish up there." He paused and looked gravely around the group.

"When we turned around after the rockslide, we followed our same trail back down a ways. Cat saw them first—a couple of big paw prints." He cast Cathryn a look of appreciation. "You have some trail smarts, Cat. I haven't seen a cougar up there for at least three years. I'm guessing she has a den, maybe cubs still with her. We didn't see her, just footprints. Once we got off the ridge and took the path down into the trees, she left us alone. We were lucky today."

Jessie turned to him wide-eyed.

"Didn't say anything ... didn't wanna spook Jaimie."

Jessie nodded.

Josh looked at Cathryn with admiration. "Cat was smart, and brave. She rode the rear, keeping an eye out and not saying anything even though she was in a dangerous position."

Cathryn smiled at the compliment, and at the new nickname.

Jack eyed her with wonder.

Adam added, "That's why we bring guns on the trail. Cougars, bears, snakes, coyotes, even the occasional determined badger—we need to be ready if there's something we can't avoid. Today was drama, not disaster," he said, summing up the day in a dry voice.

"Well, with all those dangers, Cathryn is right—this rain definitely *is* lucky." Gwen snuggled against Adam.

"Get a room!" Josh hollered, and everyone laughed and clapped.

Amidst all the noise and the steady patter of rain on the metal roof they almost didn't hear the phone. Josh took the call and then relayed the message.

"Sterling says Blaire's knee is sprained or something, I dunno. Anyway, she's in the hospital overnight cuz she also hit her head. She's on some strong pain pills and they wanna watch her. Fielding and Jaimie will stay in town."

He looked at Jack, who just nodded.

"Heavy rain supposed to hit soon. Sterling's staying in town and wants everyone to stay here for the night, you know, in case of flash floods. He said he *knows* where the honeymooners will stay, although they may not sleep—ha! Cat, you're welcome to either guest room in the main house. And we can eat him out of house and home, as long as we don't drink all his brandy." Josh laughed and the others joined in.

A short while later the storm let up some and they traipsed up to the main house. A tasty if disorganized meal was rustled up, followed by a rowdy hour of Crazy Eights. By then, drowsiness was setting in after the day's adventure.

The newlyweds headed out the door amidst a shower of birdseed and congratulations. Then Josh and Jessie made for their own cabin. The main house was tranquil for the two who remained.

"Another?" Jack asked as he refilled his own wine glass.

"Just half," Cathryn answered, nestling into the deep leather sofa after he poured the wine.

He put another log on the fire and stirred the embers.

"Cat. Good nickname. What do you think? You *are* like a catty mare, you know. Wasn't there a song ... about a mare who's always alone ...?"

She grinned. "Yes, by the Byrds." She softly sang the first phrases.

"Yeah, that was it." He sang the next line, then asked, "Doesn't the mare jump off a cliff? And realizes she can fly?"

"Something like that," Cathryn said. "I never was sure what it meant. But he jumped *with* her; they fly together."

Jack stood near the hearth, watching the fire. He seemed lost in thought.

Cathryn stared into the flames, contemplating how she and Jack had gotten to this point again. They seemed to be traveling in opposing circles, meeting at unexpected points.

She didn't know where she stood with him—not really—because she didn't know if she could count on him, or if he had room for her in his life. Even from her hospital bed in town, Blaire was still in the way.

Jack turned to face her. "What do you want out of the years you have left, Cat? I mean, how do you see them unfolding?"

Her heart rebounded with a thump. "Wow, that's a deep question. I'm not sure I understand what you're asking? I mean, what ... how would *you* answer that?" She swirled the wine in her glass, avoiding his eye. Although she had felt confident of her feelings for him last night, after today and all the hoopla with Blaire, she wasn't sure how involved she wanted to be in such a murky and dramatic situation.

He took a drink and then came to sit beside her. "Well, I've always seen the future as something to get through without being a burden to anyone," he began in a quiet voice. "And I guess I've always seen it alone. Kind of like my life is now. Although I have been ... oh, I guess you'd call it restless these last few years, not really knowing why. I know it's impossible to apply our therapeutic wisdom to ourselves. If we could, that would sure make life easier." He looked at her for a response.

She took a drink of her wine to buy some time. Looking into the fire, she said, "I've always thought—hoped—I would live a long time. I have grandchildren I want to see grow up. And I want to keep riding, always, even if someone has to tie me into the saddle like that blind old lady in England I read about," she said, laughing softly.

He chuckled. "I can see that. I can definitely see that."

She looked at him with affection and then returned her gaze to the fire. "And I've always wanted someone to share all that with. But as the years passed, it seemed like that ship had sailed. Without me. A couple of times." She paused, then in a somber voice added, "Or sunk."

After a time she said, "Do you still see yourself remaining alone, Jack?" She met his eyes with candor.

"No ... I don't know." He shook his head. "Before now, I didn't want anyone to have to take care of me when I was old. It just didn't seem fair to the other person." He paused again, and looked into the fire. "But I'm not sure now. I think there might be something more ..."

Cathryn slowly took another drink, giving her thoughts time to coalesce.

"Jack, I know you're used to being in charge, making decisions. If I can offer some advice from the other side ... please don't make someone else's decisions for them. I've found a lot of men—and actually a lot of the kids I worked with—make that mistake. They assume they know the whole situation, see the whole picture, know how the other person feels; and based on that they make decisions without giving the other person a chance to weigh in and make their own choice. I made that mistake myself once. Assumed I knew. It didn't turn out well." Her eyes misted over, remembering her last goodbye with Bob once she'd decided to marry Steve.

Jack rose and paced about the room. "I guess that's kinda what I was asking. I've thought a lot about what you said about 'an ever fixèd mark.' And how I have all these houses, but they're empty—of life, also like you said. The only place I really feel at home is my cabin on the Moody River. And even that was much nicer with you there."

She warmed at that.

After pausing for another drink, he took up pacing again. "Jaimie has always been important, and I think that kept me distracted for several years; but now her priorities and focus are changing, as they should. She's off into the world, making her own life." At the fire he stopped and looked hard at her. "Being around you ... well, it's gotten me thinking there might be something more than just riding on alone."

She took a few minutes to reflect on what he'd said.

"Jack, you know that finding meaning, or a purpose, is a big part of healing. For both of us, our kids have given our lives meaning and purpose, and probably distracted us from feeling so alone. And we both had a lot of healing to do.

Right? But once my kids were on their own ... well, I felt sort of ... adrift. Kind of without purpose, you know?" She paused a moment to feel her way through. "But I believe you're right. I, too, hope there's something more. I'm seeing that things change over the years—what's important, what's meaningful, it changes. Like in that song from *Charlotte's Web*, about how the seasons of life change, with Mother Earth and Father Time. Did you ever see it?"

He smiled. "Jaimie loved that movie. We must have watched it at least fifty times."

Cathryn's thoughts drew together and a new understanding emerged from the fog, taking shape even as she spoke the words.

"I think love changes at this stage of life. Our kids move on; their focus changes and so must ours. It's a new season. Another chance at reinvention and renewal. At least that's what I'm discovering." She felt open and strong, like when she was helping children. Or riding. She felt like her authentic self.

His searching eyes connected with hers. "Such a wise and beautiful spirit." He sat down next to her again. Their bodies touched and his warmth beckoned.

If he can set Blaire and his secrets aside ... can I? She set her glass down and studied his face.

He took her hands in his and leaned in to kiss her, gently at first, then deeply, fervently. The potent flame of longing engulfed them in mutual surrender.

And that rainy night was spent—not in the future, not in the past—but very much in the present.

With no impediments.

CHAPTER TWENTY-THREE

*T*hey woke entangled body and soul. A connection had been made, a bond forged. After a renewal of last night's tenderness in the pale light of dawn, Jack stretched and sat up. "I'm hungry."

Cathryn grinned at his boyish spirit, wishing he'd allow it free rein more often. Wrapped in the sheet, she recalled the sweetness of the night. She wasn't sure what it meant, but was surprisingly comfortable with it just being what it was. Being answerable only to herself and for herself—and not for the other person—was so freeing. She glowed with contentment.

After he'd showered and dressed, Jack leaned down to kiss her before heading to the kitchen.

Stepping out of her own shower minutes later, Cathryn heard tires on the gravel, the slam of a car door, and then the bang of the screen door. Others were awake and about. A new reality was here, and their coupling would likely become known. While she braided her hair, she examined her feelings around that newness between herself and Jack. It was unfamiliar, to know someone on this level. Emotional turbulence began to pull her into its well-worn whirlpool. For a moment she panicked. Then the teakettle whistled and she heard Jack bustling noisily about the kitchen.

No, I won't let fear pull me under. This time, I will swim.

In the kitchen Sterling boomed a hearty "Good morning!"

Jack replied, in a chipper voice, "And good morning to you, Sterling. What a great day!"

Cathryn couldn't help but smile as she made her way to the kitchen. The warbling birdsong coming in through the windows was not unlike the melody playing in her heart.

"And here's our lady, lovely as the sunrise, " teased Sterling as she entered the kitchen.

Jack turned to her with a look of affection.

Sterling discerned the truth at once. "Or shall we say *your* lady?" he added, grinning at Jack and flicking his eyebrows.

Jack laughed good-naturedly, and all enmity between the two men seemed curiously absolved.

Her puzzled look caused Jack to explain. "After we loaded Blaire into the truck yesterday Sterling and I had a few words. Seems Blaire was feeding us both false information."

"To leverage more money," Sterling added. "Big surprise."

Would Blaire's presence always hover around them? Cathryn walked to the window to clear her mind.

"What's the weather doing, guys?"

"Clear and sunny, for now," Jack replied. "How do you want your eggs, Cat?"

"Scrambled please." She poured herself some coffee and stole a glance at him as he whistled over the stove.

"Cat, is it?" Sterling asked on hearing the new name so Jack related the story of the cougar.

Sterling helped himself to coffee and gave her an admiring look, holding his mug up in silent salute. His eyes sparkled in collusion and she grinned.

She and Jack had now taken things to the next level, but she wasn't sure what that meant in their day-to-day world. They had not spoken of permanence or parameters.

'Let his behavior be your guide,' again echoed in her mind. Austen was usually of some comfort. She frowned. Had familiarity become a barrier to true comfort? To love? Would Jack's behavior continue to be erratic? After all, she was still ignorant of the truth of his situation. Then something stirred within her. Why depend on his behavior as a guide? What of her own heart? Didn't Austen also say it was best to have many holds on happiness?

Jack interrupted her reverie. "Food's ready. Let's eat."

Sterling pulled out a chair for her as Jack placed a pan of scrambled eggs, a tray of sausage links, and a plate piled with toast on the well-scrubbed kitchen table. The simple fare was unusually satisfying with the fresh air wafting through the kitchen windows.

"I must warn you," Sterling said with mock seriousness, "Blaire will be joining us this morning. Fielding and Jaimie will bring her here as soon as the doctor releases her. I'm thinking she'll head back to Fullerton today. Since it's her left knee, she might be able to drive. What about you two? What are your plans for today?" he asked, piling jam on another slice of toast.

Jack and Cathryn looked blankly at each other. Having been so completely and uncharacteristically absorbed in the present, they hadn't talked at all about what would happen today—or any day going forward.

Cathryn was due back at work in two days—a dismal reality that now seemed shockingly removed from the present. She sighed.

"I need to start back today. Gwen mentioned moving her things out here; I thought maybe I could help her and leave after that."

Before Jack could respond, Adam and Gwen knocked at the screen door and came in.

"And here's our newlyweds," Sterling announced. "Gosh, I'm surrounded by romance. I must say it leaves me feeling a bit singular. Have some coffee. Did you eat already?"

"Thanks, we're set for now," Adam said. "Although we could use some help moving Gwen's things out here from town." He looked at each of them in turn.

Cathryn responded first. "My things are still at Gwen's. I could leave from there or from here. Anyone have a plan?" she asked, taking another sip of coffee.

The sound of tires crunching on gravel distracted them.

Adam glanced out the door. "Fielding."

They all watched the young couple help an unsteady Blaire maneuver herself and her crutches out of the truck.

"Painkillers," muttered Jack.

"So much for driving herself," Sterling said, with a glance at Jack. "I'll get her settled in the recliner in the den for now while we figure something out." He opened the door and a bleary-eyed Blaire hobbled across the threshold, accompanied by a worried Jaimie and the irrepressible Fielding.

With Blaire settled in the den, Jack urged Jaimie to join them to formulate a plan of departure. Josh and Jessie had joined the group after hearing Fielding's truck. Sterling started another pot of coffee and the expanded group gathered around the larger table in the dining room.

Adam began with practical concerns. "How many pickups do we have? Any clean empty trailers? I'd like to get Gwen moved in before the weather changes again."

"I really only have a few bigger things, Adam: that hall tree, my cedar chest, probably a dozen boxes, and some artwork," Gwen explained. "Oh, and my new mattress and bed. Sorry Adam, but yours has seen better days."

Adam smiled ruefully.

"At least your new one will see better nights," Josh quipped.

The group laughed.

Adam and Gwen exchanged smiles.

Sterling calculated, "So two pickups, one pulling a trailer? Who's all going? We'll need packers and muscle."

"I'll be part of the muscle," Jack offered, "but my truck is still hitched to my trailer."

Cathryn's eyes darted to him across the table. First to commit to an activity? This was a new side of Jack.

"Oh, and my plants," Gwen exclaimed.

"When I load my bags into my truck at your place, I can bring your plants out here, Gwen," Cathryn offered.

"Good, then I can just leave my car here."

"If it's okay, I'll stay here with Mom," Jaimie said.

Sterling chimed in. "And I'll stay here to supervise invalid care. I hope I don't come to regret that choice." He and Jack exchanged a look.

"We'll come for muscle and packing," said Jessie brightly. "But remember Josh, you've got two horses that need work later today."

"No problem; this move won't take long with so much help. We can use our truck too."

Adam rose from the table. "I'll hook that old two-horse to my truck, it's the cleanest trailer I guess. It's 8 o'clock now. Can we head out in fifteen minutes? Does that work for everyone? Jack and Cat, you two wanna ride with us?"

"Sure," Cathryn replied, with a look at Jack.

He nodded.

Sterling summed it up. "Good. Plan Number One is ready for action. We'll figure out how everyone's getting to their own homes once we have Gwen moved. By then, we'll have a better idea how Blaire's doing." He stood. "Plan on lunch back here. I shall play host *and* chef," he said, sweeping them all a bow.

He turned to Jaimie and winked. "You can help me, right Jaimie? You know I don't cook!"

A smile broke over her somber face and she nodded.

"Cat, are you ready?" Jack was holding the screen door open for her.

She was baffled. "We have plenty of ...

He tipped his head toward the door with an urgent expression, so she grabbed her purse and followed him out.

"I was hoping we'd have some private time to talk first ... you know ... before we're so much in company," he said in a lowered voice as they waited in the yard. "I feel like my mind is going everywhere at once." He hesitated, then asked, "How are *you* feeling this morning?" He pushed his hair back and repositioned his hat.

She had grown genuinely fond of Jack, in spite of his moods and mysteries. And was astonished to find herself feeling more amiable than anxious—quite the opposite of what she might have expected after last night.

"I feel quite content," she said.

"Content ... uh, good," he said, looking at her with a crooked smile. "That's good, right? I was hoping it wasn't just me feeling so ... yeah, I like your word, content."

Cathryn rose on tiptoe to kiss him on the cheek. His face was scruffy but it was a good look on him. She took his hand in both of hers and said, "So we're all leaving today?"

"Yeah, I guess so."

She watched his face progress from surprise to consternation and then to thoughtfulness. He looked at her as if to speak, but just then Adam pulled up with the truck and trailer. Gwen was already in front so Jack and Cathryn got into the back seat.

"Isn't this a little different for country folk?" Cathryn joked. "You know, you go to a party and all the men are in one room and all the women in another. But I guess we have newlyweds here."

Gwen laughed. "Am I sensing other newness as well?" She looked at them in the rearview mirror. Her brow was arched but her eyes were twinkling.

It was a merry trip to town.

The women packed with haste and efficiency. Gwen had already boxed some of her things in preparation for her impending move. The men loaded the trailer and trucks. The plants plus Cathryn's bags were situated in her pickup and then she and Gwen walked back inside for a once-over.

"What will your niece and nephew think, Gwen?"

"Actually, I've been pretty open about Adam all along," Gwen admitted. "When he proposed last week I let them know the date but they were already committed to a golden anniversary party for his grandparents in Colorado. So they're expecting this. We've planned a special dinner for next

Sunday, inviting a few others to celebrate. I'll just leave a note for now." Gwen found a pen and paper and scribbled a message. Then she stood and looked around the place that had been her home for the past ten months. Cathryn's gaze followed. This place had set the stage for Gwen's new life.

"This has been good," Gwen pronounced. "And now on to even better. Isn't life a grand adventure? Let's go."

Cathryn admired Gwen's ability to embrace change without apparent trepidation or the second-guessing that seemed to plague all her own decisions. Gwen found joy in the ever-changing present—in the same kinds of changes Cathryn had taken such care to deny, avoid, or control. Yet the very things she longed for—including love—were ironically contained within those changes.

Was knowing how to adapt more useful than trying to plan for things beyond one's control? In the saddle, you couldn't plan for everything that might happen. Instead, you had to trust in your ability to ride.

It dawned on Cathryn that Gwen was a real Jane Austen heroine; not unlike Anne Elliot in *Persuasion*, who embraced a second chance at life with her beloved Captain Wentworth.

Cathryn followed Gwen out of the house and strolled to her own truck, lost in the nuance of endings and beginnings.

"Keys?" Jack spoke from the driver's seat, startling her out of her woolgathering. "It *is* okay if I drive?"

"Oh, sure. I don't particularly care for driving, and I have a long enough journey ahead." She walked around the truck and climbed in on the passenger side. "You know, I don't think I've ever been a passenger in Big Red—that's what my grandkids call my truck. This is a first."

"And I've never driven you anywhere, in anything, well ... except on Ben." He shot her a glance, which they both knew referred to last night. "Lots of firsts, yeah? Come. Sit by me," he urged, patting the seat next to him.

"Last night was lovely," she said, not caring that she was blushing. She slid over next to him and buckled up. "The whole week has been amazing. I feel ... well ... kind of brand new. I'm starting to believe things happen *exactly* when they're meant to; when we're ready. Especially if one doesn't push the river."

At his curious look she related some of Deb's advice from months earlier. They talked about that and about the events of the past few days, and then he became quiet and his brow furrowed.

"What's the frown about?"

"Oh, just thinking ahead to the trip back, for all of us. It's gotten complicated. Jaimie won't be able to ride back with Fielding like she wants. She'll have to drive her mom at least as far as Cedar Gulch."

So Jack was a planner—a trait she found refreshing in a man. She was weary of that role. She noted with amusement that today she hadn't given a thought to what would happen next other than knowing she had to leave. Another first—for her. Jack would likely drive Blaire on to Fullerton. So much for staying at his ranch again.

But as to his comment about Jaimie, she had an opinion and voiced it. "Driving her mom might be good for Jaimie."

"Really? Why?"

"Well, you know how some horses do best when they have a job?"

"Yeah."

"It's the same with people, including kids—especially kids. They often feel unimportant and powerless. Kind of useless, like so much extra baggage." She paused a moment, choosing her words carefully. "Jaimie seems younger than her years, don't you think?"

He tilted his head and seemed open so she continued.

"I think an opportunity to step up and take charge would benefit her. She'll learn she's needed and important—and capable; and she'll have some practice making decisions for herself instead of trying to please everyone around her to keep the peace. In my humble opinion."

He considered for a few minutes. "Yeah, I can see the wisdom in that. And I've thought before that I might be

overprotective of her, especially where Blaire is concerned—
you know, when Blaire drops the ball. Which is often. It
really is hard to be objective about your own situation."

"Of course it is. Isn't that one of the first things we learn
in our profession?"

"Right. And I'm used to being in charge. It's hard to step
back."

Her body stiffened. "Really?" she blurted, before she could
stop herself, recalling all the times Jack had stepped back and
away from her. And had, in fact, disappeared.

"Huh?"

"Nothing." She hoped he couldn't read her thoughts.

They rode in silence for a while. She wondered what he
was thinking or if he thought her peevish. She couldn't gauge
his mood. His face was flat, almost stony.

Eventually he spoke again. "You know, it's only hard to
step back when I *know* what to do. Like in my work, or with
horses, or in a match. But when I *don't* know what to do, like
with Jaimie, or with ... well, then, yes, it's easy to step back, or
just keep doing what I've always done. It's tough when I can't
see my way ahead, or at least have my eye on a promising
path." He looked at her in exasperation. "Being a parent is
tough; especially the weird position I'm in with Jaimie and
her mother."

That being a situation Cathryn still didn't understand, she
couldn't address it. Instead she said, "Jack, some of this is
typical. Jaimie's at an age of transition and that's tricky for
lots of parents; especially those in your situation, with
parents separated. And then for you—knowing you're not her
real dad—probably even more so, with that being a secret and
all. But I've found that whether with a child, a horse, or a ...
friend, sometimes we have to step back and let them struggle
a little to find their own way. Haven't you done that with
horses? Repeat the cue until he finds the answer, finds his
own comfort spot? He'll never truly know it until he finds it
for himself. You can't teach it, and you can't force it.
Although sometimes you can model it."

Then she laughed. "Here I am, rattling on in my counselor chair. Sorry."

"A chair well-suited, I'd say."

With a quizzical look he added, "I know we haven't spent a lot of time together yet, but you are so consistently kind. It sets me a little on edge."

"On edge? Why?"

"I've been waiting for the bitch to come out. It always does. Or always has, in my experience. Except for ..."

She arched her brow. "But you haven't been with *me* before, Jack Stone," she reminded him, with a teasing light in her eyes.

Jack Stone. She enjoyed saying his name out loud, right to his face. It made all of this seem more real.

He looked at her, then chuckled and put his arm around her. "Right again. Are you always right? That might take some getting used to."

She laughed, but said nothing. She was busy listening to her heart.

Jack turned the wheel and drove into the yard of the Lazy S.

CHAPTER TWENTY-FOUR

G wen's things were quickly unloaded at Adam's cabin, then the group headed to the main house for lunch. Gwen and Cathryn lagged behind the others.

"Cathryn—or Cat as you're now called (and I do really like the nickname)—your visit here means a lot to me. I *did* want a fresh start, and I got it. In spades. But I also didn't want to leave everything behind from my former life. I was part of Quinn for a long time, and it was part of me. Lots of wonderful memories. I didn't want to lose all that. You're like the bridge between my old life and my new life. Continuity can be good. Will you come visit again?"

"I would love that, Gwen. Of course I will. It *has* been quite a week. Transformative, actually. Life in Quinn will be very dull now, as if it wasn't before ..."

They shared a laugh, and a hug.

"I'm really happy for you, Gwen."

"And I for you. Things seem to be progressing with ... well, in some areas you thought were a little ... stagnant? But you said transformative—how so? You do seem changed. And not just from things with Jack ..." Gwen paused a moment in thought. "You seem more 'you,' if you know what I mean."

"That's it; that's exactly it, Gwen. I do feel more 'me.' A deeper, richer me. A stronger me. I'm seeing things differ-

ently. And feeling more at ease. Certainly nothing is settled in
any way between Jack and me, or even predictable. Still lots
of secrets there. But now ... well, I'm not so much about
predicting or controlling things. Because no one can. I've
known that before—in my head—but never really felt it in
my heart. And that made me restless, or nervous, trying to
control so much, which didn't work either. Even reading
Austen over and over wasn't helping."

With a mischievous look Gwen asked, "I wonder if there's
such a thing as reading too much Austen?"

Cathryn laughed. "Could be. Or maybe I was focusing on
the wrong aspects and not seeing what was right in front of
my nose. Like Emma feeling doomed to blindness. You've
been such an inspiration, Gwen—a real live Austen heroine
yourself. Thank you."

"That's one of the greatest things friends do for each
other—inspire. And I think you've instinctively picked
helpful mirrors for yourself. You know, when you talked about
your friend Deb, I was struck by how similar to *me* she
sounded—in being direct and decisive; and how we're both
very different from you. You've always been more intuitive—"

"And indecisive, and confused," Cathryn interjected.

They laughed.

"Maybe being around the two of you brought out my ...
strength? Confidence?"

"You've always had those, Cathryn, but maybe just needed
practice using them among adults. I've seen you inspire lots
of kids."

Cathryn thought fondly about the kids she'd worked with.

"I think I needed the courage to take a chance ... on me.
And to believe, in my heart, that I could manage, no matter
where the river flowed."

Gwen linked arms with her and they walked to the main
house.

Sterling turned as they entered. "Lunch is served, ladies.
Help yourselves and then join us in 'the situation room'." He
lifted an eyebrow.

The women filled their plates and entered the dining room. Jack caught Cathryn's eye and indicated the empty chair next to him. She walked around the table and sat down.

"Thanks, Jack, that was sweet of you to save me a spot."

His eyes said all she needed to hear.

The morning had been hungry work and everyone dug into the array of sandwiches and sides; there was little conversation at first. As they were finishing, Jaimie rose and carried in a tray laden with pies, still steaming from the oven.

"I didn't make them," Jaimie demurred, with a dimpled smile. "Sterling's cook makes pies in big batches and freezes them. We have blackberry, cherry, and apple."

Everyone tucked in eagerly for a second round.

Jack took a big bite of blackberry pie and then addressed the group after wiping his mouth. "We need to make some decisions on how everyone is getting home. Sterling, what's the report? Blaire doing any better?"

Sterling shook his head. "Nope. She's in la-la land. Wouldn't you agree, Jaimie?"

The girl nodded. "So I'll have to drive Mom's car to Cedar Gulch?"

"I think that's our only option, babe," Fielding replied, looking at her with affection.

She shrugged. "Well, that's it for my part then. I'd better get Mom ready to go." Jaimie carried her dishes to the kitchen and then headed to the den.

"Can we caravan as far as my ranch?" Jack asked. "Jaimie might need some help managing with Blaire, like at a rest stop or something. Or maybe we could all stop at the diner in Cedar Gulch for early supper. Cat?"

Leaving. They were actually leaving. Her gut clenched. It was like the end of summer camp—a slice of life that would never happen again. In spite of the lump in her throat, she swallowed a mouthful of cherry pie and said, "I can do that. Then I'll need to drive on."

Jack leaned into her ear and whispered, "You can always stay at the ranch with me."

Cathryn squeezed his thigh, pleased he had remembered —and repeated—his earlier invitation. She whispered back, "I think you'll have your hands full with your 'companion.' But maybe another time?"

He leaned back with a disgruntled look, folding his arms over his chest.

Sterling clapped his palms on the table.

"Sounds like we have Plan Number Two ready to roll out. Destination: Cedar Gulch. For you five, that is." He looked a little sad. Was the Lazy S as lonely as Quinn was at times?

The men went out to ready the trucks and trailers and load the horses. Gwen and Jessie headed to the kitchen to restore order there.

Cathryn rose to gather her few things from the guest room, wishing the return trip could be different. Another night at Jack's ranch would have been ...

As she made her way toward the hall bathroom she overheard voices from the den. It was easy to identify Blaire's shrill angry tone—she remembered it from River Run—only now it was irregular and slurred from her pain medication.

"I will *not*, Jaimie, no ... Jack ... I'll ride with him ... to take care of me ... all his fault ..."

"But Mom," Jaimie said, in a placating tone, "Jack's got a trailer full of horses. You know that's not easy, especially coming down out of the hills. He can't manage you too, especially in your condition."

Cathryn stilled her breath. She hated eavesdropping but Blaire had already endangered them all on the trail. There was no telling how much more havoc she could wreak, especially in her present state.

"Condition ...? what d'you know anyway ..." Blaire's anger far outstripped her ability to speak coherently. "He should pay ... Jack ... owes me ... if he didn't bring her ... stupid trail ride ... stupid horse ... my knee is all his fault ... scheming little ... he won't leave me ... not for her!"

"But Mom, you're not with him. You haven't been ever

since I can remember. Why are you so mean to him? He's my dad, and it hurts me when you hurt him."

"Dad? Ha!"

Cathryn shrank back.

"Did he ever tell you—?" Blaire sneered.

"No, of course not, why would—"

Blaire cackled. "You don't know ..." A wicked laugh escaped her. "He's *not* ... not your dad ... bound to find out ..."

"What? What are you saying? You're confused, Mom."

"Don't you say ... not a word, young lady ... nothing to anyone ... secret ... it's our little ..."

"What do you mean, not my dad?" Jaimie's voice cracked.

Cathryn winced.

"Nobody's business ... mine ... ours ... *is* a business ... he pays me ... need that money ... don't tell," Blaire hissed.

"If Jack's not my dad, then who *is*?"

Blaire broke into maniacal laughter.

Cathryn had reached her limit. She couldn't stand by and allow any child to endure this. As she reached for the door handle, Jaimie burst out of the den in tears. Her eyes widened seeing Cathryn there and she stopped short and buried her face in her hands, shaking with silent sobs. Cathryn reached for her shoulder and led her into the bathroom where the weeping girl collapsed in her arms.

Once her tears had subsided a bit, Jaimie pulled back and looked at Cathryn with a dubious expression. "Did you—?"

"Yes, I'm afraid so. Anything I can do?"

"What can anyone do?" she wailed. "Was Mom telling the truth? I don't know what to think. Should I tell Dad ..." (more tears) "or what? I hate her! I just hate her! Do you think it's true, what my mom said?"

The girl had such a lost expression that Cathryn began to tear up too. She thought for a minute, then said in a measured tone, "Let's not tell anyone now, Jaimie, okay? We need some time to think it through. This isn't the time or place. It's going to be hard, but you need to drive your mom to the diner, as we all planned. Can you do that?"

Jaimie faced her. "I think so." She took a deep breath. "Actually, I'm glad you heard it. Otherwise, I would think I was going crazy."

"Oh, you're not crazy," Cathryn reassured her. "It's the situation that's crazy. I know it seems very ... complicated, but for right now let's focus on getting to the next stop, the diner. We'll talk there, after we've had some time to think. You and I can take a walk while the guys handle your mom. I'll tell them you need a break. You're not alone with this, okay? I'm with you."

Jaimie took another trembling breath, set her jaw, and nodded at Cathryn.

"Now, have the guys get your mom into her vehicle. I'll be out in a minute. Oh, what's your cell number?" she asked, pulling her phone from her back pocket. Numbers were exchanged. "We can do this," she said, giving Jaimie a quick hug. "*You* can do this."

Then Jaimie left and it was Cathryn's turn to reel in shock. Badly done, Blaire! And yet this corroborated what Jack had said, that Jaimie was not his child. But why would Jack pay Blaire to keep *that* a secret? Why not just be rid of her? Cathryn hoped a solution would present itself after having some time to percolate. She left the house and joined the others on the porch, pulling her own feelings back and focusing on the moment at hand.

Now it really was time to leave. Many goodbyes and hugs were exchanged. Cathryn embraced Sterling and thanked him for his friendship and his encouragement.

"I wish you luck, Cat. You've been pulled into a mess; but from what I've seen, you'll make it through just fine."

"Thanks. I appreciate your confidence, and your honesty. You know, you kinda had me scared there for awhile, so charming and then so ... scheming."

His eyes lit up and he chuckled. "Never meant to scare you that way."

"You know any more details about the situation? Or have any advice?"

"No details, sorry. But wait," he said, reaching into his pocket, "here's my card. Text me or call any time. As for my advice ..." He arched his brow. "I always recommend the high road." His smile was kind, and genuine.

"That's usually my instinct, too. Great minds ..."

They laughed at that and then she turned away, grateful to know the real Sterling, the one far beyond her contradictory and inaccurate first impressions. She was also thankful for everything else she now saw more clearly, and walked with confidence toward her truck.

Jack had been watching her from where he stood by her driver's door. "You and Sterling squared away?"

"Yep," she said with nonchalance. "He's a lot different than I had thought at one point. He actually has all the good-ness as well as the appearance of it."

Jack looked puzzled.

"Oh, that's sort of an Austen quote. Anyway, I was mistaken about him. And about a lot of things. It's been an amazing week."

Jack's brows knit together as he glanced toward Sterling, then he handed Cathryn into her truck. "Fielding and I will be in the lead, with the trailers. You follow Jaimie, if you would, in case she has trouble. We'll meet at the diner." He shut her truck door.

Leaning out the open window, she gave him a saucy smile. "Kiss me, Jack. We never know where the road might lead."

His eyes widened but he cupped her face in his hands and kissed her, deeply. They looked at each other and said "Stirrup kiss," in unison.

The sun was past its zenith and tracking westward. Trucks fired up and, one by one, the caravan left the Lazy S behind.

Cathryn had come to Wyoming in search of a new perspective on her stagnant life. The adventures and revela-tions and new friends she'd found were everything she'd hoped for, and promised more possibilities ahead. She felt her good fortune and was grateful.

They were all heading back to their own homes and lives;

two in a state of confusion, and two others soon to join them. Cathryn wasn't sure how much stake she had in the whole affair. After all, no promises had been made, no future alluded to.

Blaire alone was blissfully unaware of the tempest she had set in motion.

CHAPTER TWENTY-FIVE

*T*here was no sign of conversation in the vehicle ahead. Cathryn sighed. She knew Jaimie was depending on her. But she also knew it was best for Jaimie to face this thorny situation on her own.

Contemplating Jaimie's problems had temporarily pushed aside Cathryn's questions about Jack, but eventually her mind returned to her own predicament. Jack hadn't mentioned anything beyond meeting at the diner. He had seemed like a planner. Didn't she figure in his plans, or in his future?

Should I let this particular river flow on by?

Then it hit her, and she laughed at herself. That's all she—or anyone—could ever do. With or without her, that river would run its course. Control was simply an illusion. It was rather like working with a horse. A person was never really in control of a horse. The rider could only earn its trust and ask for its cooperation—and then trust the horse in return. She found some satisfaction in that analogy.

But a specter of uncertainty lingered, along with a murky undercurrent. Blaire's revelation had cleared up a few questions, but also gave rise to new ones. And what of her threats? Idle? What kind of stakes would cause someone to threaten another person? To what lengths would Blaire go?

Jaimie now knew the truth about Jack, or at least part of

the truth. Clearly Jack needed to know that this knowledge had been forced on Jaimie; it was just a matter of when and where to tell him.

A great wheel had been set in motion.

Cathryn slowed to take a sharp curve and the valley of Cedar Gulch opened before her, golden in the glow of early evening. The tranquil view ran counter to her present state of mind. She didn't know anyone's plans beyond supper. Were they all heading back to Fullerton? Spending the night at Jack's ranch? If so, it would be awkward for her to join them there. She was still an outsider. That rankled.

At the diner she parked her truck, hopped out onto the pavement, and slammed the door a little harder than she'd intended. Walking over to Jaimie, Cathryn made the effort to set her own issues aside for the present.

Blaire still dozed in the passenger seat.

"Was it a quiet trip?" Cathryn asked in a low voice when Jaimie slipped out to join her.

"Yes," Jaimie whispered, relief apparent in her face. "But now what?"

"Well, I for one am stiff and could use a bit of a walk. How about you?"

Jack was headed their way. She gave him a smile, which he returned. But his smile turned to a scowl when she suggested he and Fielding get Blaire into the diner while she and Jaimie took a short walk to stretch.

A shrill whine came from the green SUV.

"Jack, oh, Ja-a-a-ck, ... help me, Jack."

He shot Cathryn an irritable look, which she ignored; she had more important fish to fry, and soon—unbeknownst to him—he'd be in that frying pan himself. She took Jaimie's arm and they headed down the street.

"Are you and Dad—I mean Jack—are you going to deal with this ... well, together? Or maybe that's none of my business—"

"No, you definitely need to know all the players on your team. It's a good question, Jaimie. But I'm not sure if I'm really part of the team; some of that depends on Jack. Either way, I'm here for you now," she explained, trying to be specific yet appropriate. "Does that give you enough information?"

"Yeah. So you're not engaged or anything?"

"Oh, no!" The emotion in her reply was too revealing, so she chose her next words with care. "We both like and admire each other. Jack's a good man. But compatibility of character takes time to determine. And his unusual situation with your mom kind of muddies things for us."

Jaimie nodded.

Cathryn decided to press Jaimie. "So what did you come up with during the drive? What do you need to do right now? What are your questions?"

Jaimie's eyes widened, but then she plunged in. "My questions are: Who is my real dad? Why have they not told me before now? When and where should I tell Dad—uh, Jack—that I know, or should I not tell him?"

"Good. You've defined the problem ... prob*lems*. That's the first step. The 'real dad' thing, is that something you can put on the back burner for now? And just deal with telling Jack what you know first?"

Jaimie pursed her lips as they turned and crossed the street, then nodded.

"Okay, so when to tell him ... what's your feeling there, Jaimie?"

"Tell him now," she said emphatically. "I don't like keeping secrets from him. And as far as I know, he's always been honest with me, except for this." Her eyes flashed. "It makes me mad that he lied! Why would he do that?" She pushed back tears with her sleeve.

"He must have a good reason. We just don't know what it is. Yet."

"Well, I don't think it's to be mean or anything. That's just not like Dad ... Jack."

It was Cathryn's turn to nod and, by her silence, encourage Jaimie to continue sorting things for herself.

"I want him to know that I know, right now."

"Before supper or after?"

Jaimie pondered as they walked. "After. I'll feel calmer once I've eaten."

"Good." Cathryn prodded her on gently. "What will you say after we eat? How will you tell him?"

"He'll probably be shocked that I know, right?"

"I think so!"

They exchanged a little laugh and the mood lightened.

"Maybe he'll need some time to figure out how to explain all the rest to me? That might take awhile, and this really isn't a good place for that, is it?" Jaimie mused. "Especially with Mom here, and in her condition."

"I agree. What about later tonight? At his ranch?"

"I think Dad might go on to Fullerton. I suppose the horses could stay at the ranch for a night, but they really live down by Sedgeway. I have classes tomorrow, so I need to get back to my apartment tonight after supper. Dan can drive me. He only lives about thirty miles from here, and he needs to get his own horses home too. Mom should probably just get to Fullerton. But who will drive her?"

They were nearly back to the diner.

"How will Dad get Mom's car *and* his truck and trailer to Fullerton?"

"Maybe you can leave that for him to figure out. Now here's your plan, as I heard it. After supper, you and Jack take a walk and you tell him what you know. Then you go back to your place, driven by Dan. Are you going to tell Dan yet?"

"Hmm ... no, not yet. I want to give Dad time to explain first. Then I can tell Dan the whole story all at once."

"I like that. Probably best for you and Jack to sort things out first. Can you ask Dan for support or comfort without telling him what's troubling you? You might be upset."

"Yeah, he's wonderful that way." She sighed dreamily, then returned to the less-than-dreamy situation. "He knows it usually involves Mom and all the trouble she stirs up."

Cathryn smiled to herself. A good man. Reliable.

"So this is just between you and Jack for now. I'm sorry I overheard, and I'm not going to say anything to Jack. It's for the two of you to sort out."

Jaimie looked over at her. "I'm not sorry you know, Cat. I'm not sure how I would have handled it otherwise—"

"You've handled it just fine. But it can help to have someone to bounce ideas off of. I'm glad I could be here for you." She reached her arm around Jaimie's shoulders and gave her a squeeze. "Let's go eat."

Fielding was at the door to meet them and took Jaimie's hand. Cathryn admired his open love for the girl and was pleased Jaimie had his support.

When Cathryn reached the table Jack stood and motioned her to the empty seat beside him. "How nice, thanks."

He leaned into her ear. "Is everything okay? What's going on?"

Cathryn turned and looked at him. "There *is* something going on, but let's eat first and allow events to unfold."

His eyes narrowed. Likely it was difficult for him to not know, to not be in control, to not fix it immediately. She tilted her head at him and raised a brow.

He sighed, then covered her hand with his.

A warmth filled her heart. He trusts me.

The waitress approached so they gave their attention to the menu. Blaire sat on the other side of Jack and he helped her order. Jaimie was across from Cathryn, next to Dan. Friendly conversation accompanied the meal for four of the five diners, particularly buoyed by Fielding's lively banter. Blaire was so quiet they barely knew she was there. She had no opinions and made no remarks.

When they were finished, Jack rose. "I'm getting this." He walked over to the cashier's station and pulled out his wallet.

Cathryn nodded at Jaimie, who joined him.

Seeing them head for the door, Fielding stood but Cathryn motioned him back into his seat. "I think Jack and Jaimie need a little time, Dan, if you don't mind?"

"Oh, sure, they need to say goodbye." He smiled his warm, affable smile. "I'm the lucky one. Living out here, I see her often. And in the future, I'll see her all the time, hopefully." He stole a look at Blaire, who was still groggy and silent; she hadn't eaten much, and her head was propped on her hand. It looked like she was asleep. Fielding's remark had not penetrated her drug-induced fog.

"Can you help me get Blaire to the restroom, Dan? Don't worry, I'll help her once we're *inside* the ladies room."

Reaching into his pocket, he threw a fistful of bills on the table for a tip, then maneuvered a wobbly Blaire to the ladies restroom.

"I'll wait here by the door. Holler if you need me."

Cathryn managed to help Blaire with the task at hand, and Blaire didn't resist. She simply stared at Cathryn with a dull expression and mumbled, "Why are you helping me?"

"Because your knee and your medication make it difficult for you to manage alone right now." Was it the pain or the pills that were subduing Blaire's usually-irascible disposition? Cathryn wondered about the medication dosage.

"Ready," she called to Fielding, and he opened the door.

"I've got her, Cat. I'll get her into the truck. Can you get the doors for us?"

They succeeded in getting Blaire safely buckled in again, this time in Jack's rig. He would have to deal with Blaire. And whatever he decided to do, he'd need the horses with him. Fielding transferred Jaimie's bags to his own truck and Blaire's extensive luggage into Jack's.

Jaimie and Jack approached. His arm was around her. Both appeared thoughtful. Jack walked Jaimie over to Fielding's rig and gave her a hug before she climbed in.

Cathryn stood by Jack's truck, watching in silence.

Fielding started his engine and Jaimie looked over to her and waved.

Jaimie will be all right; she'll get through this and grow.

But how would Jack feel being saddled with two vehicles,

plus Blaire and the horses? A chuckle escaped her although she felt a bit mischievous for her amusement.

He approached and looked her in the eye. "How can I thank you for helping Jaimie? This had to be a huge shock to her, and yet she's handling it much better than I'd have predicted. I think that has something to do with *you*, Cat."

"I just served as a sounding board for her. Jaimie has a lot of strength and intelligence, and good values. I think that has something to do with *you*, Jack. She just needed a little encouragement to pull it all together. She'll get through this and be the better for it. How did it go with you two?"

"Well, it wasn't what I expected. Not at all! I thought she was going to tell me she was engaged to Fielding. So I was completely blindsided. I did tell her what I could, for now. She's promised to keep it secret a while longer. Unfortunately, there are still others who would be hurt deeply by the whole truth. I have to revamp now. My old plan is crumbling. Please, don't say anything to anyone?"

"Cross my heart, Jack. I would never have interfered, but I kinda stumbled into it."

"I trust you, Cat. We'll figure it out together." He pulled her close and kissed her hair.

Insistent tapping on the glass interrupted their tender moment. Blaire was awake.

Cathryn looked at her, then back at Jack. "Do you think she knows what she's unleashed?"

"If she's lucid enough, I'll ask her. Later." He grimaced.

Cathryn did not envy him that conversation.

"Fielding got her into your truck, and her stuff is in there too. Her keys are still in her car. How will you manage two vehicles? And the horses?"

Jack thought a moment, then pulled out his phone and made a quick call. "All handled. My cousin will come get Blaire's car and bring it to the ranch. He has to go to Fullerton on Thursday so he can bring it down then, and ride back here with me. I need to return for the weekend to finalize arrangements for winter." Jack frowned. "It'll be one long ride to Fullerton unless Blaire sleeps most of the way."

"Jack, about her meds ... do you think the dose is too high? Is she inclined to take too much? I was concerned when I helped her in the bathroom, she was so out of it."

"I'll check into it. She's not one to abuse meds. But she does have other ... problems that could aggravate things. I've got a lot to consider now." His expression grew dismal.

Tap. Tap. Tap. Even medicated, Blaire did not like sharing Jack's attention.

With a sigh they made for Cathryn's truck. Once there, Jack didn't reach for her again. He looked back at Blaire, then stepped forward to open Cathryn's truck door.

Reluctantly she climbed in and leaned out the window to say goodbye. Like she'd done at the Lazy S.

But this time Jack stayed a good step back. Out of reach.

"Well, I'll see you when I see you. Text me when you're back in Quinn?"

A shadow took shape in her mind. Her new confidence wavered. Had this been just a holiday fling to him? And now they'd go their separate ways? Anger simmered in her chest. She gripped the steering wheel and started the engine. 'I'll see you when I see you'? No stirrup kiss or sweet words of farewell? No mention of when or if he'd see her again?

In a cool detached voice she replied, "Sure, Jack, I'll text you. Good luck."

She refused to look into his eyes. She didn't want to see what might not be there. Recalling the line from *Northanger Abbey* she cringed. 'Beware how you give your heart.'

Cathryn pulled onto the highway and sped east into the growing darkness.

CHAPTER TWENTY-SIX

*U*pon reaching Quinn, Cathryn texted Gwen and Jack of her safe arrival. Both responded, Jack with: *"Glad to hear it. Still driving. Talk soon."*

But after that brief message she heard nothing from him. Not a word. The whole interlude at the Lazy S was beginning to fade, like a dream does at the encroachment of dawn. Blaire's outburst had affected many, and the ripples were ever-widening.

After spending the next day wondering about Jack, and another day mourning him, Cathryn decided it was time for action. She would seek a voice of wisdom; she would consult her wise and beloved Austen.

Over the next few days and evenings she read the books and watched the films. It seemed Austen heroines mostly waited: for the man to make a move or for circumstances to change; in other words, for fate. Of course, contacting the hero was much more difficult in Austen's time; even writing a letter was inappropriate unless the couple was engaged. The heroine who had waited the longest—Anne Elliot in *Persuasion*— was understandably the one most determined to do more than wait. After rejecting Captain Wentworth's original marriage proposal, Anne spent seven years regretting her choice while Captain Wentworth was gone at sea.

Cathryn frowned. I don't have that much time.

When Wentworth returned to Anne's neighborhood and snubbed her at their first encounter, she tried to resign herself to that loss being permanent. As the oldest of Austen's heroines, Anne had lost her bloom—after all, she was twenty-seven. Her options were narrowing and time was closing in on her. Cathryn knew that feeling.

For Anne, fate stepped in and put Wentworth within the sphere of wonderful friends that had replaced her own rejecting family. Anne took full advantage of that stroke of luck and, after some struggles, placed herself more or less "in his face," albeit in a lady-like manner.

But Jack isn't in my circle of acquaintance. Now that we've all left the Lazy S, I may never see him again.

She *could* call him. What was her hesitation? Well, she'd *always* been the one reaching out, managing the relationship, sometimes even *creating* the relationship with a reluctant suitor. This time, she wanted a man who knew what he wanted. A man who would step up and declare he wanted her in his life—and back that up with action. A real hero. This time, nothing less would do.

She pursed her lips. She had little experience with heroes. Bob was the only one in her past who qualified. Are real heroes that scarce? Was Jack just another wrong man? Did she even *want* to call him after that non-committal goodbye, and now no contact?

But there was something else she saw in the books and films. Each of Austen's heroines had gained from something that changed her understanding of the situation and of herself; that helped her see it all in a different light. Cathryn recalled Gwen's question at the Lazy S: 'Why give up before you even know what's going on?' So logical. And practical. And it had actually been helpful; even empowering. Like she had shed an old skin up there in the mountains.

It was time for action. Cathryn called Deb.

"Sure I want to hear all about your trip," Deb said, eager for more details. "And did you connect with Josh?"

"I did. He was in on a big adventure with us. I'll tell you all about it when we get together. When are you free? You want to do lunch? Or plan a ride?"

"Actually I'll be in town today for supplies. Wanna grab a sandwich? We're movin' cattle this weekend. Could use another couple hands, if you can join us."

"Lunch today works; and my weekend is ... free." Her voice dropped a few levels. She had no plans with Jack, or anyone else. Would her life now revert to its pre-Wyoming tedium? Would she allow that?

∼

The two friends met at Brews.

"What fun!" Deb exclaimed as Cathryn wound up the tale of her trip—including the night at Jack's ranch, and the events at the Lazy S. "So when do you see this guy again?"

"Well, that's the rub. I haven't heard from him since we parted. And those parting terms were vague—again! I asked him to text me when he got back to Fullerton. But he didn't. I'm not sure what to do. Is he ghosting me? Frankly, I'm ready to walk away from the whole muddy mess."

"This is the in and out guy, right?"

Cathryn nodded.

"Did you talk about why he was like that before, Cathryn? Or shall I call you Cat? Great nickname, by the way. Always thought Cathryn a tad formal." Deb took a bite of her roast beef sandwich.

"He said he hadn't known what to do before because of his strange situation with the so-called daughter and her mother, so he didn't do anything. Didn't want to drag me into his quagmire, as he called it. But we were thrown together so much by coincidence that things blossomed. At least I thought they did. But when we said goodbye after supper at the diner, he said, of all things, 'I'll see you when I see you.' What kind of farewell is that after the week we had?" She stabbed at her salad.

Deb pondered for a minute then asked, "Anyone else around when you said goodbye?"

"Yeah ... Blaire, the mom, was nearby in his pickup."

"Would a more romantic goodbye have ... complicated his dealings with her? He was gonna be shackled to her for awhile on the trip back."

"Hmm, I hadn't considered that. Yeah, it probably would. I guess I was stuck in my own head. But he didn't call me when he got home either."

"So he was hauling horses and had a change in his ranch schedule because of this woman—plus he had to deal with her and her situation, get his horses home and settled, and get back to his job. Not to make excuses for him, but there's a lot on that plate." She paused. "You know, one time I was loading horses and my phone worked its way out of my pocket. I drove over it; smashed to bits." She laughed. "Wasn't funny then. Something like that coulda happened. Why don't you just ask him?" Her eyes twinkled at Cathryn.

"You think I'm being old-fashioned by not calling him at his office?"

"Not old-fashioned. But if it was you and me parting, and I didn't get back to you, what would you do?"

"Call you, of course. But that's different. In my relation-ships with men I've always been kind of the 'mother' and I don't want to repeat that. I want a man who takes initiative," Cathryn said, taking a huffy tone.

"And how would a friendly text or email—if you're not wanting to actually talk—how would that hurt anything? I say treat him like any other friend. Then leave it to him to take it up a notch. Or two." She took a bite of pie and smiled.

Cathryn considered. "Like any other friend ... that does make sense."

"If you want some ... I don't know ... guidelines? expecta-tions? for the two of you, just tell him. If he cares, he'll do it. If he objects or can't be bothered, then he's not worth your time. Did you talk terms?"

"No," Cathryn admitted. "That seemed too ... needy."

Deb folded her napkin and leaned back. "Depends on how you look at it. Is it needy or just honest because you value your own feelings and your own time? Hey, your lunch hour's almost over."

"Yikes! I better run. Thanks, Deb, great to see you and hear your words of wisdom."

Deb laughed. "So this weekend then? Wanna ride Mac?"

"Sure. Text me the details," Cathryn called over her shoulder as she hurried out the door with a wave.

~

While driving home at the end of her workday she mulled over Deb's perspective—a simple, practical perspective.

Maybe I make things too hard, too full of symbolism. Surely things happen that have no hidden meaning. Am I creating drama that doesn't exist? Like Catherine Morland in *Northanger Abbey*? She chuckled. Maybe it *was* possible to read too many novels.

She would stop speculating and take action. She would send Jack a friendly email and get back to being the Cat she had become at the Lazy S. Whether he was in or out would be up to him.

Once in the door at home and after letting the dogs out, she poured a glass of iced tea and sat down at the keyboard in the den, typed a few friendly lines to Jack, and pushed 'send.' She was about to close out and fix supper when she noticed her inbox loading dozens of emails. Two were from Jack. Taking a deep breath, she opened the most recent one.

"What's going on? I hope you're okay. Did you get my earlier email? Missing you. Jack"

Hastily she clicked on the earlier post.

"Sonny stepped on my phone. Didn't have your number memorized, had to dig to find your last email. Been thinking about you and all that happened. When can we get together? I'm trying not to do nothing this time! Gotta get to the phone store

tomorrow. Mom's in the hospital again so been hard to find time. Miss you. Jack"

Cathryn leaned back and let out a big sigh. Good thing my email to him was friendly! It will be obvious I hadn't gotten his yet.

Oh, I'd better answer him. She thought for a moment, then typed:

"Glad to hear from you, Jack. I just now got both your emails, some kind of server delay. Sorry about your mom, will she be okay? Hope Sonny didn't cut his foot. I'm moving cattle to winter pasture this weekend with Deb and Bill. Got any cow-y horses? Let me know if you want to join us. Deb said they can always use more hands. Can't wait to see you again. 555-3373

Affectionately, Cat"

She tossed a salad, topped it with avocado and egg, and sat down with her iced tea, but before she could take a bite her phone rang. She looked at it and grinned. Jack.

By the time they finished talking, her salad was soggy but their plans were firm—he would ride with her at Deb's, and he sounded excited.

For the first time Jack would be in *her* sphere.

CHAPTER TWENTY-SEVEN

*J*ack arrived with the dawn. The pale sunrise promised a clear day. Cathryn heard his truck and trailer rumbling down her gravel road as she packed snacks and drinks. At the front window she watched him check on his horse before he headed to her door.

She greeted him with a smile and a hug.

"I've missed you, Cat." His eyes wandered tenderly over her face, as if he had not seen her in a long time. Then he kissed her.

The dogs, barking initially to protect their mistress from the threatening contraption out front, now followed at Jack's heels after witnessing the friendly greeting their owner bestowed on this stranger. As Jack sat down the dogs gathered around expectantly; one cat jumped into his lap and the other wound around his legs.

"They like you. That's a good sign. Meet George and Emma (she indicated the dogs), and that's Elinor in your lap and Marianne at your feet. "Cup of coffee?" she asked.

"A hot brew would be great. It's crisp out there."

She headed into the kitchen and returned with two cups of fresh coffee.

As they sat at her tiny table, steam rising from their cups,

Jack said, "Tell me about this ranch we're going to, and about your friend, is it Deb?"

"Well, Deb and I have been riding together for years; you know, just casual trail riding. She and her husband Bill run cattle west of here; I don't know how many. It's a really pretty area, nestled up against a kind of plateau called the Vision Hills. Deb is practical and down-to-earth. Bill seems to be the romantic one. I think you'll like them. Remember, Josh is her nephew, and he *is* a great deal like her."

"Josh. Good guy."

They sipped their coffee in comfortable silence, listening to the morning songs of the birds. Although she agreed with Austen that good company consisted of clever, well-informed people who have a great deal of conversation, she also believed good company knew when to be quiet. Jack was definitely good company, by any reckoning.

He looked around the cottage with interest. "This is cozy. Small, but ... what's the word? ... charming. Feels like you."

The remark filled her with pleasure. "Thanks. I love this place. And it's the first house I've lived in without anyone else; just me."

"Kind of the same feeling as my cabin at the ranch, yeah?" He smiled at her.

"It is," she replied. "I like cozy."

When their cups were empty, he carried them to the sink and rinsed them. She let the dogs out, gave all the animals fresh water, and brought the dogs back in for the day. Her neighbor Harry would stop by to check on them later.

Jack turned to her. "Shall we head out?"

"Yes, it's a good thirty minutes from here. I've packed some snacks and drinks; I didn't know if you were bringing your own or what. I don't even know what you like."

"We'll learn those things as we spend more time together —lots more time." He winked at her and picked up the snack bag, then held the screen door while she said goodbye to four questioning faces and closed the main door. No one in Quinn locked doors. At the truck, he handed her in, made one last check on Sonny in the trailer, and they were off on their first outing as a couple. She looked forward to a memorable day.

The morning mists lifted as they drove west on the gravel, leaving behind a touch of pink in the sky.

He said his mom was doing better and was back at home.

"That's good." She paused. "I have to ask: how is Jaimie? And Blaire—is she healing?"

"Jaimie is okay. I talk to her every few days. She's got a lot to deal with now, after what Blaire told her." His jaw tightened. "I haven't talked to Blaire directly, except during the drive back to Fullerton. Luckily, she slept most of the way. Jaimie hasn't said much about her mom."

"I'm glad—about Jaimie that is. It *is* a lot, but I think she can manage. I'm guessing it's not like Blaire has ever been a kind and loving mother."

"Definitely not. I wish I could get the rest of the mess sorted out, but some of it's out of my hands. Unfortunately, I don't think we've heard the last from Blaire." He gave her a rueful look. "She's still pretty steamed, and I'm not even sure why. She sent me some nasty emails, threatening all kinds of things. I didn't respond, other than to advise Jaimie to talk to her mom's doctor about the medications she's on; they can be pretty addictive." He stared ahead, expressionless.

What had happened in Blaire's past that she would treat her own daughter in such a way? Cathryn knew well the problems that parent/child breaches created. Had Jack's influence over the years been steady enough to counterbalance the ill effects of such a mother? But that was a topic for another day. No sense putting a blight on today. She rested her hand on Jack's thigh and his smile returned.

When they pulled into Deb's farmyard folks were milling about and tacking up horses. There were at least a dozen people, but only a few that she recognized. Bill motioned where they could park. As she jumped out of the cab she saw Deb headed her way with a welcoming smile.

"Glad you could make it, Cat," she said, grasping her by the shoulders.

Jack came around the truck and reached out to shake Deb's hand. "Jack Stone. Thanks for inviting me. No doubt ..." he nodded at Cathryn, "no doubt! you've heard about me." He laughed when the women exchanged a meaningful look.

Deb shook his hand heartily. "So you're a polo player. Ever pushed cattle?"

"I have. My brother ranches in Wyoming and I've helped him change pastures a few times. And I've sometimes had cattle at my own ranch near Cedar Gulch."

"Then you know what you're doing. Thanks for coming to give us a hand."

Cathryn looked about her. "You have quite a crowd; must be at least twenty riders now."

Deb pointed out a few people. "You know Nancy and her daughter; there's her husband Tom. Then there's Heidi and Ray. Pete even showed up to help today—always nice to have the law around."

Cathryn followed Deb's gaze. Pete was a wizened old guy, lean as a whip, sitting astride a four-wheeler with a rifle mounted on the front. He was not in uniform.

"And there's several others, and some brought friends. It's a good bunch. The weather is with us. There'll be a big barbecue when we return. Oh, I see Bill's getting everyone organized to head out. Come on, Mac is saddled for you."

After Jack unloaded Sonny, he followed Cathryn to where Mac was tied. "Nice little horse," he commented, then gave her a leg up and checked her tack.

"You know all the duties of a gentleman," Cathryn remarked with twinkling eyes.

"There's a lot to be learned from books," he said with a sly grin as he made final adjustments to Sonny's tack.

As she settled into the saddle, Cathryn noticed a man staring at her with narrowed eyes from across the yard. She'd never seen him before. He looked to be in his thirties, had a stocky build, and was riding a paint horse. His bright blue baseball cap was conspicuous in the sea of orange hats and vests (it *was* hunting season), and he sat off by himself. He made her uneasy; but then she remembered Sterling had made her uneasy—and how wrong she'd been about him. Setting her misgivings aside, she turned to Jack. "Ready?"

Sonny was dancing about with all the activity, but Jack was relaxed in the saddle. "He doesn't like waiting. When Sonny has a job he likes to get right to it."

Cathryn laughed. Deb would appreciate Sonny's attitude.

Unlike the trail ride at the Lazy S, no one here needed instruction. Most of these folks had ridden together often; the local ranchers regularly helped each other move cattle from pasture to pasture, and it was a tight-knit group. The newbies, like themselves, just followed along.

The riders headed out, aiming toward the bluff. The cattle would be herded down to a winter pasture just east of the big barn—more protection and easier to feed them when snow covered the ground and drifted high. Bill rode in the lead. Deb trotted over on Crystal to join Jack and Cathryn, who were riding at the back. Jack was chatting with a younger man next to him.

Cathryn looked over at Deb who raised her eyebrows and tipped her head toward Jack. "So he's decided he's in, huh?" she said in a low voice.

Cathryn's smile was answer enough.

"About time." Deb laughed heartily, which caught Jack's attention so she said, "This ride is pretty easy, other than the switchbacks. We'll drive the cattle back the longer way, across a couple of pastures and down the road. Well, I'd better mosey on and check in with everyone. Catch you later."

Cathryn noticed the guy who had stared at her was riding next to others but wasn't really talking to anyone. She had forgotten to ask Deb who he was. He wore a pistol. Bill and a few other men, and Nancy, also sported guns of various types.

When the riders came to the fork in the road, the four-wheelers headed south and the horses moved directly toward the bluff. From a distance, it had looked to be almost straight up, but seen closer there were easy paths that zigzagged across the face. The group negotiated the switchbacks and made it to the summit without incident. The view was spectacular, with more bluffs climbing on to the west. The wide valley they had come from sprawled below them to the east.

Jack and Cathryn were knee to knee and face to face as they gazed about.

"Beautiful up here, huh?" he remarked.

"Isn't it? Legend has it that Native Americans sent on a vision quest would come here. They call these the Vision Hills. Deb's ancestors are from this area. She's a tribal member and has told me some of the stories and traditions."

They were silent for a few minutes, reflecting. She treasured how Jack loved the land as much as she did. She enjoyed being with him, but still wasn't sure if she could really count on him.

"Deb and I haven't ridden exactly here before, but we did once climb a bluff further south by Nancy's place. She hosted the EST ride a few years back."

At Jack's quizzical look she explained. "It's an annual weekend ride for women only—EST is for estrogen."

Out of the corner of her eye, she noticed the guy in the bright blue hat watching her again.

"Jack—" she began, but was cut off by Bill's voice.

"Now listen up folks. Here's our gate. Ride in, find a spot, and hold steady. Once we're all in I'll give the signal and we'll start moving them, nice and slow. The four-wheelers will meet us at the far gate. Stay out of holes and stay in the saddle." He laughed and leaned down to open the gate.

The group filed in amongst the cattle. Jack moved up on the right flank with some of the other men. Bill closed the gate and loped to the front. He raised his arm and they all began to move. The west wind was in their faces, fresh but not too strong, and the sky was a clear blue.

Nancy rode over beside Cathryn as they walked behind the herd. "So that's the polo player?"

Cathryn's eyes widened.

Nancy grinned. "Deb told me. Good rider. Nice horse."

Cathryn had to laugh. No secrets here, just like in

Austen's English villages. "Yes, that's Jack. Hey, Nancy, who's that guy on the paint, wearing the bright blue baseball hat?" She motioned toward the man who had been watching her.

"Hmm, don't recognize him. Must be someone's brother or nephew. Why?"

"Hey, mom, over here." Nancy turned toward her daughter, smiled and moved off with a wave, leaving Cathryn to puzzle over the odd attention from the stranger.

She found herself, two other women, and one man riding at the back of the herd. Everyone seemed to know their job, and the riders and cattle passed through three pastures without incident, although the last gate was narrower and took them through some ditches to reach the road. She stayed in the back as part of the drivers and let the others, including Jack, ride the flanks and bring in the strays. She admired his work in the saddle—calm and easy but on top of any situation. He fit right in.

A few heifers tried to escape at the back as the group approached the road, so Cathryn and the back riders did have their share of work. Soon all were gathered on the road and the gate was shut to let the grass rest until next summer.

As the group moved off, Jack shot her a look of pleasure.

She nodded and smiled. This was a keeping day, as Grandma Esther had called them; a day to keep in your memory, a day to treasure forever.

After a few more strays were redirected, and a calf stuck in the fence was rescued, the cattle drive was concluded with no harm to human or beast. She was thankful for the sensible mount Mac proved to be. It was a joy to ride a good honest horse. Her Henry would have enjoyed this day. He had known many such in his time. Why must they grow old so much faster than we do?

The riders could practically follow their noses back to the ranch—the savory aroma of the barbeque carried on the breeze. A few non-riders had stayed back to grill the meat and prepare the feast. Tables were laden with side dishes and a tantalizing array of pies and the usual desserts—brownies, lemon bars, and marshmallow treats. Once in the farmyard, the riders dismounted and secured their horses.

Cathryn had just tied Mac to the trailer when a sharp sound cracked through the buzz of conversation. She looked around. A truck backfire? Others appeared confused.

A sense of dread washed over her. *Where is that man in the blue hat?* Before she could locate him, she heard the sound again. *Is that a shot?*

People hollered and ran for cover. Horses whinnied and stomped.

What's going on? Where is Deb?

Out of nowhere, Jack dived at her, pulling her to the ground. Carefully they lifted their heads and surveyed the scene. Peering over his shoulder her eye caught a movement out by the road: a flash of bright green, moving past the machine shed.

"Jack!" she cried, indicating with her head.

His eyes darted toward the spot, then back at her, filled with alarm. "Stay here," he ordered. With one swift move he was up running, and leapt onto Sonny.

"Jack! No!"

As he galloped toward the road, a third shot rang through the farmyard. Two other men on horses tore out behind him, along with Deb. The green vehicle took off, speeding down the road to the north. A four-wheeler blasted out the lane behind the horses—Pete!

Looking around wildly, Cathryn found a bucket to stand on. She untied Mac, leapt into the saddle, and raced after Jack. The north road turned a sharp bend and dead-ended after a quarter mile. She and Deb had ridden there often.

Another shot rang out ahead.

Slowing to a trot, a grim realization flashed through her mind. *It's me Blaire is after. No better way to hurt Jack and get her revenge on me too.* Cathryn turned Mac off the road and urged him around behind a huge stone outcropping the size of a farmhouse. *Maybe if I can distract Blaire ...*

From behind the stone she heard another shot. Mac's ear

twitched but he remained calm; he'd likely been hunted off in the past. She side-passed him over closer and snuck a look around the boulder from behind a big honeysuckle bush.

Jack had dismounted and was facing Blaire, who now stood a little way off from her vehicle with her back to Cathryn. Jack's hands were outstretched, showing he had no weapon. He was speaking but the wind carried his words the other direction. Blaire was waving a pistol at him. The others stood further back, motionless. Pete was partially hidden beside a big shrub. He saw Cathryn and nodded, almost imperceptibly.

She backed Mac behind the boulder, then slid silently from the saddle, dropping his rein to ground tie him. With a deep breath she stepped out boldly into plain sight and cried, "Jack, it's me she's after. Right, Blaire?"

Jack dropped his hands and stared.

Blaire whirled around and narrowed her eyes. "You're right about that. Dead right, you conniving little bi—"

When she aimed the gun at Cathryn, the whole scene erupted. Jack dove at Blaire, causing her shot to go wild. The other men plunged into the fray, trying to immobilize Blaire. Pete roared up on the four-wheeler. Cathryn darted back behind the boulder and buried her face in Mac's mane, aware for the first time that she was trembling.

Mac nuzzled her arm.

Blaire screamed and another shot echoed off the rocks.

"Arrgh!"

"Got her."

"It's over."

Cathryn peered around the protective stone. A struggling Blaire was pinned on the ground by two men. A pistol lay on the ground just out of Blaire's reach. Pete held his rifle on her. Jack leaned against Blaire's vehicle, wincing as Deb wrapped his arm with a polo wrap.

Cathryn took Mac's reins and strode over to Deb, who aimed an eye at Blaire.

"Is this the woman?"

"Yes!" Cathryn gasped. "But I never suspected she'd—"

Deb elbowed Cathryn. "Ha! Bet she didn't think we'd have the law right here with us."

Pete handcuffed Blaire and pulled her to her feet. Her eyes were wild, but she now looked weak and confused. She began to sob.

Cathryn walked over to Jack. The worst was behind them, but she was still shaking. She eyed him with concern and touched his shoulder.

"I'm fine. Just grazed my arm. And you?"

"All this time I thought her threats were idle nonsense. I never dreamed ... how on earth did she find us? Oh, never mind. Let's get you to the hospital."

He grimaced. Then he turned to Pete and his doctor persona took over. "Blaire is recovering from a knee injury and has been taking some serious pain medication."

"Thanks. I'll tell the doc. We'll transport her and meet you at the hospital. Can your woman there drive you in this ... geez, what a color!" He looked askance at the bright green vehicle teetering at the edge of the ditch.

Jack peered in the window. "Keys are still in it. You can drive, right Cat?" Then he walked over to check on Sonny.

Deb took Mac's reins from Cathryn. "I'll get your horses squared away. Call me if you need anything."

Gingerly Cathryn slipped into the SUV and shifted to neutral. Two men pushed the vehicle back until she had traction on all four wheels. Then she shifted again and deftly turned it around so Jack could get in.

"Your arm's a bloody mess."

He leaned back against the seat and caught her eye.

She shook her head and sped toward the nearest town, a stoic Jack at her side.

CHAPTER TWENTY-EIGHT

The blaze of a bonfire welcomed Cathryn and Jack back to the farmyard at Deb's, and those gathered around it turned at the approach of the pair. Deb gestured to two empty chairs beside her and fetched plates of food for the worn-out couple. Several people came over to shake Jack's hand. Clearly he was seen as the hero of the day.

"What happened to the shooter?" someone asked.

Jack cleared his throat. "She's being transferred to the state hospital for observation." His voice was steady as he continued. "The person targeted was actually Cathryn here, although that wild shooting could have injured anyone. We're sorry to have put any of you or your horses at risk."

Turning to her he took her hand and said, "You knew Blaire's true purpose and took a huge gamble for me, and for all of us. How can I ever thank you?"

She was glad the firelight hid her blush. "I simply did what had to be done."

"She's a real heroine," someone added.

A heroine. *Me?* Her head swam but she felt pride welling within her.

Jack nodded, then looked back at the others.

"Our thanks to everyone who helped lock down the situation."

The sheriff added, "You risked your life to contain the shooter, Jack. And Cathryn, likewise, stepping out to distract her like you did. You both have our appreciation." He eyed those around the campfire and the folks assembled nodded their heads. Everyone seemed satisfied with the explanation and the outcome, and the low murmur of friendly chatter resumed in the flickering firelight.

Deb leaned near. "You must be exhausted, Jack, and probably in some pain. Don't drive back to Fullerton tonight. You two can bunk here. Or, if you want to drive back to Cat's, your horse has hay and is settled in. You can come back for him tomorrow."

Jack stared at the fire, then looked at Deb. "You're right. I'm not up to loading, driving for hours, and then unloading. I really appreciate your offer to stay here, but I do think I'd be more comfortable at Cat's for the night. By morning I should be okay to drive; we'll come back for Sonny then. The sheriff said we can drive Blaire's SUV tonight, and then leave it in Quinn for him to transport to impound," Jack explained. "So it's okay if I leave my truck and trailer here?"

Deb nodded. "Come for a late breakfast, why don't you?"

Cathryn had been watching Jack with concern; he was tiring. "Shall we take off?"

He stood and offered her his free hand, then turned to the group again. "It wasn't a typical end to a cattle drive, but I enjoyed meeting all of you. Our thanks again to all who helped, and to those who kept things going here—the food was great."

Cathryn became aware of someone at her side; someone in a bright blue baseball hat. With all the excitement, she had forgotten her misgivings and eyed him now with caution. He was still squinting, but up close it was not menacing.

"Hi. Jimmy Unger. Remember me?" His friendly grin glowed in the firelight.

She stared at him but no memory came to her. She had never seen him before, she was sure of it.

"Aren't you Mrs. Wilson, the music teacher?"

She laughed with relief. "Jimmy, you're not the first to mistake me for Mrs. Wilson. She's my sister, and lots of people think we look alike. I'm sure *she* would remember you. Shall I say hello to her for you?"

"Sure, could you?"

"It's good to meet you, Jimmy. Who are you here with?"

"My uncle Aaron, over there," he indicated. "It was nice to meet you, too, both of you. And good luck with your injury," he said, turning to Jack.

"Thanks. I'm sure it will heal fast."

The couple started for Blaire's vehicle, but Jack stopped in his tracks. "Wait. I need to look in on Sonny."

"Sure. I'll go with and say goodnight to Mac. Thank goodness he was so calm and sensible amidst all the shooting. Sonny too."

Sonny was munching hay and nickered a welcome to Jack, who responded by scratching the horse behind the ears.

Cathryn walked over to the big half door in the back— Mac and another horse leaned over for attention and she rubbed both their faces.

Jack stroked his horse's withers. "I'll be back in the morning for you, Sonny. Looks like you're all set for the now."

Another nicker voiced the horse's approval of the plan.

With that the couple made for the green SUV, climbed in, and headed back to Quinn with Cathryn at the wheel. Moments after they left, Jack was dozing. She hoped that meant the pain had lessened, and saw it as a good sign.

Her cottage at Quinn was veiled in shadows as Cathryn pulled into the driveway. The new moon had set early and wooly clouds wrapped the earth in sleepy softness.

Jack drowsed next to her. The rhythm of his steady breathing was comforting. When she cut the engine, his eyes opened. "Are we there yet?"

A laugh burst out of her. After the day they'd had, his sense of humor was especially welcome. His deep laugh joined hers. It was good to be safe, and home.

They were met at the door by wagging tails. One cat

slipped in from the outdoors, then both cats joined the dogs in approaching for greetings.

"I see what you mean, Cat. It's really nice to be welcomed home like this." He reached down to pet each of the animals with his free arm.

With a soft grin she said, "It is." After letting the dogs out and back in, she gave the four animals bedtime treats and read a note from Harry. He always left one so she would know he'd been there and how they all were. Helpful neighbors were one of the blessings of a small town.

Jack sat down and she pulled off his boots and placed them by the door. Then they moved to the bedroom where she helped him out of his clothes. This time it was her turn to prepare the bed, and she created a comfortable nest for him with plenty of pillows to cradle his injured arm.

The night passed in a hush until they were jangled awake by Jack's phone.

Cathryn peered at her clock—five fifteen. Was he on call?

He mumbled a groggy "Hello," then bolted upright. "What?!" His tone was urgent.

She switched on the lamp.

"Oh, God! When? Are *you* okay? Did you call 911? Who is there with you?" He fired the questions at his caller faster than could be answered. "I'm about two hours away, at least. Let me know when Jeff gets there, okay? I'll get started now and call you in a little while. Yes, I love you too. I'll be there as soon as I can, Mom."

He clicked off and stared at his phone. Cat propped the pillow under his arm again and waited until he was ready to talk. It wasn't long.

"My dad is dead. Dead! Mom woke when she heard a noise—he had fallen out of bed. She couldn't rouse him. The ambulance just left. Jeff's only twenty minutes away. Luckily she had the presence of mind to call him first. She's amazing." He looked at Cathryn, or rather through her. She could almost see the gears of his mind engaging.

"So what needs to happen next, Jack? What can I do?"

He took a deep breath. "Well, I need to get there, fast. But I also need to get Sonny home and unloaded. Geez, that'll take a lot of time ..." He frowned.

"Can I drive Sonny? You could drive Blaire's car to the authorities in Fullerton. Does it have to stay in this county?"

He gave her a penetrating look. "No, that's good. They said I could drive it to Blaire's county of residence, but I told them I had to drive my horse back, so yeah, that would work. Then I could leave straight from here. But you haven't been to the farm down in Sedgeway."

"Just give me directions. And what do I do when I get there? Where does Sonny go and all?"

"There's a hired man there—his name is Troy—so if you can just get Sonny to Sedgeway, Troy can handle the rest. I'll call ahead and alert him. He can park the trailer and unhitch my truck so you can drive it back to town. Hmm, so I need to call Troy, and the sheriff from last night, and my brothers ..."

He flopped back against the pillows with an enormous sigh and a bewildered expression. "I still can't believe it. After all the trouble he's caused. This changes everything," he muttered.

Everything? Cathryn longed to ask him what that meant but didn't want to complicate the present crisis.

"I'll call Deb to alert her I'm coming, and ... let me call the sheriff. You take care of your family calls."

He sat upright and nodded, but still looked dazed.

"You want a quick bite to eat?" she offered. "Nothing is open here this early."

"Can you make me a travel mug of coffee? That'll hold me."

"Jaimie." He leaned forward in agitation. "I need to call Jaimie too. Man, I just can't believe this. It's so unexpected. I mean, neither of them are ... were ... in good health, but I had been worried about *Mom*, and now it's Dad instead. He's ... gone." He leaned back on the pillows with a whistle and closed his eyes.

She reached for his hand. He grasped hers with both of his, then winced from stretching his arm.

"How is it?" She nodded toward his arm.

"It'll be fine. I'll get it looked at again once I get Mom taken care of. I don't want her to be alone with all this."

"Of course not."

She kissed his cheek then pulled on her robe and padded to the kitchen to start the coffee. It was cold this early in the morning so she switched on the heater to take the chill off the cottage. She could hear Jack talking on the phone to his family, one by one. In a few minutes she returned to the bedroom to help him dress. Once they were in the front room, she knelt to work his boots on for him.

"Helpless as a baby!" he cried, but his wry smile showed his appreciation. He rose and opened the blinds, peered out at the ashen sky, then turned to her. "Cat, could you ... do I ask too much for you to stay with me a few days? In Fullerton? I know you're not, well, part of the family ... but I want you with me. Will you come?"

At first she was taken aback. She didn't belong at a family event yet, especially a tragic one like this. Then Deb's words ran through her mind: 'like any other friend.'

"You'll need *someone* to dress you, won't you, Jack?" she said with an arched brow, which earned a smile from him. "Of course I'll come. I'll arrange work, have Harry take care of my animals, and pack some clothes. Do you think ... will I need anything dressy?"

"Probably. Kind of. Law office stuff. Bring riding clothes and boots too. I want you with me as long as possible ... or as long as you can put up with me." His easy smile returned.

"As you wish."

He was chuckling in the front room as she returned to the bedroom to dress, then she heard him on the phone again.

She entered the kitchen and poured coffee into a travel mug, then walked Jack out to Blaire's car beneath a low canopy of gray. The birds were still asleep but the wind was stirring in anticipation of dawn.

"Watch for fog along the river roads," she cautioned. "It can be thick."

"Will do." He pulled her close. "I'm so glad you're with me, Cat." The embrace was intense, prolonged.

She stroked his cheek. "Text me when you reach Fullerton, so I know you're safe. Are you sure you can drive?"

"Yeah. And to be honest, I'm relieved to not have to drive the trailer one-handed. Let me know your progress with Sonny. By the time you're done at Sedgeway, I should have some things settled and will meet you ... somewhere. You're okay with seeing my mom? I guess you know her from years ago, but ..." He opened the car door and eased himself carefully onto the seat. Cathryn closed the door for him.

"Sure. She always seemed so sweet and kind."

"She is. In that way, you remind me of her. Come here."

Cathryn stood at the window on tiptoe as he leaned out and gave her a goodbye kiss.

"Are you familiar with the tradition of the stirrup cup?" she murmured.

He nodded.

"Your feet aren't actually in stirrups but you are departing, so that was a stirrup *kiss*, a new tradition—*our* new tradition."

"As you wish." He kissed her inner wrist tenderly, then backed slowly out of the driveway. Soon the green SUV was swallowed by the fog.

'As I wish.' It certainly seems so. A little hard to believe after all these years.

Back inside Cathryn sank into her big chair by the window with her own coffee in hand. She inhaled the rich aroma and wrapped her chilly hands around the steaming mug. So many things were spinning around in her head, each commanding attention. But she noticed something new, something different. She wasn't tense or driven. Now she could just sort of drift, and simply enjoy the memories and experiences, not feel driven to interpret them or evaluate them, or see them as precursors to a future that she needed to control or direct. This was so much easier! It was a new kind of ... detached caring. At least it felt detached to her. Especially as involved Jack. No more ruminating or obsessing, no more trying to ferret out hidden meanings. She would just trust—in what he said and did, and in what she felt. *And*, if he should prove false, or even just change his mind, she knew she would still be okay. She could ride on. Yes, this was very nice indeed.

As she finished her coffee, the sky brightened. She rinsed out her cup and went to fetch her weekend bag.

~

"Locked and loaded," Deb said as the women closed and latched the door to Jack's horse trailer. "Bill and I will get your truck back to Quinn later today."

"Thanks for your help, Deb." Once again, Cathryn was grateful for a friend like Deb—so calm and confident in any situation. And was pleased to think maybe some of that was rubbing off on herself.

"Hope things go well in Fullerton. From what I know of Jack, I like him. You're right, he's a good horseman and seems like a good guy. Might be a few tough days ahead though."

They walked around the trailer to take a last look at Sonny who was pawing in his eagerness to get on the road.

"Yes, I imagine so. I'm not sure what my role will be since he has his brothers there, but I'm taking your advice—to just be a friend. And be there for Jaimie, too," Cathryn said, thinking out loud as she climbed into the cab.

"Call if you need to." Deb pounded on the hood. "Now off with you."

"Bye. And thanks," Cathryn called out, then focused her attention on maneuvering the long truck and longer trailer through the farmyard and out onto the gravel road. Not long after she turned onto the oil road, a text announced Jack's arrival in Fullerton.

Her own journey there would give her plenty of time to think about how the next few days might unfold; but driving

the unfamiliar truck and trailer with Jack's beloved horse
aboard kept her thoughts very much in the present as she
made for Jack's place near Sedgeway.

His words from this morning were still turning around in
her mind.

'This changes everything!'

What could he mean?

CHAPTER TWENTY-NINE

The late-morning sun played hide and seek with the clouds as Cathryn pulled into the farm lane at Sedgeway. Troy was on hand, as arranged, and was as helpful as Jack had promised. She forked some fragrant hay over the fence to Sonny, who was happy to be in his own paddock, while Troy parked and unhooked the trailer. She leaned on the pitchfork and looked around, surprised at the number of trees. Many were evergreens of good size, not so common on the prairie. Who had planted them? Pine Grove Ranch was an apt moniker.

She sent Jack a quick text of her arrival and reassured him that Sonny was safe and settled. Within moments she had his response:

"Thanks. We're at Mom's apartment, here's the address."

It was an exclusive retirement center in an older part of town that Cathryn was familiar with. After thanking Troy for his help, she climbed back into Jack's truck for the short drive to Fullerton. She would now be in Jack's sphere, and with his family at a rather crucial and private time. How would that go over? When she reached the complex, she parked, slipped out of the truck, and closed the door.

Just breathe. After all, Jack asked me to be here. She

entered the building and walked down the hallway, looking for apartment #7.

"You made it." Jack was waiting at his mother's door and folded Cathryn into his arms. It was just the kind of welcome she'd hoped for. After an affectionate hug, he guided her into the dining area where a small group sat around the table.

"Cathryn, you remember my brother, Jeff?"

Jeff stood and extended his hand. "Long time. Nice to see you, Cathryn. And this is my wife, Natalie." The women exchanged smiles and nods. "And our kids Tyler and Glory." More smiles and nods. The teens looked to be a few years younger than Jaimie.

Jack then led Cathryn over to his mother. "And of course you remember my mom, Bonnie." They had only met a few times, at school events or in the neighborhood, but Bonnie looked much the same. Her hair was now white, but her face retained the soft, pleasant expression Cathryn remembered.

"Yes, I do. It's so good to see you again, Bonnie. Though I wish it wasn't in such sad circumstances," Cathryn said.

Bonnie reached out her hands and Cathryn took them graciously, surprised to feel Bonnie squeezing her own gently.

Jack sat down by his mother and indicated the seat next to him for Cathryn.

"We were just saying that Joe and his family set out from Wyoming this morning, and Jaimie and Fielding are on their way too. The funeral arrangements are proceeding as far as we can, with what we know. Dad was a great—but secret—planner. We're waiting for the attorney to call back to set the time for the reading of the will which, in an odd kind of twist, also includes the details of the funeral plans. We've discovered he didn't share those with any of us."

The awkwardness around the table was palpable. No one knew what to talk about. Was this due to her arrival? Or was it just the situation? Jack was doing most of the talking, something she knew he did when he was nervous. Everyone was somber but no one was deluged with grief. Was this the typical mid-western stoicism where friendly civilities

disguised deeper feelings? There were no tears. No fond remi-
niscing either, but maybe it was too soon. The visit limped
along, propped up by small talk among the adults about the
weather and jobs. The younger ones were occupied with their
phones, oblivious to the conversation. The ringing of Jack's
phone was a welcome interruption.

"Yes. Okay. Tomorrow at nine? Does that work for everyone?" Jack looked around the table and got a few nods. "Is
your office still on Downing Street? Okay. We'll be there."

"So, tomorrow morning at nine. You remember where the
attorney's office is, Jeff? Then it sounds like the burial is set
for the following afternoon. The particulars will be described
at the reading of the will."

He glanced at his mother. "Mom, are you okay with this?"

She looked at him and then at Jeff. "Yes, it all sounds fine.
I'm sorry I can't tell you what your dad wanted. Every time I
brought it up he'd either holler or stomp off. I guess we just
have to wait until tomorrow." She placed her hands delicately
in her lap. Then she looked up at each son again.

"Can we all have supper together tonight? I'd really like
some company this evening."

"Sure. We'd like that too, Mom. It's nice to be together
like this. Jack, do you think Jaimie and Fielding will be here
by then?"

"I think so. But Joe's group probably won't arrive until
later. They'll stay at my old place on the lake next to you Jeff,
and Jaimie and Fielding will stay at River Run with me. And
speaking of eating, I'm hungry. What do we want to do for
lunch?" He looked around the table.

"The ladies from my card club are bringing in potluck
today and will lunch with me, so you all figure out where you
want to go," Bonnie said. "I'll see you again for supper."

～

The brothers chose a café downtown. The adults sat by the
window and the teens sat at their own table. Conversation

varied from quiet to lively, with no discussion about their father.

Jeff's cane was slung over the back of his chair. "So, what's the story with you two?" he said, shooting a grin at his brother.

Cathryn looked at Jack.

He leaned back and put his arm around her chair. "Well, I asked her here because she feels like family to *me*, although there's nothing official." He tossed her a sly look. "Not yet. I've still got a few ... shall we say ... riddles to solve, but we've recently been through some exciting adventures together." He patted his injured arm.

"He took a bullet for me," Cathryn remarked, with a playful look at Jack.

Jeff and Natalie gasped.

"It's been a regular wild west adventure. Twice!" Jack laughed and proceeded to tell them about the fire at his place on the Moody River, the trail ride at the Lazy S, and then the story of the cattle drive.

Jeff and Natalie enjoyed Jack's colorful storytelling, and cast a few admiring glances at Cathryn.

"I would never have guessed you were so brave, Cathryn. Or ... Cat. You always seemed so quiet and demure in school."

"Probably because I was. I'm definitely not the life of any party."

Jack looked at her with affection. "Still waters ..."

Then Jeff turned to Jack with a skeptical eye. "So Blaire's *still* in the picture?"

Jack frowned. "Unfortunately, yes. But that chapter might be coming to a close now."

They all stared at him, waiting for clarification.

"Sorry. Can't say more but the miserable mystery will soon be over, one way or another. And I, for one, will be relieved."

∽

Supper at the apartment was a quiet affair, with the same group at the dining table as earlier; Jaimie and Fielding had been delayed. Cathryn felt a little easier with Jack's family after the shared lunch. She spent some time talking with Natalie while the brothers visited with their mom.

~

Later that night at River Run, Cathryn and Jack settled themselves in the big chairs by the living room window with glasses of wine. He didn't speak of his dad, or of the miserable mystery, and she didn't press it. The fire crackled cheerfully and the quiet was soothing after all the recent events. She reflected again on the satisfaction of being in good company.

Soon Jaimie and Fielding arrived. Jaimie was tired and a little out of humor, but Fielding was his usual ebullient self.

When the men retreated to the family room to watch the video of the Lazy S polo match, Cathryn followed Jaimie to the bedroom.

"Don't want to watch the video?"

Jaimie shook her head, her mouth drooping.

"Want some company?"

At her nod, Cathryn entered and sat on the antique trunk at the foot of the bed. Jaimie sprawled across the bed, surrounded by her unpacked bags.

"What's going on?" Cathryn asked gently, sensing Jaimie wanted to talk but didn't know how to begin.

Jaimie closed her eyes, then bolted upright. "It's everything!" she exclaimed. "First Mom getting hurt on the trail ride, then telling me about Dad ... uh, Jack ... and now Grandpa. It's just too much." Tears rolled down her cheeks.

Cathryn opened a few drawers searching for tissues, then moved to the bed and sat next to Jaimie, who was now slumped over with her legs tucked under her. As she handed Jaimie a tissue, she said, "Of course it is. Jaimie, that's a lot to happen in such a short time—for anyone." Cathryn edged closer and put an arm around her.

"And then the whole shooting thing—it's freaking unbe-lievable! I'm so sorry, Cat. I could tell those pain meds were making her even more angry than usual. But I never thought she'd do something like ... so crazy. My own mother." Her body shook with sobs.

Cathryn handed her another tissue. "How is she now?"

"Well, I think she's off those pills, but I'm not sure. I can't trust her about anything. Oh, it's all such a mess," she wailed, dissolving into tears.

Cathryn sat quietly by while Jaimie had her cry-out. When the worst had subsided, Cathryn had to subdue a little smile. This scene was very like Marianne's cry-out in *Sense & Sensibility*, where well-meaning Mrs. Jennings had offered olives to a distraught Marianne as a possible cure for her broken heart. Olives indeed!

After Jaimie drew a tremulous breath, Cathryn asked, "So what do you want to do? What helps when you're over-whelmed?"

Before Jaimie could answer Jack appeared at the door. "Hey Jaimie, I'm really craving some ice cream. Will you come with?" His smile was irresistible.

She brightened a bit. "Okay, Dad ... I mean, Jack."

Cathryn noticed Jack didn't respond to the subtle ques-tion—so subtle that Jaimie was possibly not aware she'd asked it.

Jack looked at Cat. "Any special request?"

"Chocolate chip for me please."

"Mint chocolate chip for me," added Fielding, who had just come around the corner.

"Hey Cat, wanna play cards while they're gone?"

"Sure, I love to play cards, and can never find anyone to play with. You two hurry back and you can join us. What's the game, Dan?" she asked as they wandered off to the family room.

Fielding dealt the cards but then set his hand down and looked squarely at Cathryn. "I'm going to ask Jaimie to marry me. I told Jack—you know, the old traditional thing—and I wanted to tell you too. I'm not sure, are you and Jack ... like, are you a couple? He seems to consider you family. And Jaimie feels close to you, so I wanted you to know too." His face lit up with a jubilant grin.

"Dan, that's wonderful! Have you talked about marriage before? When are you going to ask her?"

"We've been in love since we met at that big horse expo three years ago. We've kinda talked about it, like in the future. I can't imagine my life without her. Oh, I'll wait until after the funeral. She's had a lot to deal with lately, with her mom and now her grandpa," he said with quiet understanding. "Although it would be great if we could announce it to the family while we're all together," he mused.

Cathryn fingered her cards. "What does Jack say? I'm sure he'd know what would be best for the family."

"He said after the burial."

"That makes sense. You certainly have my support. From what I've seen, you and Jaimie are great together."

Fielding picked up his cards. "Good. I thought you would approve. Now I just have to figure out how to approach Blaire ..." He paused for a moment, his face clouded by an uncharacteristic frown, but it was gone in an instant and he was his usual cheerful self again.

"You and Jack have any plans in the works?" he asked, with a mischievous twinkle in his eye.

"Wouldn't you like to know!" Cathryn quipped as she arranged her hand.

Nearly an hour later, Jack and Jaimie returned with a selection of frozen delights. When four bowls were heaped with ice cream the two couples retreated to the comfort of the living room. Cathryn liked the casual lifestyle Jack seemed to lead—no pretension, no fussiness, no standing on ceremony. Both Jack and Jaimie now appeared more relaxed, sitting comfortably together on the sofa enjoying their ice cream.

While she ate, Cathryn pondered that change—along with Fielding's remark about Jack and herself. The cool creaminess of the vanilla, punctuated by chunks of deep, dark chocolate, was delightful and she slowly savored each spoonful. She caught Jack watching her, and colored at being discovered in a private reverie of pleasure.

His big grin eased her back into the present and brought a smile to her face. When Jaimie and Fielding went to the kitchen for second helpings, Jack moved next to her on the loveseat. His warmth was comforting.

"Did he tell you?" Jack asked.

"Yes, he did. I was surprised he did. Can I assume you gave your consent?"

"Of course." He chuckled. "I think they're good for each other and have a fine chance of happiness together." He stole a look at her. "And Cat, I'm kinda liking this whole happiness together idea ..."

She gave him a warm smile and nudged him. "Me too!"

CHAPTER THIRTY

The aroma of freshly brewed coffee curled its way into Cathryn's lingering dreams, accompanied by baritone humming and the steady spray of water. The first light of day was softened by steam from the big mug on the bedside stand. She wriggled deeper into the covers for a few more minutes, then threw them back, sat up, and walked over to the window for a better look at the valley. *Her* valley. Hers and Trinity's. The river was still swathed in mist, and the fields were beginning to take on a rosy glow.

The attorney's office. That's where we're headed this morning—and soon. She pulled out what she would wear, took a sip of coffee, and knocked on the bathroom door. "Save me some hot water!"

Jack's muffled voice replied, "Too late, sleepyhead. Better hop in here now before it's gone."

Sure that he was teasing about the water, she opened the door. Their playful shower was short but sweet and set a mood of affectionate unity that would likely be needed for the day ahead. She wrapped her hair in a towel and pulled on her robe, thinking how peculiar it was that no one in the family knew the contents of the will, or even the burial arrangements. Why would his dad refuse to share that? 'A rich man used to having his own way' came to mind ... he must have been a difficult man indeed. Poor Jack. Hopefully the facts would be revealed today. Facts could be horrid things, but she hoped it would not prove so for Jack.

Wrapped in terrycloth from head to toe, she dropped into the big chair near the window to finish her coffee and watch Jack dress; his arm slowed him down but he managed, even buttoning his shirt one-handed. Does he know how handsome he is? He glanced up, a tinge of color in his face. Still some of that shy guy from school. She gazed at him fondly.

"Want some eggs?" he asked.

"Yes, please, scrambled, with some toast and juice?"

"Coming right up, ma'am," he said with a mocking smile and an elaborate bow.

Then he gave her a serious look. "I *do* want to get there early to talk with Mom before it all begins."

"Don't worry; I dress quickly. I'm low-maintenance," she assured him as she stood and pulled the towel off her head.

He was rooted to his spot, looking puzzled.

"Ingrid Bergman ... *When Harry Met* ..."

"Ah yes, I remember now. Low maintenance—are you sure about that?" he asked with a sardonic lift of his brow. He was chuckling as he headed for the stairs.

They left in good time and were near the edge of town when they saw the flashing lights. Traffic was backed up in all directions.

"Oh, no!" Jack gave her an agonized look. He stopped the truck and handed her his phone. "Call Joe or Jeff. Tell them we might be late." Then he shot out the door and trotted toward the nearest police car.

Cathryn tried to keep an eye on Jack while she searched his phone for Joe or Jeff. Jack first spoke to an officer, then leaned into one of the damaged cars.

"Hello?"

"Joe, hi, it's Cathryn. McNeil. Jack and I are on the way,

but we're blocked by a car accident. Jack has gone up to the scene. He wanted me to tell you we might be late."

"Oh, you two are okay though?"

"Yes, we weren't actually in the accident."

"Well, that's just like Jack to jump in and do what he can. Is the ambulance there yet?"

"No ... well, I hear a siren now."

"We won't start without him, of course. Just text when you're on the way again. Hey, it'll be good to see you. Been a long time."

"Yes, it *has* been a long time."

"Thanks for letting us know."

Cathryn watched Jack move about the accident scene. While the officers directed the ambulance, he maintained close contact with the injured. After he spoke with the emergency crew he stepped back. Yes, I admire him very much indeed. She couldn't wholly say that about any other man from her past, except for Bob. Jack was exceptional in many ways, yet completely unpretentious, doing heroic things without expecting to be called a hero, or even be noticed. He truly is the best man I know. The officers began directing traffic and Jack sprinted back to the truck.

"Jack, do you know how amazing you are?"

He gave her a curious look. "Just doing what anyone with my training would do." But his smile told her he appreciated her compliment.

"Are the people badly injured?"

"No, I don't think anything life-threatening." He took the wheel and wove the truck into the slow-moving lane of traffic.

" Joe said they'd wait."

Jack nodded in reply.

She sent Joe a text that they were on the way again.

When they turned into the small parking lot at the attorney's office, Cathryn drew a sharp breath. There was the odious bright green SUV.

"Oh, no! Jack, is that—?"

"Yes," he said, through gritted teeth. "I expected she'd be

here since Jaimie is. That's usually her excuse to worm her way in. And who knows? Dad was so eccentric, he may have left his entire fortune to her." He laughed. "No, that's ridiculous." Then he looked at her with wide eyes. "At least I hope that's ridiculous ..." He came around to open her door and hand her out.

She loved those little things he did, the small tokens of affection. How different it was to feel like a treasure rather than a burden. They entered the brick building hand in hand.

As expected, everyone else was already there. He squeezed her hand. She knew he was concerned that he'd been prevented from talking to his mother before the reading. Fortunately Bonnie had saved the two seats beside her. Jack pulled out Cathryn's chair for her, then eased himself into his own and put his arm around his mother.

Cathryn looked at the faces gathered around the massive walnut table. Bonnie appeared calm and not at all distraught. Perhaps there was not much affection left in the case. Jaimie and Fielding sat across the table from Jack and herself, and Jack's brothers were present with their wives. Blaire was perched next to Jaimie, and looked like the cat that had swallowed the canary—or was about to.

The attorney droned on with opening remarks, all familiar to Cathryn so far. She'd participated in scores of will proceedings. Names were being called, a sort of roll call, and she refocused her attention.

"Excellent. Everyone is present as summoned. Do we have any persons in the room that were not specifically summoned?"

Jack spoke up first. "This is Cathryn McNeil. My brothers and my mother know her from years ago."

Cathryn smiled at each of them and received nods or smiles in return—except from Blaire, who kept her haughty eyes on the attorney.

Jack nodded to Jaimie and she spoke next.

"This is my special friend, Dan Fielding. Everyone here knows him."

Fielding flashed an affable smile. He was so welcome everywhere, it would not have surprised Cathryn to hear applause.

Jack's brothers then introduced their spouses.

No one introduced Blaire, who preened in her chair. She must have been summoned. Dressed immaculately and in high style—all in black—she even sported a small hat with a demi-veil. Why would *she* wear widow's weeds? What an affront to Bonnie. But Cathryn had to admit Blaire looked stunning in black.

The attorney went through the burial arrangements. No one reacted with any surprise.

"And now for the bequests. My client directed that I read the following statements—one for each beneficiary. Please save all comments and questions until the end of the reading, in its entirety." The attorney cleared his throat.

Cathryn glanced at Jack. His jaw was tense. What is he expecting? Wasn't it all quite predictable? But clearly Jack anticipated something. His fingers drummed on the back of his mother's chair and his heel was bouncing up and down. She had an urge to reach over and lay a comforting hand on his thigh, but resisted.

I had much better sit and watch.

"To my patient and loving wife and excellent mother to our sons, I bequeath my five agricultural parcels in Manning County and all the assets in our joint accounts 35957 and 35958 at Fullerton Community Bank and Trust."

Bonnie remained expressionless. There was probably nothing unusual in that part of the finances.

"To my three sons, I bequeath my five commercial buildings, the farm parcels they each currently manage, including the polo field, all farm equipment and livestock, and the assets remaining in operational account 35950, on the condition they find an equitable way to divide up these proceeds among themselves, after which they will have the proper papers drawn up at their own expense."

The brothers exchanged knowing looks, as if this kind of

challenge had been set for them before. It was fortunate they got along so well. Cathryn had seen that kind of condition cause outright war in families and tie up proceeds for years.

The attorney cleared his throat once again.

Blaire sat up very straight and lifted her chin.

"Next, I bequeath my seven rental homes in Fullerton, the investment account at Community Federal Savings, and the ranch at Holland Grove in Pierce County to my beloved daughter, Jaimie Stone."

"Daughter?" Joe blurted.

Every face whipped around to stare at Jaimie.

Blaire smirked.

Jack leaned toward his mom, whispering to her. She still appeared composed. Had she known? Was that what Jack had wanted to talk to her about? And last night—was that what he told Jaimie when they went for ice cream? It all began to make sense, in a convoluted way.

The attorney rattled his papers to regain their attention.

"And to my daughter's mother, Blaire Burgess, I bequeath the enclosed one dollar bill to invest in her favorite gambling machine. I wish her the best of luck."

Now all eyes locked on Blaire. Her lips were pressed into a tight, thin line. Her face flamed with fury. She slammed her fist on the table.

"That old jerk! After all I did. After all I put up with ..." She flew from her chair and limped her way to the head of the table. "Give me that!" she commanded, ripping the crumpled and worn dollar bill from the attorney's hand. She turned an icy stare on the group. "You'll all regret this!" She stormed out, her leg brace barely slowing her down.

There was a moment of stunned silence. Then everyone talked at once.

"Hold on; hold on everyone." Jack leapt to his feet in a move for silence. "Let's go somewhere to talk about this."

"River Run is closest, Jack."

"Is that okay?" Jack received nods all around, and the flustered group swept out of the law office.

Back in the truck, Jack let out a long slow sigh. "At last! At last it's all—well, almost all—out in the open. Now everyone can hear the rest of the story." He threw his head back and laughed with abandon.

Cathryn joined in his laughter, feeling his relief. And nursing a compelling curiosity about the rest of the story.

He reached over, took her hand, and squeezed it. "Let's go home."

Her heart jumped. Home. He had said it like it was their home. Together.

No, no ... he couldn't mean anything particular by that. River Run was, after all, *his* home.

Not *her* Pemberley.

CHAPTER THIRTY-ONE

"Fielding, pick up some more ice cream!" Jack bellowed into the phone, then clicked off with a grin. He looked at Cathryn. "What? Too celebratory?"

Not sure if he was joking or serious, in a guarded voice she said, "You know your family best."

Striking a more sober note, he said, "Yeah, and there's still more to be said. I'm not sure how everyone will take it." He pursed his lips as he drove up the driveway for River Run.

Once parked, he turned to her. "You are unbelievably patient with all this, Cat."

Forbearing. Yes, I flatter myself I am. That saying from *Pride & Prejudice* amused her and she pressed her lips together to subdue her smile.

Jack misinterpreted her poorly concealed merriment.

"No, really, I mean it. I told Jaimie everything last night— well everything that's appropriate for her to hear without denigrating her mother, which wasn't easy. I really did want to tell you everything too. You have *no idea* how much I've wanted to confide in you. But Mom still hasn't heard it all either. I wonder if the others have any tales to tell?"

"Jack, of course you should tell your family first. All this has been going on for years ... long before you and I ever, uh, bumped into each other."

He frowned. "You and I are way more than 'bumped into,' aren't we?"

"Jack, we are 'hell and gone from Cartagena' beyond bumped into." She slid out of the truck.

He closed the door and looked at her intensely. "*Romancing the Stone,*" he cried. "Hey, wasn't he Jack, too?"

As they stood laughing at the romantic parallel, a soft rain began to drizzle down on them. He took both her hands in his. The light in his eyes was so powerful she was sure no storm could extinguish it.

"I love you, Cat."

The rain pattered gently while a flood of emotions rose in her throat. She pulled his face down and kissed him, long and deep, then touched his cheek and said, "I know."

His befuddled expression tickled her. She arched her brow in reply, wondering if he'd get the film reference. When they reached the porch, she looked at him. "Well?"

He gave her a wicked look. "Where's your blaster, Princess?"

They entered the house laughing.

The others arrived in a matter of minutes, with Jaimie and Fielding following a short time later bearing the requested ice cream. Jack set out bowls and spoons. Cathryn filled a pitcher with water and ice and lined up glasses and jars of nuts and other toppings. As the family members filtered in Jack said, "Get yourself some ice cream and find a seat around the table. I'm guessing there's still a lot to explain."

After helping his mother to a seat, Jack sat down next to Jaimie, stood his spoon upright in his ice cream and said, "First off, brothers, let's welcome Jaimie as our sister!"

The brothers all pounded their hands on the table in some kind of familial salute.

Cathryn looked around in amazement. How was such unity possible after having such an odd—or *mean* as Jack had once said—father? She felt a little envious of the brothers' solidarity.

Jaimie blushed and her eyes filled with tears.

"So, where do we go from here?" Jack asked, patting Jaimie's hand and looking around at the group. "Do you want to ask questions? Should I just talk? Oh, and by the way, I explained things to Jaimie last night. I had been wanting to ever since her mom told her a few weeks ago that I wasn't her father, but didn't tell her who *was*. Once Dad was gone, I felt Jaimie would be safe from any retribution he might inflict. I wanted her to have the full story because, well, obviously ..." He grabbed his spoon and took a bite of ice cream.

"My question is awkward," began Joe, "but I know it's on all our minds." He looked at Bonnie, who was eating delicately. "Mom, can I ask if you knew about this? You seem so calm. Although you've always been the calm one, even with all the raging Dad did, and all our brotherly chaos," he said, exchanging looks with his brothers. "But if you don't want to talk about it, we understand."

Bonnie was quiet for a minute, looked at each of her sons around the table, and then smiled, which puzzled the brothers exceedingly.

"Jaimie has always been part of our family and always will be," Bonnie said, her voice soft and gentle. "It's just her title that's changed. You boys know I always wanted a daughter. And now, dear," she said, looking at Jaimie, "you are a daughter instead of a granddaughter. Love is love, family is family. Titles don't mean much in my estimation. It's the person we love; it's you we love." Bonnie gazed at Jaimie with affection then resumed answering.

"Did I know? Not specifically. Not about Jaimie. But Blaire was not the first of your dad's other women, and maybe not the last," Bonnie said with a pensive expression. "There were two others that I knew about before Blaire; I believe one affair went on for several years."

"But Mom ..." Joe broke in.

Bonnie held up her hand to silence him. "Boys, you have to understand that our marriage happened in a different era; a time when women had very few choices. In those days many couples stayed together even after the love was gone—and sometimes it had never been there in the first place, being only the result of a poor choice made one night. I know that today couples often don't stay together when there is discord or an affair. I'm not sure if that's good or bad. But women can now earn a living and usually have more options."

"When your dad and I fell in love—and we were *very* young—neither of us had a penny to our name. He was a Sand Hills cowboy with nothing going for him but his charm and his determination. We struggled along together as we had you three boys, and we were very much in love. The early years were good. Very good. Then he discovered his knack for making money in land speculation. And he started making money hand over fist. You have all benefitted from that, and I'm glad, but it changed him. He became—oh, how shall I say it? Grasping. Greedy. Money was his only focus. All he could think about was the next big deal." Her face was troubled.

"He started moving in different circles, and became attracted to high-powered women who could give him an edge in business. One was an attorney, and they made a lot of deals together. The other made her way up in the banking world with his help. Blaire was in real estate, which I'm sure was convenient. But by the time she entered the picture, I was so far removed from his business and his life, I have no idea what deals they made together, if any."

"My dearest wish was that you boys be taken care of properly, and that I would not be a burden to any of you in my old age. I had an attorney set things up the way *I* wanted. Your dad signed it all—I think because he knew that I knew, although we never really spoke of it. That was many years ago. That's when it ended, for me." Bonnie stared at her hands clasped in front of her for a few minutes.

No one broke the silence.

Then she looked up again, her expression clouded. "Hopefully none of you knew, but I developed a special friendship with someone else. I'm not going into the details, and he died a few years ago, but I was not lonely all those years, if that is any comfort. He was a wonderful companion, especially as you boys got older and moved out of the house, busy building your own lives. So, although I have twinges of regret at times, mine has not been an unhappy life. Not at all. You have each made me so proud, and you all seem happy, or on the verge of happiness"—she eyed Jack—"and that lets me know I've done well by you. Your happiness gives me the greatest joy." Bonnie's eyes welled with tears.

She looked at each of her sons again, focusing last on Jack. "I'm guessing you've paid a bitter price in this situation, am I right? Trying to protect me. And Jaimie."

Jack shook his head. "Say nothing of that. It was done for good reason, and it is finished now. I hope."

He turned to Jaimie and said, "I'm guessing your mom is very angry about now, after the will. I don't think any of us were expecting how that went, what he left her. I'm hoping there are no repercussions toward you. None of this was your fault. Don't take any of it on yourself, Jaimie. Just know we welcome you as our sister now and forever."

"Oh, Dad ... uh, I mean, Jack," she stammered, tears filling her eyes.

"You've called me Dad your whole life," Jack said with affection. "Call me whatever you want. Dad is fine with me. Why change it now? If I could, I'd adopt you as a daughter, but I don't think I can legally adopt my half-sister. I wish there was something ..." he trailed off.

Cathryn hesitated to speak, but then quietly offered an idea. "You could have a ceremony to celebrate and confirm your bond. Like the hand fasting ceremonies in Scotland at Gretna Green, only it would be an adoption, not a wedding."

"I'm not sure what Gretna Green is, but I love that idea. Jaimie?"

"Oh Cat, yes. Can we have it soon, Dad? While all the family is here?"

"I don't see why not." Jack looked around the table. "Any objections?"

Joe answered for the group. "Of course not. Anything for our sister!" Hands pounded on the table again.

"Ok, we'll figure out the particulars after the burial. Now, are there any more questions that should be answered?" he asked, then devoured a spoonful of his melting ice cream. "Anything else that needs to be set straight? After today, I'd like all this to be left in the past. So speak now or forever hold your peace."

In a tentative tone Jeff asked, "Um, Jack, how did you know Jaimie *wasn't* your child? I mean, you *were* paired up with Blaire for a while, weren't you? I guess it's not really any of our business, but ..."

"Nah, I look at this as the family's business. And as I said, I have shared all this with Jaimie already. So here's the thing. Blaire and I had been broken up for almost a year. I had seen her with Dad at restaurants a couple of times, but I figured they were cooking up real estate deals. And, as you all know, I was still kind of a mess from losing Ellen and the baby. Being with Blaire hadn't helped my mental state *at all*."

He took a deep breath, and then continued. "Well, I stopped at the house one day—Mom and Dad's house—unannounced, looking for some photos to copy and frame. It was Mom's card club day so she was gone, but I found Dad and Blaire in—shall we say—a compromising situation, so then I knew it was more than a business relationship. I was shocked. At both of them. A short time later Blaire came to me, saying she was pregnant. So with that time frame, I knew the baby wasn't mine. Dad was denying paternity, but Blaire was determined to go after him, even if she had to blackmail him."

"At my suggestion, the three of us met at a restaurant. I was hoping the neutral location would keep them both civil and we could work something out. She threatened if he didn't support her fully plus support the child, and write them both into his will that she would tell Mom plus she'd bring a huge paternity suit and ruin him."

"I've never seen him so angry. He was roaring right there in the restaurant. Part of it, Mom," he said, looking at Bonnie, "was that he actually *was* concerned about the whole mess hurting you; he didn't want you to be dragged through all that. Of course, he also thought it would hurt his reputation as a businessman. That's when they both looked at me. I was the perfect pawn. People knew I'd been with Blaire at one point. If I claimed to be the father, all suspicion would be off Dad, and Mom would be protected. So would the baby. Dad agreed to set up a trust for the baby, large enough for the interest to be used as generous child support. He also made arrangements to pay Blaire an additional monthly stipend, buy her a car, and fund special trips that she wanted. It all worked well for a few years."

Spoons clinked against bowls and he continued.

"Blaire and I never got back together, although she tried to manipulate that. I think a lot of people thought we were together, which was what Blaire wanted. I *hated* that part. But I really loved being your father," he said, beaming at Jaimie.

"After a time, Blaire began to pester Dad for more money. He got cranky and threatened to stop paying anything. She brought up her lawsuit again. It was getting ugly."

Jaimie broke in. "I was about twelve by then, and I know why. Mom had started gambling. Online. She's been addicted for years. Our high-society lifestyle was a sham. We were broke. We lived off credit cards. Mom wasn't even selling much real estate. All she did was gamble. I overheard her tell someone on the phone that we might lose our house. I was scared, so I talked to Dad about it—meaning Jack of course—because I didn't know ..."

"So I stepped in and made a deal with Blaire," Jack continued. "I would help get her out of debt if she would get treatment and quit gambling. I didn't want to see Jaimie's life turned upside down. I give Blaire credit, she got help, and did quit for a few years."

"Yes, she did," said Jaimie. "But I think she started gambling again when I left for college."

Jack took a long drink of water. "I had set myself up, really. But I didn't know what else to do at the time. These last few years have been really tough, trying to keep Blaire at bay. She went after anyone I tried to date. I suppose she figured if I got married, I'd stop bailing her out, and Dad might stop paying her too. She really had her claws into me and I didn't see a way out. I was caught between her and Dad. If I outed either of them, Jaimie and Mom would pay the price." He hung his head.

Bonnie put her hand on his shoulder. "Oh, Jack. Is that why you've been such a loner all this time? I was so worried you'd never find happiness after losing Ellen and the baby."

There was silence around the table for a few minutes as it all sank in.

"Well, no more worries now, Mom," Jack said. "We've all been released, in a way, by Dad's passing. I know I'm ready to move on." He looked directly at Cathryn.

Several of the others glanced her way and she could feel the color rising in her cheeks. All she could think to do was smile at Jack.

"Well then, that's that," Bonnie said calmly. She stood and began gathering the dishes. Everyone joined in the cleanup. The delicate and perplexing matter was placed firmly behind them. The miserable mystery was resolved.

A sense of relief permeated the room, evident in how everyone moved in harmony and in the easy comfort between them all. There was true gentility here, wealth or no.

I like Jack's sphere.

It feels like home.

CHAPTER THIRTY-TWO

*C*athryn was grateful that the next morning dawned crisp and clear. River Run, past and present, was lovely in the fall.

Jaimie and Fielding had retreated to the deck while Cathryn and Jack prepared sandwiches and lemonade. Lunch together outdoors would give the newly-defined family a chance to sift through the recent revelations together. While neither she nor Fielding were part of the family in any official way, Cathryn felt a sense of belonging, something she had not known in a long time.

'Sometime in the morning ...' She began to hum the tune as she plated the food. Then she became aware of Jack, standing very still, watching her. As she met his gaze, her throat filled with emotion and her voice fell silent. His look was so full of affection that she couldn't help returning an equal amount to him.

When he spoke, his voice was deep and low. "Cathryn McNeil, do you have any idea how happy I am right now?"

She closed her eyes for a moment and took a deep breath. "Yes," she replied, opening her eyes and taking in the sincerity of his expression. Joy bubbled within her, filling her with light. She looked back at him, her heart full of love. "Yes, I believe I do."

Their ardent interlude was interrupted by whoops of joy coming from the deck. They exchanged a curious look and promptly carried the food out.

"She said yes!" Fielding proclaimed, his face shining with happiness as Cathryn and Jack joined the young couple on the deck. Gathering Jaimie into his brawny arms Fielding whirled her around as she dissolved in giggles and tears.

Jack and Cathryn shared a knowing look. Cathryn had anticipated Fielding wouldn't wait long. She adored his *carpe diem* attitude and enthusiasm for life. The excitement of the young couple was contagious.

Jaimie was radiant. "I'm so happy. I wish everyone could be as happy as me."

"You two are a good match," Jack said. "I can't think of a more perfect couple in the world. Well, maybe there are a *few* others ..." He winked at Cathryn.

She stretched up on her toes and kissed him on the cheek.

He kissed her forehead and then exclaimed, "I'm hungry!"

Fielding echoed the sentiment and the men tucked into their sandwiches without further comment while the women shared a smile.

Cathryn still had concerns. Would Blaire try to derail all this? It was known she didn't approve the match between Jaimie and Fielding. Jack might need to play the hero—or the arbitrator—a bit longer. Did Blaire have any ammunition left? Even if she did, Fielding's determination to protect Jaimie might prove a force to be reckoned with. Especially if joined with Jack's.

The young couple decided to keep the engagement a secret until after the burial, although in the kitchen after lunch Jaimie confided to Cathryn that she *so* wanted to wear the beautiful amethyst engagement ring Fielding had given her to seal their love.

"Why not wear it on a chain around your neck, hidden inside your clothes for now? That way it will be close to your heart. And a precious secret between the four of us for just a little longer."

"Oh, Cat," Jaimie said, rushing over to give her a hug. "You have the best ideas. I hope ... well, I'm glad you're here, and ... I hope you stay." There was a light in her young eyes.

"I'm glad I'm here too," Cathryn assured her.

She didn't feel it necessary to mention there was a funeral to attend today.

Jed Stone had ordered a private, family-only service and burial at Pine Grove Ranch, his farm south of town by Sedgeway. It was the place he and Bonnie had called home for many years until their health issues required a move to town. Pine Grove was where Jack had moved to in junior high. It had been the place dearest to Jed in spite of all the other acquisitions and wealth he had amassed. Jack would own it now; he had been managing it for the last several years, and kept his polo horses there.

Gray clouds cast a somber mood as the group walked out to the site chosen by Jed. The foreman had already dug a grave there, and the boulder chosen for the headstone was close by: a rugged stone, unmarked. Cathryn was moved by its beauty, and wondered about this man who had been so belligerent and egotistical during his life. These quiet and humble end-of-life choices seemed to reflect a different man. Perhaps the simple cowboy that Bonnie had fallen in love with? Maybe that man had 'died' years ago but was just now being buried? Such a long goodbye.

Bonnie held a handful of flowers picked from what was left in the farmyard garden, mostly coneflowers and zinnias that looked a little tired. Cathryn saw the sorrow now. Bonnie's face was drawn, her eyes downcast. They were indeed burying the man she had loved—and lost many years ago. Had she been living with her loss all this time while the cantankerous Jed lived on, stirring up trouble?

Tears stung at Cathryn's eyes and she looked downward so they would fall freely, unseen by the others. Once again she was the young girl who had suddenly lost Trinity, and that pain seared through her. Then the shock and hopelessness when she discovered Bob's death burst into flame within her. She too had borne her losses long, and alone.

Knowing how loss triggers other loss, she looked over at Jack, who stood beside his mother, his head down. Was he saying goodbye to Ellen and his unborn child again too?

Farewell had been drawn out for all of them.

Bonnie's sons stepped forward and slowly helped lower the coffin into the grave. Joe, as the eldest, said a few words. Each of the sons in turn threw a shovel of dirt into the grave.

Then Bonnie stepped forward with her flowers and dropped them onto the coffin, tears filling her eyes. Her gentle voice could barely be heard. "Rest in peace, you rascal."

She blew him one last kiss and then turned away, walking slowly through the stubble of the shorn hayfield to the house.

Jack and his brothers stood together and watched their mother settle herself on the porch swing. No one spoke. The foreman fired up the bobcat and filled in the site. Together the sons rolled the boulder into place.

The man was gone. Along with all the chaos and heartbreak he had created. What remained was a stone. And peace. Cathryn saw it in Jack's eyes when he looked over at her. His peace had also been a long time coming.

The small group walked around the farmyard together. Jack pointed out special places to Cathryn, and the brothers shared fond memories with their wives and each other. She smiled at the antics they remembered. She had always wished for a brother. These would have been fun brothers indeed.

Bonnie joined them after a time. The clouds continued to create a low gray ceiling, promising an autumn shower. Golden leaves—poplar and cottonwood—swirled in the breeze as the group departed for dinner at River Run. Bonnie had requested Jed's favorite meal for the occasion: steak, American fries, green beans, and peaches. Nothing fancy. It was very much a family meal, eaten quietly at Jack's large dining table as rain tapped softly at the windows.

The mood lightened when Bonnie brought out dessert: a large yellow cake with chocolate frosting that she had made herself. Jack served the remaining ice cream, and the group had no trouble consuming everything amidst fond recollections and easier conversation. Everyone helped clear things away and put the kitchen in order.

When the others moved out to the living room, the four secret-holders in the kitchen exchanged conspiratorial looks. Jaimie touched the chain around her neck and Cathryn nodded. Her heart warmed as Fielding removed the ring from the chain and slipped it onto Jaimie's finger.

Jack winked at Jaimie. "Go on."

The four joined the others in the living room, and when everyone had settled into the comfortable sofas and chairs Jack asked, "Is it too soon for something joyful?" He looked candidly at his mother.

With no hesitation at all Bonnie said, "Joy is always welcome. And I've had an inkling of something going on." Her eyes sparkled.

A glowing halo seemed to surround Fielding and Jaimie as they stood in front of the fireplace. Unable to contain himself any longer, Fielding shouted, "We're getting married!"

Jaimie held out her hand and the amethyst ring gleamed in the lamplight.

Everyone jumped up to offer hugs and congratulations.

Then Jaimie walked over to Bonnie, whose eyes were brimming with tears. She stood and held Jaimie in a long rocking embrace.

It was everything Cathryn had wished for them all. Now the family's attention could focus on a happy event.

Jack put his arm around Cathryn and said, "Did you ever think things could turn out this great?"

"I'm always hopeful; and very happy my wish was granted this time." Cathryn basked in the warmth and love she felt all around. Just like in the song.

Jack led her over to the window where the rivulets of rain were transforming the smooth glass into lace. She smiled at the aptness of the design. As he pulled her close, she looked up at the face that had so often been tense and drawn. Tonight all traces of brooding and pain were gone. He was relaxed; he was happy; and he was here with her.

He caressed her hair with affection. "I never thought I'd be this lucky." Taking her hands in his, he drew them to his chest. Looking deeply into her eyes, in a thick voice he whispered, "Marry me?"

Cathryn's heart leapt. "Jack!" She reached up and touched his face. "Yes. Oh, yes."

His mouth met hers with tender urgency and she melted into the river of love flowing all around her.

Then her mind clicked and she pulled back. "But, Jack ..."

He put a finger to her lips. "Sshh ... this will be our secret for now. We'll give them their time."

She nodded and they gazed at Jaimie and Fielding.

Jack smiled and wrapped Cathryn in his arms.

Those arms felt like home.

CHAPTER THIRTY-THREE

"What did you and Jaimie decide to do for your ceremony?" Cathryn sat next to Jack as they drove to the event. He'd reserved a private room at a restaurant for brunch while Joe and his family were still in town.

His face registered mild surprise. "We didn't really plan anything. It's simple. She's my half sister, raised as my daughter, which I acknowledge by—what was it, hand-something?"

"Hand-fasting. It dates back hundreds of years. It occurred in many cultures, usually as a betrothal or marriage ceremony. It was well known in Scotland, most famously at Gretna Green. Some took a vow of eternity; some for 'as long as love may last.' Anyway, it's a show of unity, binding two people together as loving and willing spirits. So it symbolizes both intent *and* consent. Did you see it in *Braveheart?*"

He nodded as he turned onto Horizon Drive.

"How do you know all this stuff?"

Cathryn threw her head back and laughed. "I've always been fascinated by other cultures and their ceremonies. I guess it goes back to my research on families and children, birthing traditions, and how different cultures raise their children. There's often wisdom in the old ways. We're taking a little creative license here, repurposing it but, in my opinion, all important life events deserve ceremony and recognition."

Jack drove on, deep in thought. "So, I'm thinking I will make my promise to continue to be the father in her life, and ask her to continue to be my daughter. How's that sound?"

"It sounds simple and sincere, just as it ought. Did you and Jaimie talk about it at all?"

He looked dubious. "No. Guess I didn't think about that. There's been so much going on. It's not like anything is changing between us. Well, I guess it is, more for me. She's already thought I'd always be her father, while I had thought of raising her only for a time. This will make it a forever—"

They drew a sharp breath at the sight of the green SUV.

"You think she's here to cause trouble? Have you talked to her since the will was read?"

He remained tight-lipped.

"Maybe she's here to mend fences now that Jaimie's getting married?" Cathryn asked, ever hopeful. "Jaimie has no other father now."

Jack gave her a doubtful look. "I won't go on the offensive, but I will be prepared to defend Jaimie in whatever she chooses to do." He set his jaw.

"Maybe now everything is exposed to the light, Blaire is seeing things differently."

He still looked skeptical. "How can you think so well of people?"

Cathryn squeezed his hand. "How can I not?"

He opened her door. "We still have the protection orders in place. She's the one violating them by being here."

"True. But let's not invoke them unless she makes trouble. She's on probation and probably getting treatment. People do change, Jack. And often need some wiggle room to do it."

Jack rolled his eyes and sighed. "I know. I'm just so tired of the whole business with her."

He took Cathryn's hand and they walked into the restaurant together.

They were shown to the room and found everyone seated at a large round table. Blaire wasn't there. Could it be a coincidence she was dining here with someone else? Jack sat by

Jaimie, with Cathryn at his other hand. The room was filled with friendly chatter but went silent as a tomb when Blaire entered. She was dressed with great care and took a seat across from Jaimie, returning nods and seeming sincere, her demeanor neither haughty nor bitter.

Food orders were taken and beverages poured.

Blaire ordered nothing.

Jack dinged his spoon on his water glass and all eyes turned to him. "You all know we're here to confirm and celebrate the bond I have with Jaimie. This is an adaptation of something called hand-fasting, and since Cat just explained it to me again, I'll let her explain it to you," he said with a merry look. "Cat?"

Faces full of anticipation turned her way. She was surprised, but pleased to share her information. There were nods of interest all around as she spoke, although Blaire's face held no expression; it was immovable, rather like the porcelain face of an old-fashioned doll.

When Cathryn finished her explanation, Jack and Jaimie rose and faced each other. He took her hands and said, "Jaimie, I've raised you as my daughter. Today I promise I will continue to be your father as long as I live, because I love you with all my heart. Will you accept my promise?"

Cathryn's eyes welled with tears.

Jaimie was tearing up too, but she drew a deep breath and looked into Jack's face. "Yes I will. I've always loved you as my father. You're the only father I've ever known. I accept your promise, Dad, and I will live as your daughter for as long as I am here on earth."

Then, to Cathryn's surprise, Jack pulled a small box from his pocket and lifted out a delicate chain with a tiny amethyst stone. He fastened the necklace around Jaimie's neck. Then they turned to the group and he grabbed her hand, raising it in celebration.

Congratulations flew about the room and the table was well pounded. Cathryn thought it one of the happiest ceremonies she'd witnessed. Her thoughts flew back to Gwen and

Adam's impromptu wedding. So much love lately. It really was all around.

When father and daughter were seated, Blaire stood. An expectant silence blanketed the room. All eyes were on her. Cathryn thought briefly of the shooting, but Blaire made no sudden moves; she simply stood with her hands folded gracefully in front of her.

"Jaimie and Jack," she began, "I support you making this commitment." She sniffed delicately. "Jack, although things have been difficult between us at times in a number of ways, I have always appreciated how you were there for Jaimie, as a father. And Jaimie, you couldn't have had a better father. You are a wonderful daughter and I'm happy for you both." Then Blaire came around the table, gave Jack a smile of sorts, and kissed Jaimie on the cheek.

Jaimie stood and threw her arms around Blaire, who responded by stiffly patting her daughter's shoulder. After a long look at Jaimie, Blaire quietly left the room.

Cathryn was filled with admiration. This must have been incredibly difficult for Blaire, but she had done it with dignity. Hopefully this meant Jaimie's wedding could now take place without disruption or drama.

The looks the others exchanged varied from puzzled to amazed to amused, their eyes coming to rest on Jaimie.

"Things seem to be turning around," Jaimie admitted. "All the secrets are told. Plus, I think Mom realizes she's now dealing with an independent, soon-to-be-married woman and," she said with a laugh, "that woman's very determined soon-to-be-husband." She looked gratefully at Fielding. "I think Mom is recovering from more than just her knee. Oh, and she has a special new companion of her own. Some doctor she met in Wyoming. I think that's softening her attitude too."

"It sure is," Fielding chimed in. "We're doing the wedding our way. Neither of us wants a big society wedding, do we?" He glanced at Jaimie, who shook her head. "It will be a simple ceremony. It's the marriage that's important."

That elicited many cheers and more table pounding.

As the food was brought in, Joe asked, "Have you set a date yet?"

"Yes," Jaimie said. "We'd like to be married two weeks from tomorrow if that works for everyone—especially for your family, Joe, since you have to travel so far."

He checked the calendar on his phone, as did his wife, who spoke up first. "That date looks fine for us, right dear?"

Joe nodded.

"Granny B?" Jaimie said, looking at Bonnie. "Oh, is it still okay to call you that?"

"Of course it is, dear. It's what we're all used to. Why change now? I'm sure that date is fine for me."

"My best friend Krista will be my maid of honor, and Dan has asked Sterling to be his best man."

Fielding explained. "Sterling and my dad were best buds, and since I lost Dad, Sterling's been kinda like a father to me. Of course, you all know I lost Mom when I was a kid, and Dad never remarried. I guess their love was that once-in-a-lifetime kind."

There was a pause of silence.

"They'll both be with us in spirit," he said, managing a small smile.

Jaimie kissed him on the cheek then added, "The wedding will be at that little country church out by Dad's new place, and the reception will be at River Run." Her face was flushed with excitement.

The group chattered happily while they ate.

Cathryn was delighted to be part of it all but in the back of her mind her own departure and return to daily life in Quinn loomed. She thought back to that November day, standing in Gwen's old driveway; the day she became aware of change entering her life—rather against her will at that point.

Things were still changing. When she departed tomorrow would this new sense of belonging disappear like the morning mist? It was all just too good to be true.

Wasn't it?

CHAPTER THIRTY-FOUR

*S*team rose off Henry's back as Cathryn curried him. Today's ride was likely their last of the season. At his advancing age, he was not so nimble at negotiating icy spots. A fall could be serious, for Henry or herself. She grimaced. More changes. Sometimes she wished she could freeze time.

She missed Jack. Besides his work, he was getting livestock and equipment situated for the winter at his different locations. On the prairie, winter could arrive without warning. Although they talked nearly every day that just wasn't the same as being together, watching his eyes and being comforted by his touch.

Having agreed to keep their own engagement secret until after Jaimie's wedding, Jack and Cathryn hadn't made any plans or even talked about how their daily lives would alter. No wedding date was set. It was all very vague. A familiar sense of uneasiness crept in and she frowned.

Many more changes were on the horizon, especially for her—if this wasn't all a dream. She found it unsettling, and had difficulty focusing on daily life in Quinn and the mundane details of her job. She longed to work with children again. That was one change she would welcome if she could find such a position, which she likely could in Fullerton. Certainly she would join Jack at River Run, wouldn't she?

Another wrinkle was her beloved cottage in Quinn—she was not eager to leave it. That would be another big life change. But that was what she wanted, wasn't it? The idea of change, of moving on had seemed good. The reality was something different. She recalled how Gwen had embraced it all with equanimity.

Cathryn turned these thoughts over in her head while she walked Henry to cool him down. As she threw his blanket over his back and worked the fasteners, she decided she would fall back on her new philosophy: don't push the river. Jaimie's wedding was this weekend. She would focus on that for now. And on how Austen's heroines had moved forward in various ways, embracing change to achieve their dreams. She then remembered that Austen's books and the many films ended with the engagement or the wedding. Nothing beyond. No wisdom to be found there unless one looked at the few secondary characters who thrived in good marriages.

As she opened the gate to Henry's paddock, Mortimer, a mule also enjoying his senior years, ambled over to greet his buddy. After they nudged noses Henry turned and nickered at Cathryn, knowing there was always a piece of carrot for a goodbye treat.

She smiled. "Here you go guys. Henry, I'll be gone for a couple of days again. You and Mortimer stay out of trouble." The two busily chewed their carrots. As she reached for the gate Henry raised his head and whinnied.

She laughed. "I trust that's a thank you and not an impertinent remark? Don't go and abandon your gentlemanly ways just because you're old. I simply won't allow it." She kissed his nose and ruffled his forelock then slipped out, fastened the gate, and returned to her truck.

On the way back to town, Lisa rang her. There was much to say. Cathryn longed to tell Lisa of her engagement but that news would have to wait; she had promised Jack. And she didn't want to jinx anything. Jed's demise had been in the papers of course so she was able to fill Lisa in on some of those details, as well as Jaimie's wedding plans. The two agreed to meet for lunch the next time she was in Fullerton.

After a simple supper, Cathryn eased herself into a warm bath. Later, wrapped up on the sofa in her comfy robe, she checked email on her laptop but found nothing compelling. She wondered what Jack was doing. Was he thinking about her?

Soon George and Emma insisted on bedtime treats. Time for the cats to come in for the night too, bribed with a small meal. Animals took such joy in routine; they liked to know what to expect and what was expected of them. Perhaps that was something that strengthened her connection with animals, and with children. A part of her also liked to know what to expect and what was expected. And what to count on. An ever fixèd mark.

How would her animals take to the upcoming changes? How would she? There was some loss with every gain. The word bittersweet came to mind.

Cathryn climbed into bed and opened her book. It was an Austen sequel, but her thoughts wandered to Mrs. Dashwood again. She was surprised to find her own views quite different than some months earlier, now believing Mrs. Dashwood *did* find her own happily-ever-after. Was he a wealthy gentleman? Did she move to his estate? Was he among the ranks of the landed gentry, or even the nobility? Perhaps he was in her own economic sphere and thus allowed to join her at Barton Cottage? Maybe she married Sir John? Cathryn wrinkled her nose at that idea.

Why did Austen write only of young heroines? Was love any simpler for the young? Cathryn's own love life had never seemed simple.

In Austen's day one expected to love only once, if that.

In Austen's day, lifespans were also much shorter.

Perhaps it wasn't that older women didn't find romance. Perhaps some of their situations were resolved in more delicate ways, such as could not be written about in that era of rigid class distinctions and strict social expectations.

Cathryn drifted off to sleep with questions tumbling through her mind. Her own situation became co-mingled with Regency tales, resulting in odd and confusing dreams.

～

Jaimie's wedding was a modest, intimate affair. Just what a wedding should be. Marriage was about starting a life with someone, not about putting on a show. How did weddings ever get so off-track?

Cathryn entered the church on Jack's arm. He seated her and then returned to Jaimie. The sun streamed through the old stained glass windows, drenching the tiny chapel in holy light. The strains of the single violin, at times accompanied by Glory's clear high voice, caused Cathryn's heart to soar. The ceremony was simple and sweet. The love was true and the vows sincere.

Heavenly turned to lively at the brunch at River Run. Following the meal, a few wedding traditions were enacted, mostly by the younger ones, although Cathryn noticed Sterling was often a behind-the-scenes instigator of the merry pranks. While Sterling and Fielding did not resemble each other physically, their likeness in temperament was uncanny. Did Sterling have no children of his own?

"Cat, I'm going to throw the bouquet," Jaimie cried.

Good-naturedly Cathryn joined the group of young ladies. Blaire, the only other single woman, was off in a corner wrapped in cozy conversation with her new beau and could not be coaxed. Cathryn had just turned toward the bride when the bouquet grazed her face and landed in her arms. Whoops and cheers broke out, and Jack got many pats on the back, while Cathryn received excited hugs from the starry-eyed girls, and a most meaningful hug from Jaimie.

"Did you aim this at me?" Cathryn whispered.

Jaimie just giggled and gave her a saucy look.

Fate had provided an opening. Jack cocked his head at her. She shrugged and smiled. He made a big show of clearing his throat to command the attention of all, then held out his hand as if asking her to dance. Cathryn walked over and placed her hand in his. Taking the flowers from her, he waved them over his head. "These make it official, folks. Cat and I are engaged!"

Everyone pressed around them at once, offering congratulations.

Bonnie stood a little outside the circle, her eyes misty.

"Mom?" Jack asked, holding Cathryn's hand and moving toward his mother.

"I am so happy about this. I was praying it would work out for you two." She held out her arms to embrace them both. "To think, after all these years ... someone from the old neighborhood ..."

Sterling approached them with a sly smile. "And when did this happen? It wasn't back at the Lazy S, was it?"

"Nah," Jack replied. "I was still kinda gun-shy at that point. Oh, I knew I had found the right woman. I just wasn't sure if I was the right man. A couple of weeks ago, I realized I was."

Sterling clapped him on the back. "Glad you finally figured it out, Stone."

Giving Cathryn a knowing look, Sterling leaned in to kiss her cheek. "Congratulations! And I have to say, I knew you were the right one all along."

She reached up and gave him a hug.

Jack looked on happily this time.

A little while later Jack drew Cathryn aside. "Go put on your boots," he said. "I want to show you something."

"My boots? With my gown?"

"Yeah, we're going on a walk. I don't think those little shoes are up to the gravel, seriously," he said with exaggerated concern. "Meet me by the front door."

In a few minutes Cathryn joined him there and they slipped out together. He led her down the hill toward the road, then turned toward the river. The sun washed the land in that delicious glow of late afternoon. The trees edging the river were past full color and dropping their leaves in preparation for the long sleep of winter.

"I love autumn," she whispered.

"I love you," he whispered back.

"Why are we whispering?" she said, suppressing a laugh.

"Ssh, you'll scare the deer."

When they reached a fence, he led her around to a gate and, with a wink, produced a key. The couple slipped through and closed it again, then stealthily followed a trail through the trees to the water's edge. They picked their way among the rocks until a large flat stone rose before them. Five people could easily stand on the stone. The water lapped gently at its feet in a steady rhythm.

Jack turned to her. "Is this it? Is this Trinity Rock?"

Her eyes caressed the familiar place and her heart swelled.

"Yes," she sighed. "I don't know how long it's been since I actually stood on it." She leaned forward and touched it with the full palm of her hand. It was solid, comforting. An ever fixèd mark amidst the turmoil of love and loss, and the search for heroes and home—a long and winding road seeking something she had never found. Until now.

And at last she knew why. The ever fixèd mark was not a place; not even this place.

It lived within herself.

Had she made any different choices in life, taken any different turns, this moment might not be happening. Each turn had held a purpose, a meaning, even if she had been doomed to blindness at the time.

The breeze sent leaves of gold dancing through the air until they landed on the water, bobbing and twirling as they sailed away. She drew a deep breath.

Magic. I'm surrounded by magic, and I'm sharing it with Jack.

This time she wasn't lost in a novel or in her head; this time it was all real. She had found her way home.

Jack leapt onto the stone and reached out to help her up,

long gown and all. They stood hand in hand, silently watching the river.

She felt the power of the stone and the river surge through her, the two forces ever at odds and yet ever one. The wind ruffled her hair and she looked at Jack. "This is a first, you know. I've never been here in a gown."

He raised an eyebrow. "Ah, but you are perfectly dressed for the occasion."

She looked at him curiously.

Cupping her cheek tenderly he said, "I don't want to wait, Cat. I want to marry you right here, right now; just the two of us—with the land and the water and the sky as our witnesses."

He took her hands in his and kissed each open palm tenderly. All the right words were spoken, with loving promises made.

And every tree and stone rejoiced in the perfect happiness of the union.

The End

〜

SONNET VII

Is love a fancy or a feeling?
No it is immortal as immaculate Truth.
'Tis not a blossom, shed as soon as youth drops
from the stem of life—
for it will grow, in barren regions, where no waters flow
nor ray of promise cheats the pensive gloom.
A darkling fire, faint hovering o'er a tomb,
that but itself and darkness nought doth shew,
is my love's being,—yet it cannot die.
Nor will it change, though all be changed beside;
tho' fairest beauty be no longer fair,
tho' vows be false, and faith itself deny,
tho' sharp enjoyment be a suicide,
and hope a spectre in a ruin bare.

HARTLEY COLERIDGE

Thank you for reading Love & Stones!

Please consider leaving an honest, spoiler-free review at reader/fan page sites. Your review can help others decide if they, too, might enjoy this story.

~

OTHER BOOKS BY SALLIANNE HINES

Available now
Her Summer at Pemberley (2020) is a sequel to
Jane Austen's beloved novel *Pride and Prejudice*,
being the story of Kitty Bennet.
Available everywhere books are sold.
For more information, go to author's website
for a convenient 'buy here' button.
https://www.salliannehines.com

Coming Soon
The Pleasure of Her Company is a sequel to
Jane Austen's *Sense and Sensibility*,
being the story of Mrs. Dashwood, the mother
of young heroines Elinor and Marianne.
Look for it early 2021.
Visit the author's website at
https://www.salliannehines.com
for more information and to
sign up for the mailing list to get
updates on all her upcoming books.

ACKNOWLEDGMENTS

So many people helped me along this path.

Thanks to my beta readers and cover consultants *Betsy Anderson, A.W. Bailey, Dr. Steven J. Carlson, Allie Cresswell, Edwina Edwards, Elena George, Abigail Goetz, Elizabeth Goetz, Mikiya Goetz, Heidi Herman-Kerr, Susan Joyce, Cheryl Krutzfeldt, Jessica Lankford MS, Mary Lee, Jean Liestman, Adrianne Wagner.* Thanks to *Noreen Young* for use of her equine facility and her horse Little Fancy for the photo shoot. Polo expertise appreciated from *Jodi Wright, N.W., and Karen Turner.*

My thanks to members of the James River Writers group and The Park Avenue Authors and members of many online writing groups for their support and feedback.

Thanks also to my son Dan Goetz and all my family members for their ongoing support.

And much appreciation to *Miss Jane Austen* for being an endless well of inspiration for so many.

ABOUT THE AUTHOR

Sallianne Hines is a great fan of all things Austen. And J.R.R. Tolkien, Mary Stolz, Georgette Heyer, Marie Kondo, and many more authors.

In March 2020 she launched her first novel, *Her Summer at Pemberley*, a *Pride and Prejudice* sequel telling the story of Kitty Bennet. Several more novels are in progress for her Austenesque "Mothers, Sisters, Friends" group of books. The next one, *The Pleasure of Her Company*, which is Mrs. Dashwood's story, will launch in 2021. Two nonfiction books are also in progress—learn more about these at her website https://www.salliannehines.com.

Sallianne is a lifelong horsewoman, parent of three, grandparent of eight, and shares her home with a boss cat and two dogs (who give way to said boss cat). They all live in a little house on the prairie. Really. She is an advocate for animals, children, and simplicity, and believes it's never too late to become a heroine.

To learn more about Sallianne and her books, visit her website at https://www.salliannehines.com.